T0171169

OVER
THE
HOLIDAYS

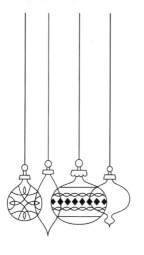

OVER
THE
HOLIDAYS

SANDRA HARPER

Pocket Books

New York   London   Toronto   Sydney

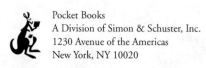

Pocket Books
A Division of Simon & Schuster, Inc.
1230 Avenue of the Americas
New York, NY 10020

First Pocket Books trade paperback edition October 2009

POCKET and colophon are registered trademarks of Simon & Schuster, Inc.

For information about special discounts for bulk purchases, please contact Simon & Schuster Special Sales at 1-866-506-1949 or business@simonandschuster.com.

The Simon & Schuster Speakers Bureau can bring authors to your live event. For more information or to book an event contact the Simon & Schuster Speakers Bureau at 1-866-248-3049 or visit our website at www.simonspeakers.com.

Designed by Akasha Archer

Manufactured in the United States of America

10   9   8   7   6   5   4   3   2   1

Library of Congress Cataloging-in-Publication Data

Harper, Sandra A.
    Over the holidays / Sandra Harper.—1st Pocket Books trade pbk. ed.
       p.   cm.
    ISBN-13 978-1-4391-5870-8
    ISBN-13 978-1-4391-6670-3 (ebk.)
    1. Family—Fiction. 2. Christmas stories. I. Title.
PS3608.A776O84   2009
813'.6—dc22   2009016864

Acknowledgments

Happy Holidays to my wonderful editor, Kathy Sagan, and my amazing publisher, Louise Burke—thank you for giving me the best present of all. To my incredible agent, Nicole Gregory—may your days be merry and bright. To Jean Anne Rose, Ayelet Gruenspecht, Jessica Webb, Kerrie Loyd, and everyone at Pocket—I thank you every day of the year.

Season's Greetings to my writing group: Greg Chandler, Lori Gunnell, Craig Hilary, and Peggy Miley—Monday nights are always festive with you.

Happy New Year to Michael Polaire and to my equine experts, Carolyn Doran and Alwynne Hellfach.

Love and joy to my mother, JoAnne, and to my sisters, Catherine and Nancy, and to all those holidays of yore.

Peace on Earth to Tracy Tynan, who understands the yuletide better than anyone.

And a special Christmas wish for Eric and Jackson: let it snow, let it snow, let it snow.

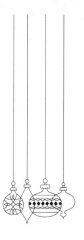

1

It was only December first but Vanessa Channing felt like it had been Christmas forever.

In late September, she had spotted trussed and tinseled Christmas trees at her local mall in Sherman Oaks. Then, seconds after the Halloween candy and superhero costumes had been slashed to half price, the drugstore shelves were restocked with cobbling elves and icicle lights and Santas that jived to "Jingle Bell Rock" when you clapped your hands.

You'd think that with all these visual cues, Vanessa would be further along in her own holiday preparations—her tree, her gifts, her dinner, her general plan of attack—but instead she was shot through with doubt and indecision.

Hard as it was to believe—Vanessa was, after all, a thirty-eight-year-old wife and mother—she hadn't done a lot of Christmases. And, for the last few years, they'd flown East, to Massachusetts, where her sister-in-law presided over her own seasonal pageant.

But this year, owing to finances and Vanessa's reluctance to yet again cross the country in the worst possible month with people under the drinking age, she had suggested to her husband that they stay home. Save money. Keep it simple.

"And maybe we could put more meaning into this," she'd told him at breakfast that morning. "Find a connection."

"I connect with snow and a fire in the fireplace," JT said pointedly. "And sledding. And skiing."

"But now you live in California," said Vanessa, wishing, not for the first time, that all the East Coast transplants would let go of the whole white Christmas thing. "And if you really missed the snow so much . . . you'd still be living in Wenham."

SHE PULLED UP TO THE GOODWILL. As she reached into the back of her dusty green station wagon and slid out four bags of old clothes, she was overwhelmed by all the giving she had to do: to friends and neighbors; to the postman and the teachers at school; to her husband and children and relatives; to the charities that were saving the world.

There was so much to do, so much giving to be dispensed,

that Vanessa reached into her purse, uncapped a plastic bottle of Tylenol, and washed down two caplets on the strength of her saliva alone.

Okay, I don't mind giving to Goodwill, she thought humbly. In fact, on the long list of Things to Do at the Holidays, this was the one act that was free of any other baggage.

Goodwill didn't open for another hour, so she stacked the bags next to the door marked DONATIONS and jumped back in the car. Her day was jam-packed. There was the grocery shopping, the housecleaning, the piles of laundry, and a parent meeting at school. And most important, she had to reserve energy for a job interview later tonight—some New York playwright who might need her help with his script.

I wish I felt more spiritual at the holidays, she thought, driving through Studio City towards her market. More joyful . . . and filled with love for humanity.

But it didn't really matter what she felt, because Vanessa Channing had twin boys, aged nine, and so Christmas was mandatory. It was hurtling towards her and it simply had to be braced, like uterine contractions or an earthquake.

Even this early in the morning, the lot at the supermarket was jammed. Parking her car in the hinterlands, she crossed the asphalt, keeping time to the ring of a jangling silver bell.

"Help the needy," said the bell ringer, an older gentleman with a thin Midwest accent. He had the straight posture of a former marine and was fixed next to the red Salvation Army bucket.

Vanessa rummaged through her purse and opened up her wallet: there was a five and a twenty. Fingering the five, she reminded herself that things were not *that* dire. With a smile for the bell ringer, she pushed the twenty into the pot. He gave his bell an extra tinkle.

Okay, she thought with relief, I do have some love for humanity. And, as she entered the grocery store, she mentally checked off *charitable donation* on her holiday list.

ALTHOUGH DRESSED IN HEAVY COTTON LEGGINGS and a zippered gray wool sweater, Thea Clayton did not look casual. Perhaps it was the black muslin scarf wrapped just so at the neck or the dark sunglasses or the way she attacked the beach with a sense of urgency. She was hoping this walk would give her some inspiration. God knows, she needed something.

I used to glean energy from this ocean but now I gaze at it and feel nothing, she thought dully. And the pounding of the surf sounds like white noise, like elevator music—tuneless and forgettable. Her Venice neighborhood, which once seemed avant-garde, felt more like a catch basin for tourists, derelicts, and the many exhibitionists who presented their tattoos and body piercings as some kind of declaration of independence.

Didn't someone once say there's nothing so conventional as a rebel? she thought idly.

And could I twist that into some kind of art?

Leaving the sand, she cut through the alley and over to Pacific Avenue, passing a seedy couple caged behind a shelter of discarded beach debris. Two shopping carts, a battered blue boogie board, and a string of T-shirts had crafted their fortress. A yellow shade umbrella perched atop, like a turret.

As she approached the Dudley Street Diner, a muscular

surfer in his late twenties locked his bike to the pole of a parking sign. His was the timeless attire of the beach denizen: cargo shorts, sandals, and mellow mind-set.

He took one glance at Thea's clenched jaw and drew her into a lazy hug. "Hey, baby, why so stressed?"

"Because this . . . this, fucking grit isn't working," she sighed, spreading her arms wide into a dramatic arc. "Venice used to inspire me." She looked down glumly at the dirty sidewalk awash with sticky residue, cigarette butts, and splotches of tar.

Marcus opened the door to the diner. "Huevos rancheros," he said.

In a Jell-O-green vinyl booth by the window, Thea sipped her cup of bitter coffee and studied her boyfriend's pouty mouth. Not everything in Venice was annoying, she decided.

"I'm sorry." She reached across the table for his strong, capable hands. "I'm just obsessing about work."

"No worries," Marcus said lightly. "You'll think of something."

"That is so fucking not true." Thea banged down her mug. "I'm completely dry. And now it's December."

Marcus looked perplexed.

"Thanksgiving, Christmas, New Year. It's an artistic desert until January second." She toyed with her multicolored braids that tangled uneasily in her long, dark blond hair.

Marcus drummed the table lightly with his fingertips as Thea stared out at an amorphous blob of teenagers bouncing along the colonnade, leaning on one another and chatting animatedly.

"Sex is passé," she said wearily, noting a skanky girl rubbing the thigh of her skinny, kente-cloth-swaddled boyfriend. "Anyone with a computer can have that. Passion is Catholic, revenge is telenovela, and violence is CNN."

"You lost me, dude."

The huevos rancheros arrived on an enormous royal blue platter with a side of hot corn tortillas. Slicing precisely down the center of the egg yolk, she watched intensely as the stream of golden lava puddled around the rice and beans.

"I like Christmas," Marcus said. Rather than study his food, he was choking it down, fortifying himself for an afternoon of sanding and shaping surfboards. "No one rides that day. Got it all to myself."

"So Christmas for you is good surfing."

"A great opportunity."

Something inside Thea began to quicken.

Slightly.

Picking up a bottle of hot sauce from the Formica tabletop, she sprinkled a few drops over her plate. "When you were little, what did you like about it?"

Marcus gulped thoughtfully. A kinky cork of espresso hair fell over his greenish eyes and he pushed it back.

"The year I got Nintendo was life changing."

Nintendo! How adorable. She loved being with a guy twelve years younger.

"Anything bad ever happen?"

"Not bad, but Mom would always cry over whatever I gave her. Once it was a box made out of Popsicle sticks. Fuck, I think she still has that thing."

They laughed. Thea felt flushed. Marcus was so beautiful—his ease, his mocha-colored skin, his sinewy forearms.

Uncomplicated.

"I'll take you over to Christmas Tree Lane," he said brightly. "Everybody there goes ape shit on their houses. There're millions of lights and all these moving reindeer and stuff. Yeah, you got to see this."

Thea found herself caught up in Marcus's childlike excitement. His lightness chased away her bluesy mood.

"Christmas," she said, watching him shovel up the last mouthful of beans and salsa. "Okay, take me there."

AFTER BREAKFAST, THEY STOOD UNDER THE colonnade and kissed good-bye.

"Go make art," he said, lightly patting her behind. Then, unlocking the beach cruiser with the fat tires and comfy seat, he pedaled off to the surf shop. Thea wandered back home to pretend to work.

She had converted her living room into an art studio. Two stories high, it had floor-to-ceiling windows and a view of a murky Venice canal. It was spare and spacious with pure white walls and hardwood floors. She preferred the squall of gulls and the distant hum of traffic to the drumbeat of waves over on the beachfront side of the neighborhood. Confronting the daily parade of tourists, joggers, and street urchins was the price one paid for a house with a view of the ocean and the pier. Her side, the backside of Venice, was more peaceful.

Her desk, a simple white drafting table, was beside the window and overlooked the canal below. She sat down, opened a sketchbook, and drummed the pages with a black

Prismacolor pen. She gazed out at an egret poking its beak into the mud searching for breakfast. She stared back at her pad but couldn't think of anything.

After ten minutes she gave up and decided to go down to her mailbox for something to do.

At the bottom of her stairs was a bank of four mailboxes. With a small key, she opened up her compartment and extracted a fistful of missives, mostly postcards from Realtors extolling the property value of her neighborhood.

Back in her kitchen, she tossed the junk mail into the recycling bin, then stared intently at the holiday card from her dentist.

It was a nineteenth-century image of a horse-drawn sleigh on a snowy path. The message inside read, *May the Peace of the Season be with you.* Underneath was printed *Dr. Felton and Staff* in embossed gold lettering.

When did this happen? Thea mused. That we all became enthralled with an image of a time that probably never existed?

She sat down again with her sketch pad and doodled holiday images from memory. Bethlehem and holly berries; stars and dancing snowmen.

She imagined making some kind of statement about, what? Hopes, dreams, gifts, misery?

Christmas was bigger and better than either sex or violence, she decided. But after another hour with her sketch pad, she couldn't connect the dots.

So telling herself she was doing "research," she ambled over to her laptop on the coffee table and flopped on her couch.

She checked her email (another great time waster), then

scrolled through her bookmarks to her favorite art grant websites. She cast a wide net: culture, rituals, and religious icons.

She rubbed her hands. She could feel a video art piece/installation coming on.

She got to work.

"I'VE GOT SOME IDEAS FOR A new series," said Thea. Perched on a chrome bar stool in Vanessa's kitchen, she idly watched her sister tear open a box of mushroom risotto. Although the two bore a striking resemblance—tall and slender, with long blond hair and brown eyes—Thea seemed wilder and darker than her younger sibling.

The room was cluttered and friendly with a black-and-white linoleum floor, paned-glass cabinets, and a scratched butcher-block island. Through the doorway, Thea could see into the adjacent dining room furnished with a pine dining set and china hutch. The table was cluttered with lunch boxes, mail, and empty glasses. From beyond that, in the living room, came the sound of a blaring television and the war cries of boys engaged in video games.

"Here," Vanessa said, handing Thea a wedge of Parmesan cheese and a grater. "Make yourself useful."

While Thea shaved the cheese onto a white dinner plate, Vanessa dumped the rice and the contents of a flavor packet into a hot nonstick skillet.

"I've been thinking about Christmas. And its impact on society," said Thea. "Its importance, culturally and spiritually."

"Since when do you care about Christmas?"

"Since I realized that everyone has a relationship with Christmas whether they like it or not." Thea began to sample the shavings. "Which sort of fascinates me."

"Well, you'd better be careful," said Vanessa. "People take this holiday very seriously. You don't want to offend anyone."

"Gee," Thea's eyes gleamed. "I never thought of that."

Skimming the directions on the box, Vanessa realized, with alarm, that she'd forgotten to add liquid. She ransacked her cabinet for chicken broth, came up empty, and decided to just substitute water. Filling a measuring cup at the sink, she dumped it over the rice in the pan, which had crusted and burned. "I have an idea, why don't you do something with the twins during vacation? Take them to the batting cage, or to a movie. This is your chance to be an aunt."

"Yeah, well, I'm kinda busy right now . . ." said Thea, wishing that Vanessa wouldn't pressure her about her nephews. "So where's JT?"

"He's playing basketball with the other unemployed crew guys. He promised to be back by eight so I can get to the theater." Because, Vanessa added silently, unlike everyone else's sisters, you never offer to babysit.

"He's still not working?"

"No, and it's always slow in December."

"The freelance life's a bitch, I know."

Vanessa glanced with dismay at Thea's handiwork: The platter was empty. "Don't eat any more Parmesan! That's all I have for dinner." Snatching the diminished wedge, she began to grate the cheese herself. "Go to the stove and stir the risotto!"

Thea scooted up to the sturdy Wedgewood and obediently

swirled the rice. "So are you going to your in-laws' for Christmas?"

"I don't know. We can't really afford the airfare right now."

Resting the spoon on the rim of the pan, Thea strolled over to the pantry and sorted through Vanessa's selection of drinks. She read the contents of a bottle of antioxidant pomegranate juice.

"Thea!" Vanessa picked up the wooden spoon at the stove. "You're no more help than the kids! Anyway, I've been thinking about Christmas too . . . and how to make it more meaningful."

"Everyone talks about making it meaningful," Thea said thoughtfully. "But is it?"

"Oh Thea," *you can say things like that because you're a self-absorbed artist with no kids,* she almost blurted, but managed an earnest, "I want it to be more than just buying gifts."

Thea twisted off the bottle top and took a tentative sip. "How are you going to do that?"

Vanessa tapped her spoon. "I was thinking about honoring the winter solstice. The waning of the light. There's this website—TakingBackThe25th.org—and they suggested recycling some of your old stuff into iconic symbols. Like, make a solstice altar or a wreath from discarded mittens."

"A wreath out of mittens—what could be more meaningful?"

"It's the idea of recycling something—caring about Mother Earth—you cynic."

Thea snorted. "Hey, from where I am, your life is full of meaning. You're a wife and a mother. I'm alone at Christmas.

No husband, no kids. I'm practically a pariah. You know more people kill themselves in December than any other month of the year?"

"You're not alone—you've got Marcus. I thought you two were happy."

Thea strolled over to the refrigerator and inspected the contents. She pulled out a plastic container of hummus and a jar of olives.

"We're happy." Twisting off the lid, she stuck her fingers down in the brine.

"Sit down if you're going to eat," Vanessa said, "you're worse than the boys." Flinging open a cabinet, she pulled down a plate, found a knife and some crackers, and placed it all on the center island. *Thea still acts like a teenager!* Vanessa thought, resuming her former position at the stove, *and that fling with Marcus is going nowhere.*

Suddenly, she whirled around, her cheeks flushed and her blond plaits swinging. "I forgot to tell you! I ran into Robin Weinstein at a school event. She told me her daughter's having a bat mitzvah."

"Okay, I don't care." Thea scooped up a generous amount of hummus on a sesame cracker and sucked her fingers.

"She said she'd been up north on vacation, and she ran into Cal Hawkins!"

Vanessa looked triumphant, waiting for her sister's reaction.

"Really?" Thea swallowed hard.

"So, silly, that's where he is—in Point Reyes. Robin said it's a really charming town . . . very rich hippies, organic, roaming cows. The women all age naturally—no one uses a razor or colors her hair. We should all move there."

Cal Hawkins. "Why do you think I care about Cal Hawkins?"

"I don't know, I sort of thought he was the missed train."

"There are no missed trains in L.A. We barely have mass transit."

"You know what I mean . . . he was brilliant. And your equal."

"No one is my equal. But I'm glad you still think I'm a loser for fucking up with Cal Hawkins."

"That's not what I meant."

"Olives make me sick after a while," Thea said, pushing the jar away. "When's dinner?"

Vanessa waggled her spoon. "Don't change the subject. We should see if he's still single."

"Why are you butting into my personal life?"

"You just said you were depressed."

"No, I said being single at Christmas was hard but that doesn't mean I want to track down old lovers."

"But aren't you curious? He was always so dreamy."

"He was an intense motherfucker with a lot of baggage."

"Right," said Vanessa. "Dreamy." She snapped off the heat under the pan. "Will you get the boys? They need to wash their hands and help set the table for dinner."

Thea strolled through the dining room into the entry hall and then stood in the archway eyeing her nephews. "Hey, guys."

Alex and Ethan, nine-year-old fraternal twins, were

bunched up on the worn brown sofa with matching black controllers.

"I killed it," Alex shrieked with enthusiasm as he aced his simulated tennis serve.

"Your shot was out," his brother insisted with a whine.

Thea took a tentative step into the room. The floor was littered with crumbs, and the bright red liquid from a juice box was pooling on the wooden coffee table.

"It's time for dinner."

The rally continued.

"So, do you guys do art at school?"

Ethan shot her a sweet smile. "Sometimes we draw our feelings. And we made papier-mâché pumpkins for Harvest Celebration."

Alex suddenly snapped to attention. He rolled back on the cushions and kicked his legs in the air. "EEEEE, art is stupid, stupid, pee-pee."

Ethan, falling into his role as supportive sidekick to his boss brother, also kicked up his heels. "We hate art!"

"Really? So you wouldn't maybe want to go to a museum or come over and paint in my studio one day?"

Alex began to gag and Ethan pretended to choke him.

Thea doubled back to the kitchen and added ice to her drink. Children are overrated, she thought. Why do people spend so much time with them?

GARY WAS WAITING FOR VANESSA OUT on Santa Monica Boulevard in front of the Back Alley Theater. A reedy man with a permanent worry crease above his right eyebrow, he swooned when she arrived.

"Thank God you're here. It's complete shit." Vanessa kissed his cheek. It was always the same four weeks before a show opened. Why didn't producers remember this?

"Neil is brilliant," Gary said. "New York, edgy, but so distant, so removed . . ."

Vanessa wondered if that was code for *he's straight and won't fuck me.*

Gary's left arm encircled her shoulders like a death vise as they crossed the lobby. Framed posters of past productions lined the chipped green walls. "It's the second act, it's always the second act," he whispered. "Where is it going? What is he trying to say? It needs something. Pathos? Bathos? Nudity?" Sweeping open the heavy oak doors, he grunted in an exasperated way.

They crept quietly into the darkened theater. Neil Cohen was slumped down in the second row, fixated on the two actors with the director up on the stage. He was scribbling wildly all over his manuscript. Vanessa slid into the seat next to him.

Glancing over at them, Neil rapped his pen on the armrest. "Gary, what's going on?"

"Neil, this is Vanessa Clayton, the woman I told you about. She used to produce for Back Alley and she's our resident dramaturge."

Neil eyed Vanessa warily. "You can sit there all night, I'm not taking any notes." Standing up, he moved to the end of the row.

Vanessa glared at Gary. "You didn't tell him I was coming?" she mouthed.

The producer threw up his hands. "Well, you see what I'm up against."

"I think I should go," she whispered. "Until you work things out. It's his play—you can't just force me on him."

The actors and director paused and glanced over at the two of them. Gary laid a restraining hand on her arm and Vanessa cringed.

She waged a mental debate over whether her sudden departure would create more or less commotion. I should probably stay for Gary, she finally decided and, quietly shuffling through her plum-colored clutch, removed a small spiral pad and pen before turning her attention to the scene in progress.

Gary handed her a copy of *Safe Deposit* and she read through the first act, growing more and more excited. It was a compelling story, intense and dramatic, with complex characters—certainly not the complete disaster Gary had intimated. But the pacing sagged here and there and it needed a layer of polish.

Twice she glanced stealthily to her left and caught Neil watching her. Her cheeks grew hot and she felt embarrassed—clearly he didn't want her there. Too bad, she thought unhappily. It's a good play and I could really, really use the money. Plus, she was enjoying the smell of dust, the creak of her chair, and the echo of the actors' voices fanning out into the dark, empty theater.

At one A.M., Jake, the bleary-eyed director, called it a night. Vanessa rolled her stiff shoulders, stashed away her notes, and walked slowly up the aisle with her producer.

"Well?" Gary ran his fingers through his shaggy salt-and-pepper mane. They stood alone in the lobby, the harsh overhead light making them appear ghoulish.

"It's really good," she murmured. "I can see why you wanted to do it."

"And?" Gary prompted.

"You're right about the second act lacking focus. But I think fleshing out the part of Sam will make a difference."

"Can you tell him that?"

Rocketing past them, Neil slammed the push bar on the entrance door and released himself into the crisp night air.

"Neil!" Gary hurried after him.

Vanessa slipped out her cell phone. While listening to voice mail, she heard the two men in a heated discussion out on the street.

"Hey, honey," JT's sunny voice was speaking from her mailbox. "It's midnight, I'm going to bed. I love you."

Vanessa smiled and dropped her phone into the pocket of her vintage tapestry coat. Continuing outside, she discovered that Gary was now alone. She touched his drooping shoulder.

"It's late, I'll call you tomorrow. And Gary"—she gave him a quick squeeze on the arm—"it's better than you think, really. Don't worry."

"Motherhood and happiness have clearly dulled your senses," he said before heading back inside the theater.

She fished out her keys and, with a quick scan of the block, hurried to her car. As she rounded the corner, she spotted Neil leaning against the brick wall of an all-night liquor store.

"Following me?" he said in a low voice.

She pointed to her station wagon. "My car." She pressed the lock pad and the taillights flashed briefly.

He ventured out, his hands fiddling in the pockets of a navy peacoat. "Where are you headed?"

"Studio City."

"Are you taking Cahuenga?"

"Why?"

"Well, my buddy was supposed to pick me up but he's not answering his cell."

Vanessa took a good look at Neil. His hair was light brown and shoulder length and his build was slight. Underneath his arrogance she detected the bruises of a poet, the sort of boy who sat in the last row of English class and always had ink on his fingers.

"You don't have a car?" She moved towards the driver's side.

Neil shrugged. "Don't need one."

Oh, brother, Vanessa thought. "Get in."

The presence of an enormous spirit climbed in next to her and threatened to deplete the oxygen level. She cracked the window and headed north towards the hills.

"Does Gary call you every time he freaks out?" he said, staring out the passenger window.

"No, every other time. So where am I going?"

"Whitley Heights, off Franklin." Neil tapped his heel nervously in the foot well.

They hit a red light and Vanessa turned to face him. "Look, Gary's a good guy. And he really loves the play. He just wanted to help, that's all."

Neil said nothing. Vanessa was about to add, *and I'm sure I could help you polish that second act,* but decided to let it go. Clearly this guy was a loner and didn't appreciate what she might bring to the project.

"Yeah, sorry to make you come out so late," Neil said.

"Oh, it's okay." It was fun getting out of the house and away from my kids for the night, she almost confessed but stopped herself. It seemed awkward, too chatty, somehow, mentioning her family life to this stranger.

Neil glanced at her profile. "So, who have you worked with?"

Vanessa named a couple of well-known L.A. playwrights.

"Never heard of them."

What an asshole, she bristled. "Oh, so you're one of those East Coast theater people who come to L.A. and then complain about how it's not New York."

"I'm from L.A.," he said.

"Oh." Vanessa shifted uncomfortably in her seat.

"I haven't lived here since high school. So I don't know a lot of locals anymore."

"I just meant . . . New York isn't the only city with great theater," she finished lamely.

"After Franklin make a right at the first signal," he pointed.

They drove the rest of the way in silence. Vanessa felt foolish for mouthing off over something so silly. *I don't have to defend my town to him!*

She dropped him off on the crest of the hill, up where you could see the 101 freeway wending its way through the Cahuenga pass.

"Well, good luck," she said.

"Thanks for the ride." He opened his door. "Rehearsal's at six tomorrow."

Their eyes met briefly. With the overhead light, she could see that his irises were a watery blue.

He climbed out of the car. "Hope you can make it."

"Okay, sure, I'll be there."

She followed his Levi's jeans, and that confident stride, as he scaled a winding stucco staircase to an arched door with an ornate, wrought-iron peep window. He slipped inside, and she put the car in drive.

The theater, Vanessa groaned. Why couldn't I have majored in business?

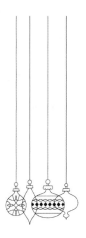

2

At four A.M. Vanessa was awakened by the *thwack thwack thwack* of the paddle attachment on the standing mixer. Reaching out with her left arm, she swiped JT's side of the bed but came up empty.

Wrapping a pink chenille robe over her nightgown, she staggered down the tiled hallway to the kitchen and discovered her husband drinking French roast coffee and watching his dough knead.

"Hey V," he said and kissed her on the mouth. He tasted bitter and anxious. His dark blue eyes were bloodshot.

"I need to sleep," she yawned. "But someone's making too much noise."

"It's the cinnamon rolls. You have to let them rise twice before you bake them."

Vanessa bit her lip. She didn't want to discourage JT from his culinary pleasure, but she sensed hysteria in every beat of the dough.

"Honey, I love cinnamon rolls. What's going on?"

"I was thinking about taking a professional chef's course. You know I love to get up early . . ."

No, she wasn't aware of that. As long as she'd known him he'd always complained that the worst part of being a gaffer was the six A.M. crew call.

". . . and cooking is creative and the results are instant. And you're helping people, feeding them. You're making a difference. You're not standing around on a set, lighting useless products that people don't need and probably shouldn't buy . . ."

Taking a sharp detour from this familiar rant, she thought instead of their dwindling bank account. The job that fell through. The mortgage payment. Christmas gifts. Plane tickets to Boston. Just butch it up, she thought wearily. Suck it up like a man!

"We need a steady income, V, the freelance life is crazy. I'm dependent on, what? two DPs for my livelihood—Dave and Jeff. And when they don't work, I don't work. Do you realize—"

She cut him off. "I took that job with Gary. A thousand bucks, and it's cash. It'll help cover groceries, gifts. We can squeak through till January. And actually, it's perfect that you're home 'cause you can take care of the boys when *I'm* working."

"There's still a chance I might get something . . ." JT sounded defeated.

Vanessa folded her arms and leaned against the counter. "Gary's calling me a dramaturge, but after meeting this guy, I'd say I'm really a glorified babysitter."

JT drew her into a hug. He kissed the top of her head and held her close. "You are the best. I'm sorry for always dumping on you."

"It's okay," she lied.

He picked up his mug. "And about Massachusetts . . . I don't think we should go." He swallowed the last of the gritty sediment. "It's too much money."

Vanessa stiffened. Any relief she felt was smothered by guilt. "We could throw it on the plastic."

"Nah, it'll be fun here, in our own home," he said, roughing up his short blond hair.

So it was decided. They were staying put. Vanessa took a tentative deep breath. "Then, you'll call your brother?"

"Sure." JT shrugged nonchalantly in that worrisome husband way which meant she'd have to remind him three times or call Richard herself.

The timer *ping*ed and he switched off the mixer. Now it was quiet. Just the two of them. He dumped the dough into a bowl and covered it with a damp kitchen towel.

"Let's go back to sleep," he said, wiping his sticky hands on his faded PJ bottoms. "Everything needs to rest."

In their bedroom, snug and sandwiched under the cotton comforter, he whispered in her left ear, "I need more control of my life."

"I know." Vanessa drew his arm tight around her middle.

"I love you, V," he said, kissing her neck and drawing up her nightgown. She heard the distant hum of traffic down on Ventura Boulevard.

Before she closed her eyes, she glanced at the clock. "If we do this, you have to get up and take the kids to school."

"Of course," he said, muffled under the covers. "I'll do anything for you."

She sighed and then relaxed into the sweetness of an early dawn.

AT SEVEN O'CLOCK, ALEX WAS SHAKING her awake. "Mom! Are you getting up?"

Opening her eyes, she saw that JT was still fast asleep beside her. She climbed out of bed and gave his broad, muscular backside a fierce punch. "Asshole!"

At Jacaranda Elementary, she parked in the fifteen-minute zone and hurried Ethan and Alex across the trampled field, past the cluster of bright yellow lunch tables, and into the third-grade classroom. Ms. Garcia, the teacher's aide with the waist-length ponytail, gave her a wide smile.

"Hello, Mrs. Channing. You haven't signed up for the Holiday Potluck!"

"Oh, yeah," Vanessa said sleepily. "I've been meaning to . . ."

The aide was at the ready with her clipboard. "We'd like every family to bring in a significant dish from their cultural tradition."

"Eggnog and scotch?" Vanessa murmured under her breath.

Ms. Garcia glanced at her sign-up sheet. "We have latkes, *Bûche de Noël*, sprinkle cookies, tamales . . ."

Vanessa brightened. "How about cinnamon rolls? Will that do?"

"Oooh, how sweet. Did your mom used to make that for Christmas morning?"

Vanessa had a sudden memory of Carol, fast asleep under her powder blue coverlet on Christmas morning. "Don't wake me before nine," she had instructed her daughters. "I'm a working woman and this is one of the few days I can sleep in!" When it was time for Vanessa and Thea to open their presents (a bride doll? Candyland?), Carol sat on the Naugahyde sofa and sobbed about how miserable she was, alone and without a husband at the holidays.

Vanessa turned to the aide. "Uh, no, the rolls are my husband's side of the family."

Ms. Garcia filled in a spot under BREADS AND PASTRIES. "Could you bring three dozen?"

"Three dozen?" Vanessa felt slightly dizzy, then remembered that JT had lots of time for this. In fact, she realized, since he's not working, we'll do the Christmas shopping together. So it will be good, this lack of money. It would unite them in the true spirit of the holiday. She imagined the two of them, laughing and holding hands as they picked out gifts in beautifully decorated stores. Afterwards they'd enjoy

a sumptuous lunch and linger over coffee and dessert with
their festive boxes and bags by their sides. They were dressed
in smart wool coats and striped scarves and they were kissing.
Somehow, as her fantasy unfolded, the background morphed
into France.

"And Mrs. Channing, about Alex . . ." Vanessa's dreamy
Christmas shopping was interrupted by Ms. Garcia's hushed
tone, a tone that implied one of her offspring was not up to
snuff.

"Have you been helping him with the lyrics for our holiday song?"

"Song? No, I don't think they've mentioned a song."

The aide frowned with the slightest contempt. "So you
didn't get the handout?"

"I'm sure I did." Or, she fumed, most likely it was JT, who
picked up the kids and then discarded the Very Important
Handout on the floor of his car or in the trash!

"Well, the Holiday Sing is three weeks away and I've noticed that Alex still doesn't know the words to our song. And
I'm not sure he's using his full potential for musical expression."

"So you're saying he's not singing?" Why did she need a
master's in education to decode this conversation?

"Could he have some kind of bias against the song?"

"I'll speak to him tonight," Vanessa assured her and, with
sudden speed, jumped aside to let the hapless mother behind
her step into the circle of admonishment and shame.

Scanning the room for her boys, she noticed they had
joined a noisy game of Hacky Sack in the corner.

She smiled; they looked so happy and full of life. They were only nine, for God's sake. Who cared if they forgot the words to "Frosty the Snowman" or whatever it was. Before she ducked out of class, Vanessa checked the December calendar posted on the bulletin board next to the door. The Holiday Sing was the Friday before winter vacation.

She made a mental note and scurried home. She was hoping to break down Neil's script before lunch.

THEA AND MARCUS WERE WALKING DOWN Santa Claus Lane, a half-mile stretch of homes where, year after year, the neighbors schemed to best one another in fantastical, electrified light displays.

It had taken four freeways to get here, in the foothills above Pasadena. The houses were mostly ranch style, although many had been scaled up with towering second stories, built-out great rooms, and free-form add-ons.

The street was legendary, and the line of cars waiting to cruise by the twinkling, moving tableaux was half a mile long. Growing impatient with the traffic, they ditched Marcus's SUV at the corner burger joint and doubled back on foot. This decision placed them alone on the sidewalk breathing in exhaust and captive to the steady hum of engines and the chatter of families inside the cars and vans. The night was crisp and clear and Thea could trace the silhouette of the San Gabriel mountains just beyond them.

"I remember this one," said Marcus, admiring a spinning,

twinkling five-horse carousel. "I used to come here with my family every year."

Thea peered through the lens of her digital recorder and slowly panned the street. Over the next hour she filmed a car full of teenagers drinking beer and singing rap versions of Christmas carols, a family munching on hamburgers while admiring a pair of marching toy soldiers, a teenage boy urinating on a brick wall, and a couple fighting about the track suit he'd given her last year when she'd told him repeatedly that she wanted a diamond necklace.

"I don't see how this is art," Marcus told Thea on the way back to the car.

"Maybe it's not," she said. "But it's compelling. Now that I'm in it, I don't know how to get out. It's interesting that our entire culture has agreed upon these images—these ideas—to represent this holiday."

Marcus smiled vaguely and Thea felt an unwelcome twinge. There were limitations to all relationships, and unfortunately, his lack of interest in ideas and issues was one of them. She'd have to talk about this with Tina or anyone who looked beyond surfline.com for a bigger worldview.

Thea thought about the first Christmas she had spent with Cal Hawkins. They'd both been seeing other people—he, a graphic artist named Melissa, and she, a guitar player named Kurt—but their loved ones had left them alone in L.A. and flown off to visit relatives in other cities.

Cal had taken her to a Japanese restaurant up in the hills with a view of the L.A. basin. They'd had sake and rumaki and pretty hot kisses.

That had been the start of their two-year affair, which neither of them could commit to full-time.

Cal Hawkins doesn't really count as a relationship, Thea
decided. It was art with sex. Because when they weren't in bed,
he painted her—often in the nude.

I gave him the best years of my body, she thought.

Marcus started the engine of his truck. "Let's get back to
the beach, get some beers at Sal's."

"Okay," she smiled. Marcus would never paint her. But he
was around, and close by, pretty much every day. And that was
good in many ways. She was certainly wise enough to know
that one person could never supply all your food groups.

Still, she warmed at the thought of those nudes. And wondered whether she looked as good back then as she was imagining she did right now.

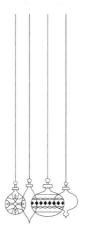

3

Three thousand miles away, in a pale yellow colonial with neat blue shutters, the Massachusetts Channings were finishing up their breakfast.

Patience Polk-Channing stirred her cinnamon oatmeal and chatted to her husband, Richard. In a buttoned-down shirt and with flecks of gray in his clipped blond hair, he was a more erudite version of his younger brother, JT.

"I think the theme for this year's Open House should be A Victorian Christmas," said Patience.

"Didn't you do that last year?" Seventeen-year-old Liberty dug into half a grapefruit.

"No," said her mother. "Last year was A Winter Wonderland, and everything was white and very simple. This year I see garlands, sashes, top hats."

Richard smiled pleasantly and then returned to *The Boston Globe*.

"Well, I'm not coming," said Libby, tossing back her thick brown hair. Her fingernails were chewed and the green polish was chipped. "I hate the Open House. I hate all your horse friends and their stupid stable talk."

"Liberty Polk-Channing!"

"Don't call me that! I told you, I hate being a hyphen. I'm changing my name to L Channing."

Patience dropped her jaw and tapped Richard's paper.

"Are you going to let her talk like that?"

Unhappily, Richard entered the fray. "Liberty *Polk-Channing*," he said pointedly, "you must speak to your mother in a respectful tone."

Dressed for the school day in sleek suede sneakers, jeans, and a belted sweater, Libby checked her cell phone. "Dad agrees with me," she whispered under her breath.

Patience aimed her sharp blue eyes at Richard. "What do you mean he agrees with you?"

"He hates your stupid Open House too. He just hasn't told you because he's nicer than me."

"Richard." Patience's voice quivered. "You hate our Open House?"

Richard adjusted the knot on his crimson tie. "Darling, I think it might be nice to take a break once in a while. Do you remember last year? The panic attack over the goose? Thank goodness you responded to Valium. Otherwise . . ." He let the implications hover in the air.

"No, no, no, you love the Open House." Patience reached for the carafe and poured him more coffee. "And this year, I promise to stick with roast beef. And I'm making you a plaid cummerbund to match the trim on my dress. I'm filling the gift baskets with potpourri today!"

"Okay, Dad," said Libby. "Speak now or forever wear a cummerbund."

"P," Richard spoke kindly, as if he were addressing one of his patients, "I love you and I'm willing to truss up like a turkey for you on special occasions. But let's be clear—I do not love the Open House." He checked his classic tank-style watch.

"You don't love the Open House?"

"I do not."

"I don't believe it!" Patience was indignant. She pushed her blue velvet headband back on her scalp and smoothed her impossibly straight dark brown hair.

"This time of year is always hectic. There are more fractures than usual—someone should do a study—and a large party with finger food and scotch and idle chitchat with people I don't care about is not as meaningful as it used to be. Now, please, can we have this discussion later? I've got pre-op at eight thirty."

"You two can discuss it all you want, but I'm not coming." Liberty bent down and grabbed her backpack off the floor. "Mom, you are totally nuts at Christmas, it's a complete horror show. I wish I was Buddhist." Swinging the black nylon sack over her right shoulder, she rattled her car keys, kissed her father, and vacated the premises.

Patience frowned. What had gotten into everyone this morning? Padding over to the kitchen counter, she placed a slice of nine-grain bread into the toaster oven. Then she stood by the bay window and watched Libby hurry down the front walk and jump into Richard's old gray sedan. She remembered when her daughter loved the Open House and would clamor to pass around the hors d'oeuvres on a silver tray.

That was at least five years ago, a nagging voice told her. She hasn't even helped decorate the house since middle school.

Patience spread the toast with just a kiss of Vermont creamery butter and placed it before her husband. I'm not going to let them ruin my holiday, she resolved. She thought about how much she loved the sight of the rental truck pulling up to the house. The stacks of folding chairs on the lawn and the pretty red slipcovers she always tied over their wooden frames. Okay, maybe she had gotten a little carried away last year. All right, she *had* sobbed uncontrollably for two hours after the last guests had gone. But Richard didn't understand how much work it was to pull off a successful event. For seventy-five guests. Year after year.

Finished with his breakfast, Richard cleared the table and headed upstairs to the master bathroom with Patience trotting behind.

"Christmas is my favorite time of year. The snow, the carols, the tree," she said. "What will I do if we don't have our Open House? Everyone expects it. My plum pudding . . ."

Richard revved up the electric toothbrush. "They'll go somewhere else."

Patience drifted into their adjoining bedroom, hung up her velour robe, and dressed in tan breeches and a dark blue sweater. She sat on the bed and pulled on her riding boots. Being short and sturdy, she loved the way they made her feel just a little bit taller.

"Beau's leg is still swollen. He slipped on some half-frozen manure last week," Patience called out. "Dr. Leavitt saw him yesterday."

"I should have been a vet." Richard crossed to the walk-in closet, eased into a serviceable navy blazer, and continued his march towards Beverly Hospital and Bibi Lunt's torn medial meniscus. "People pay up front, there are simple insurance forms, and the patients can't email."

Before heading out the front door and the promise of a nice quiet drive along a country road, Richard glanced fondly at his wife. She was pretty and spotless and he loved her curvy hips and the hint of summertime freckles in the cleft between her breasts.

"You are adorable eleven months a year," he said and kissed her. "And then there's Christmas. Have a nice day."

PATIENCE CAREFULLY STEERED HER POLISHED BLUE station wagon around Wenham Lake. The air smelled of chimney smoke and gathering clouds. The fields at Marini's Farm were empty and there was a hoary layer of frost on the ground. The sky was five shades of gray.

As she drove, Patience clung to the tidiness and order in her town. The graceful, sweeping lawns, the straight white fences and carefully crafted stone walls. The history of the place soothed her. I love Wenham, she said to herself, especially at Christmas with the candles glowing in the windows and the wreaths on the doors. Her tummy relaxed as she turned left into Apple Hill Stables.

A short hike up from the parking lot, Beau's barn was surrounded by maples and birches, stark and poised for the coming winter. Inside his stall, the planks were weathered but clean, and it smelled of hay and animal musk and faintly salty soil.

Brushing her gelding's silky chestnut coat made Patience content. With no ride today, she gave him an extralong, luxurious grooming and fed him a few carrots. Before she left, she rubbed herself against his warm, honeyed neck. She was definitely a barn girl. She preferred the scent of the stable on her jacket to any perfume.

Out in the parking lot she waved at Kirstin Weaver.

"Hi, Patience," said the ruddy-faced blonde. "I heard Beau hurt his leg."

"Leavitt says to take it easy for a couple of weeks, nothing too serious."

"Did I tell you? Michael and I are going to St. Bart's for Christmas."

"St. Bart's?" Patience couldn't imagine sitting on a beach at Christmastime. It seemed illogical.

"Yahoo! I'm free from that holiday dinner. And with the kids gone it seemed the right time to do something different. I will miss your party, though. It's always so great. Loved the whole white decor last year. You do make everything perfect. And I don't care what anybody says—the goose was fine."

Patience nodded robotically as Kirstin drove off. I've given that party for twenty years, she thought. Since we were first married. Why doesn't Richard understand?

Making her rounds—the market, the dry cleaners, the bank—she wondered what they'd do if they didn't have the Open House. Where would they go? Who would they see?

Everyone always comes over, she thought. She didn't even bother sending invitations anymore. They just all showed up. She couldn't remember anyone else offering to host an event on Christmas Eve for years.

She picked up a turkey sandwich at the Cape Ann Deli and sat on a bench by the lake, just watching the soft ripples in the water. A few errant geese were still lingering, having prolonged their flight south by a few days. They do the same thing every year, she thought, and it's good. It's tradition. It's . . . what we all do.

Later that afternoon, in her blue-tiled kitchen with the dark cherry cabinets, she patted her leg of lamb with chopped mint and parsley.

Tonight at dinner we'll talk about it again, she decided. If those two are adamant that we cancel our Open House, then they'd better have some other ideas.

She smiled, catlike.

Those two will never come up with anything.

The Open House will go on.

*   *   *

LIBBY SPENT HER AFTERNOON IN THE Hamilton High School
library, finishing her college applications under the watchful
eye of Ms. Kinley.

About a dozen or so seniors grouped and regrouped, like
synchronized swimmers, around various glowing laptops on
the reading tables. In hushed tones and occasional squeals,
they bemoaned the personal essay and exchanged tips for padding community service hours.

At the apex of this hive was Ms. Kinley, a brassy redhead
in stacked heels and a short skirt who held forth with candor
and nerves of steel. When Libby was sure that her essay con-
tained the perfect balance of both bravado and humility, she
approached the college adviser and dutifully handed over her
paperwork.

"Have you decided on your first choice?" Ms. Kinley
crossed her shapely legs and scanned the forms for errors.

"My first choice—or my parents'?" Libby writhed with
ennui.

Ms. Kinley peered over the top of her sleek black glasses.
"Sit down, Libby."

Heaving herself into the molded plastic chair, Libby laid
her cheek on the table. "My parents are ruining my life. They
are total East Coast snobs. They don't want me to go to California for college."

"And, because you are a smart girl, what will you do to
show them the error of their ways?" Ms. Kinley was impervi-
ous to teen drama. Which was why she was the only candidate
for college adviser, five years running.

Libby sat up. "I really, really, really want to go to Santa Cruz. I have to leave New England."

Ms. Kinley consulted a spreadsheet on her right. "You sent in your application to the UCs? That was due November thirtieth."

Libby nodded.

Ms. Kinley cut through the mire. "What made you decide on Santa Cruz?"

"Well, I had this amazing camp counselor, Lindsay, who went there. She said it was awesome."

"And?"

"And? Well, she said it was very diverse, and everyone was really into world culture and I just . . . know in my heart that's where I should be."

"Because?" Ms. Kinley said impatiently.

"Because . . . I love new places, and I want to see the world. Become . . . worldly."

"And their academic programs would suit you because . . ."

"Okay, okay." Libby twisted up her hair and then let it fall. "I don't know anything about their programs. But I have been to California and I just feel, somehow, connected . . . that I *have* to go there."

Ms. Kinley smoothed her yellow legal pad and wrote out some instructions:

1. Scour home page for degrees, departments, etc.
2. Find at least 2 courses that you want to study
3. Google Santa Cruz and research pertinent info. Cannot be anything to do with surfing, ratio of male students to female students, etc.

Glancing at the teen, she smiled briefly. "Start with this list and build a case. I understand you want to spread your wings. Just make it palatable to your parents."

Libby bounced in her seat. "My aunt and uncle live in Los Angeles."

"That's a three-hundred-mile start."

"Thanks, Ms. Kinley." Libby scooped up her paperwork and whipped out her cell phone.

"Oh, you're not done yet," the counselor tapped the table. "We've still got choices two, three, and four to finish up."

"I MISS MY BROTHER," RICHARD SAID as he carved the leg of lamb for dinner. "And Vanessa and the kids."

"Me too," Patience said absently. She was standing beside him at the kitchen counter scraping the roasted red potatoes from the pan into a white bowl with a navy pinstripe. "But soon they'll be here for Christmas."

"No, they won't." Richard picked up the platter and bussed it into the dining room, nicely furnished with a Chinese rug, pewter candlesticks, and botanical prints on the walls. Libby was hunched over her quilted place mat surrounded by textbooks and a messy pile of worksheets.

"Liberty," Patience set the potatoes down next to a fresh green salad. "Will you clear that away? It's time to eat."

"Who's not coming for Christmas?" said her daughter, shoving the homework toward the far end of the table.

"Your aunt and uncle." Richard poured himself some red wine. "I think we should go out there and see them."

Libby stifled the urge to shriek and remained calm. She knew better than to side with Dad this early in a battle against her mother.

Patience gathered up Libby's pile of books and set them neatly on a chair. "I don't understand," she said, taking her usual place across from her daughter. "Why aren't they coming?"

"Well, it's too expensive."

"Richard," Patience said pointedly. "Don't you think we should discuss this?"

"We are discussing this." He chose a rare piece of lamb and arranged it precisely against a half circle of crusty potatoes. Then he offered the platter to his daughter.

"Ugh, you know I don't eat anything with a face." Libby reached for the salad bowl.

"But it's awfully late to change our plans now." Appraising the meat, Patience chose a dark end cut. "And I'm sure the flights to L.A. are all booked up. Maybe we could go out at spring break."

"No." Richard sliced his lamb with a skill that was breathtaking. "It's the holidays and I want to be with family."

"I haven't seen my cousins in a year," said Libby carefully.

"What if we cover their tickets?" said Patience. "Like last time. It'll be our Christmas present."

Richard shook his head. "Vanessa feels they've accepted too much from us already."

"You spoke to Vanessa?" Patience was surprised. Her husband rarely made any social calls, or holiday plans on his own.

"She called this afternoon."

She called *you,* Patience bristled, when she knows *I'm the calendar keeper.*

"She said that JT hasn't worked much lately and that things were slow." Richard chewed thoughtfully. "I just don't understand why he stays in such an unpredictable industry. Seems like a waste of a good education."

"Well, he was always a bit of an adventurer," said Patience. "Without JT, we probably would never have mountain biked or kayaked to Plum Island," *which might have been a good thing*, she added silently. *It was hot and sticky and I was eaten alive by greenheads.*

"What does Uncle JT do again?" said Libby.

"He's a gaffer. He sets up the lights on film sets," said her father.

Film sets. That sounded interesting, Libby thought. Way more interesting than Wenham, Massachusetts.

Patience steered them back on course. "What does Vanessa think about our coming out?"

"We didn't get that far. My two o'clock arrived and I said I'd call her back."

"So she doesn't know we're coming?"

"I thought maybe you could speak with her tomorrow. Make the arrangements."

Libby slumped. Fuck! Now the ball was in her mother's court.

Patience smiled. "Of course, dear. I'll call her tomorrow."

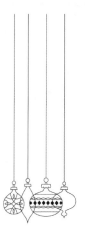

4

Vanessa was inching her car into a tight parking space when her cell phone rang. She set the brake, reached into her purse, and noted a Massachusetts number on caller ID.

Don't answer, a warning voice jabbed. "Hello?"

"Vanessa? It's Patience."

"Oh, hi, how are you?" Slumping against the seat, Vanessa stared darkly through the windshield at Neil's pink Spanish house.

"I'm fine. But Richard told me you don't want to come out for the holidays."

Why did she put it like that? Vanessa inhaled sharply. "Well, it's not that we don't *want* to come, it's just too expensive this year."

"I know, things have been hard. So how about this . . . How about we take care of the plane tickets? It would be our Christmas present to you."

Something in her sister-in-law's tone made Vanessa feel like she was standing in line at the soup kitchen. And how, in past vacations, when they'd accepted charity, Vanessa had felt obligated to defer to Patience and whatever she had planned. She recalled a long lunch at Richard's club last year and the stress of keeping two eight-year-olds occupied through three courses and wine. And there had been the Open House where she had to chat with half the population of Wenham while balancing some greasy meat on her lap (duck?). Then she remembered the year that Alex was sick with a fever from the minute they touched down at Logan airport. I'm really not up to a command performance this year, Vanessa thought wearily.

"We're family," Patience was saying. "You'll get the tickets next time."

She has no idea, Vanessa thought helplessly, that there's never a *next time* in the freelance life.

"I hope you don't mind—I went ahead and checked the airlines and we could book you into Boston the Monday before Christmas, returning on January second. Would that work?"

Glancing out the window, Vanessa flinched. There was Neil, sitting on his front stairs, watching her. Now that she was on display, she felt the stirrings of a backbone.

"No, that won't work, Patience," she said abruptly. "And unfortunately, you've caught me on the way to a meeting. But thank you so much for the offer . . . I really appreciate it. And we'll figure something out for the near future. Gotta go. Bye!"

She clicked off her cell and jumped out of the car. "Sorry, didn't mean to keep you waiting," she called out to Neil.

"I thought something was wrong. You were just sitting there," he said, contemplating her parking job, "halfway into the street."

"Oh, it was just family stuff . . . the holidays."

Neil shrugged as if he had no idea what she was talking about.

She followed him inside, through a bright white living room with a barrel ceiling and simple canvas furniture. It felt sort of like a spa or hotel lobby.

"This is beautiful," she said, wishing her own home were as clean and breezy.

"Gary's boyfriend found it. But it's a little twee," he said, as they climbed a circular tiled staircase. "I can't write in sterile environments. That's why I live in New York."

I wish my house were twee. Vanessa cringed at the thought of her grimy furniture and the patina of crushed snack food and sticky fruit drinks that kept her from any civilized, sophisticated sort of life.

Reaching the second floor, they continued down a polished hallway. "The bedrooms are too sunny," Neil was saying, "and there's a view of the hills."

God forbid, Vanessa thought, poking her head into one of the bedrooms. A spectacular view of the hills.

They ascended a second flight of stairs that led up to an attic rumpus room. Dark and windowless, it had mossy shag carpeting, crimson-flocked wallpaper, and a raised platform with a brass pole. A freestanding tiki bar and minifridge completed the frat house feel.

"This, I love," said Neil, flopping down into a sagging vinyl couch from the seventies. "Unspeakable things have happened up here."

I can't believe I'm leaving all that comfort and beauty downstairs to work in the attic! Vanessa frowned. Committing herself to the stained plaid La-Z-Boy, she wondered why she never got to work with any female playwrights.

"They brought me out for my edginess and now they want to kill it." Clearly, Neil carried the weight of injustice on his slender shoulders.

Ignoring this outburst, she opened her copy of *Safe Deposit*. His play was about brothers coping with the strange disappearance of their father, a mystery that's never been solved.

"The setup is great," she said, referring to her notes on the yellow pad. "At the end of act one, we suspect it was suicide."

Neil stretched his spindly legs onto the scratched chrome coffee table.

"But in act two it feels a little lost. I'm not exactly sure why Philip is keeping the letters a secret from Sam. I think the story turns on Philip's motives—"

"I want it ambiguous." Neil hooked his thumbs into his jeans' pockets. "The truth is ambiguous. Your truth, my truth.

Philip and Sam are both right . . . from their perspectives. I don't want to change that."

"Okay, but maybe you can help me understand their motives a little more. If there was a stronger case on both sides, it would make the story more powerful. More tragic, really."

Vanessa noticed that Neil had no script or notebook to work with. Oh I see, she frowned. He wants me to do all the heavy lifting.

"Let's take Philip. Does he want to shield his younger brother from the truth? Does he love Sam unconditionally? Or is he really power tripping, keeping the upper hand, wanting the money for himself?"

"What are you, my English teacher?"

"Sorry, didn't mean to sound pedantic," *you fucking jerk!* She tossed her hair angrily. "Look, maybe we're wasting our time, you obviously don't *need* any notes." Standing up, she tucked the play and pad under her arm. "Why don't I let you think about what you want to do. I have a couple of calls to make, so I'll be downstairs in one of those *sterile* rooms."

"But . . . I thought we were working together." Neil's tough demeanor devolved into the whine of a frustrated toddler.

"And I'd love to work with you. I think your play is really great. But you're the author and only you can decide if you want any help. I'm just here to facilitate your vision."

Neil ran his hands through his hair and looked away.

Crossing the room, Vanessa gave herself a mental high five.

It was a good thing she lived with Alex, Ethan, and JT. They had taught her a lot about dealing with boys.

PATIENCE WAS FURIOUS. HOW DARE THAT Vanessa hang up on her! And after all the things they'd done for them over the years . . . not to mention the money they'd loaned to JT when he wasn't working.

Did he ever pay it back? she wondered, whipping herself into a froth. I should ask Richard.

Powering up the computer in the kitchen nook, she consoled herself on the Internet, searching for the perfect bedroom slippers to give her husband for Christmas.

The phone rang. "Hello," she said, cradling the receiver under her left ear.

"Hello, dear, how are you?" A fractured, feathery voice creaked across the line.

"Oh, Mother, you caught me in the middle of something. How are you?"

"Just fine. But your father and I have decided to stay in Florida for the holidays. Your sister is coming down with the girls, and I hope you and the family will join us too."

Patience glanced out the bay window. There was a dusting of sugary snow on the elm tree on the far side of the lawn.

"I don't know, Mom."

"There won't be many more Christmases we can all spend together," said Martha. A steely note of guilt betrayed the little-girl voice.

"But you always come here!"

"It's getting harder for your father to make the trip . . . you know he doesn't drive the highways anymore. And that puts too much pressure on me. No, we're going to stay here and order a nice turkey from the market. And it comes with all the side dishes, too. They even have vegetarian for Libby. It's called tofurkey. Isn't that cute?"

Patience bit her thumbnail. Supermarket Christmas! Fake turkey!

Martha Polk waited for her daughter's answer. When none was forthcoming, she said sternly, "The important thing, Patience Elizabeth, is *not* what we're eating but that we're all together on Christmas."

"Of course," said Patience meekly. Then, while her mother described the latest classes at her senior center (calligraphy, no-salt cooking) and her daily routine (seven A.M. power walk through the Golden Palms complex with her Body Buddies, fixing lunch for Jim, mocktails at four with the Pattersons), Patience scrolled through her bookmarks and clicked on United Airlines. After a detailed account of Martha and Jim Polk's breakfast preferences (Raisin Bran and sliced bananas), health concerns (her father's glaucoma and her mother's IBS), and platitudes for living (Old Age Ain't for Sissies), Patience had confirmed three reservations from Boston Logan to Los Angeles International Airport on December 22.

"So," said Martha, breathless from her monologue, "why don't you talk to Richard about coming here for Christmas?"

"I will," said Patience, hurrying through the kitchen to the entry hall. On the table next to the front door was her purse. Opening her wallet she slipped out a credit card. "But I don't think he'll go to Florida," she said, returning to the computer.

"He was saying something about visiting his brother in Los Angeles this year."

"Los Angeles!" Martha said aghast. "It doesn't seem very Christmassy out there, does it?"

About as Christmassy as Florida, thought Patience. "Give Dad a kiss for me," she said, typing her Visa number onto the billing form. "I've got to run."

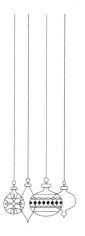

5

Ethan and Alex were standing at the kitchen counter making school lunches. Assessing their choices, Vanessa nodded with approval at Ethan's sandwich: He had overlapped slices of turkey and Swiss cheese on whole wheat bread and was carefully spreading the mayo from corner to corner.

Alex was padding his lunch box with powdery red chips, cream-filled chocolate cookies, and a plastic cylinder of string cheese. "Where's the real food?" She gave him a nudge on his shoulder.

He pointed at the cheese. "Protein." Then, finished, he

bounced into the chair next to his dad and grabbed the box of frosted wheat flakes.

"Are you driving them?" Vanessa glanced over at JT. He was buried in the sports section of the paper and sipping orange juice.

"Can't. I'm meeting Dave at the Bagel Bin. He just bid on a commercial job in Chicago."

"Really?" said Vanessa, skillfully hiding her surprise. She wondered who would be starting a shoot this late in the year.

"I think it's a Valentine's Day spot. Apparently someone fell out."

"I hope you get it, sweetheart." She kissed him and turned to the twins.

"Boys. Car. Ten." Back in her bedroom, she grabbed Neil's play from her bedside table and dropped it into her canvas tote. Passing the mirror on her closet door, she caught a glimpse of herself. Oh, no! she shuddered. I've got on that stale mom uniform—jeans, cotton sweater, clogs. Jerking off the sweater, she excavated a stretchy black tank from the bottom of her sock drawer, and topped it off with her bottle-green velvet jacket. Sweeping up her blond hair she swirled it high with four glittering bobby pins. Finally, she replaced the sturdy leather clogs with pointy black suede boots.

There, she said, satisfied. Now I look like the theater.

"VANESSA!" MS. GARCIA ALWAYS SEEMED TO catch her when she was in a hurry. "Alex and Ethan haven't turned in their food for the homeless shelter." As she watched her third graders stash their sweatshirts and lunch boxes in red cubbies, Ms. Garcia heaved the sigh of the saintly. Who wasn't concerned with the homeless at this time of year?

"Oh," said Vanessa. "What do you need?"

"Did you read the handout?" The aide sighed again, with a little less forgiveness.

"Ahhh." Vanessa searched through her tote. "I don't think so . . ."

"There." Ms. Garcia spied the bright orange flyer in Vanessa's bag and pointed at the lengthy list.

"We especially need sweet potatoes."

"Sure, no problem." Vanessa whisked out the door before any more requests could be made.

She was sliding into the driver's seat when Karen Maguire-Weinstock, third-grade room parent, waddled up to the car. Eight months pregnant, Karen was an elegant earth mother in mulberry leggings and a flowing silk jacket. Her hair was beautiful and very blond and she'd had the verve to attach a diamond-encrusted pin to her lapel. On closer inspection, Vanessa noticed it was a miniature portrait of Karen's daughter, Indigo.

"Hey, Vanessa, I'm collecting for the teachers' holiday gifts."

"Oh, sure," Vanessa reached for her bag. "How much?"

"We're suggesting forty per child. And, well, you do have two boys in the class."

"Eighty dollars!" Vanessa gagged slightly.

Karen smoothed her stomach. "We're giving Ms. Garcia a gift certificate to a day spa and Ms. Archer a handmade quilt from the Folk Museum. I mean, they work so hard all year for our kids, they deserve something special."

Vanessa prayed silently for JT to get that job and opened her wallet.

"I've only got fifteen on me. Can I give you the rest tomorrow?"

Karen snatched the money and directed her belly towards a schlubby dad in cargo shorts. "But please don't forget," she called back tensely. "My salon is insane this time of year—everyone wants extensions for the holidays—and there's a baby coming."

Vanessa nodded and slammed the car door. She'd have to make sure that JT drove the boys to school for the rest of the week. She couldn't afford to run into Karen again.

Then, jamming out of the parking zone before anyone else could shake her down, she headed towards Hollywood to Neil's house.

WHEN SHE REACHED HIS PLACE, HE wasn't outside waiting on the stairs. And she had to ring the bell three times.

Finally Neil opened the door, wearing gray pajama bottoms and a T-shirt. "Sorry," he squinted at the morning sunshine. "I was up all night working."

Following him into the kitchen, she watched him open cupboards and search through the fridge for five minutes.

"Fuck," he said. "No coffee."

Vanessa said nothing. She was making a list of all the

things she could have been accomplishing while he was stumbling around the house and wasting her time. The Christmas shopping alone was crushing her. She hadn't bought a thing.

"Could we get something to eat?" His bloodshot eyes beseeched her.

"Uh, sure."

"I'll print out the new pages," he said, disappearing to the rooms upstairs. She stood at the kitchen window and stared, trancelike, at the 101 freeway and the lines of cars inching south towards downtown.

Twenty minutes later they were seated on rickety metal chairs with steaming bowls of café au lait at the Farmers Market—a warren of food stalls and fruit vendors happily embraced by natives and tourists alike. Slowly and absently, Neil munched a scrambled egg burrito and read the *New York Times* while Vanessa pored over his new scenes.

She smoothed the pages on the table. "I'm glad you stayed up all night."

He glanced at her briefly, then turned back to the Arts section.

Really! Vanessa thought with exasperation. What is the point in meeting with this guy? We'd work just as well through email. But suddenly, she became aware of a way to make this morning worth her drive. "Let's see how it goes at rehearsal tonight before you make any more changes," she said lightly. "And while you finish your breakfast, do you mind if I run next door to the mall and grab a couple of things?"

"What kind of things?" Neil glanced at her over the paper. His expression revealed nothing. Jeez, Vanessa thought, he's so hard to read he should have been a detective.

"Just, oh, Christmas things. You stay here, read the paper, and I'll be back in a half hour."

Neil drained his coffee cup. "I'll go with you."

"Uh," Vanessa felt slightly desperate. "It's just . . . just a short thing."

"I'm done. I'd like to wander around. Check out the locals."

"But I have to go to American Girl Place!" Vanessa covered up her embarrassment with a tilted chin.

"Yeah?" Neil said. "I happen to have known an American girl or two."

Clearly, he's confusing dolls with girls, she thought. "Okay, fine." She led them through the food stands out to the main street. Then she stopped and wagged her index finger. "But when we step inside, don't say I didn't warn you."

The charm of the venerable Farmers Market vanished as soon as they crossed the invisible line separating the 1930s fruit vendors from their glitzy neighbor to the east—an upscale mall with a Main Street, USA theme.

Gazing up at the blazing two-story emporium, Vanessa left the unhurried pace of café life for a dizzying tween Gomorrah.

Riding the escalator, they passed giggling girls in wedgie sandals with butterfly clips; shrieking girls in pink cowboy boots and white patent pumps. In blue corduroy newsboy caps. In ruffled dirndl skirts.

Their overdressed, overanxious mothers were being dragged along like chum in the wake of a powerful fishing trawler.

Jumping off the moving stairs, Vanessa grabbed Neil's forearm. "We're looking for the Gold Rush Nicki Starter Kit and the Belle Époque Bakery Case to send to my god-daughters."

"I thought we were looking for dolls."

"I'll just, I'll just . . . meet you back here," Vanessa stammered.

But after fifteen minutes of wandering lost through galleries of doll displays, doll furniture, doll beauty products, a doll theater, and a doll tea room, Vanessa realized she had made a tactical error.

Circling back to the second-floor landing, she approached a long line snaking towards the Information Desk.

Waiting impatiently behind several mothers with assorted children and strollers, Vanessa wished she could wrap up two slutty twenty-dollar Barbies and call it a day. But her old high school friend Amy would expect thoughtful, meaningful gifts free of cultural and sexual bias to empower her girls. In principle, Vanessa totally agreed with that idea. But in practicality, a hundred-dollar doll with a fictional backstory in the Gold Rush broke the bank. Why not tie on an apron, cradle a corn-cob, and pretend you were Laura and Mary Ingalls? Vanessa mused. Like Thea and I did.

For the umpteenth time she counted the number of people ahead of her. Now it was down to a Hassidic mom in a head scarf, two Korean mothers with babies, and best friend moms in skinny jeans and hair extensions discussing a makeover party for their thirteen-year-old girls.

Wondering what happened to Neil, she gazed across the foyer and spied him over at the register, chatting up three salesgirls.

And one appeared to be holding a cellophane package with the word "Nicki" splayed across the top.

"Do you mind holding my place in line?" She smiled at the Best Friend Moms who were now scrutinizing each other's French-tip manicures.

As she approached Neil and his groupies, she could clearly see a gunslinging doll, in pink chaps and cowboy boots, in the arms of the fresh-faced clerk. Then a fourth employee arrived with a white cabinet filled with plastic cakes and pastries.

"Hey." Neil grinned at Vanessa. "Is this what you were looking for?"

VANESSA DROVE THEM BACK TO NEIL'S house, pulled up to the curb, and left the car running.

"So I'll see you tonight at the theater," she said as he climbed out the passenger door. "Do you need a ride?" she added quickly.

"No, Ashley said she'd pick me up."

"Oh, okay." The image of blond, pretty Ashley, the actress who played the sister, made Vanessa feel slightly jealous. She shook it off. "And thanks for helping me Christmas shop. I have to send those gifts out today."

"It was fun," he said. "A nice break from writing."

Nodding slightly, he loped up the front walk. He had a faraway swing to his stride.

Neil definitely lives in another world, Vanessa mused, as she watched him fumble with his keys and disappear inside. But I guess it's not such a bad place to visit.

As long as I'm not gone too long.

Glancing at her watch, she calculated three hours to ship the dolls, reread the play, and get to the market before dinner.

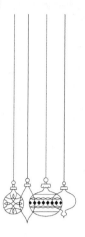

6

"V, I got the job!" JT scooped Vanessa up in a bear hug and proceeded to dance her around the kitchen.

"Honey, that's wonderful!"

"Dave's my guy. He always comes through with something."

Vanessa kissed him. Life was never better than right before JT started a new job.

He gazed into her eyes and toyed with her fingers. "There is one little thing . . ."

"What?"

"I leave Monday and we don't finish shooting until December twenty-third."

"Oh, all right," she said sweetly, thinking about a nice tidy sum in their bank account.

He winced. "Yeah, but . . . Richard and Patience and Libby are coming here for Christmas."

"What?" Vanessa snatched her hand back. "I thought we decided to stay home *alone*."

"I know, but Patience called today and she was kinda upset that we wouldn't all be together."

"She called *you?*" *When she knows I make the plans?*

"Well, I was home. Anyway, it's Libby's last Christmas before college and, well, I guess they miss us."

They miss you, she thought.

"Do you want me to tell them not to come?"

"Yeah, and make me the bad guy." Vanessa was steamed. She just didn't feel like entertaining anyone this year.

"It's only one week. And you know Richard, he'll want to watch sports on TV and find a golf game."

"Patience always wins," Vanessa shrugged. "If we don't go there, she comes here."

"V, Patience likes us."

"Likes *you*." Vanessa's eyes blurred. With JT gone, she'd have to take care of the twins—not to mention Neil—alone.

And deal with all the Christmas stuff herself.

Turning her back on him, she reached into the shopping bags and started to unpack the groceries.

"Look," he said, "I know the timing's bad, but I'll help when I get home. We'll make the dinner together. It'll be fun."

He pulled out the battered aluminum stockpot from the

lower cabinet and set it on the stove. Glancing over at his wife he looked morose. "Okay, I'm going to call them and cancel."

Vanessa felt ashamed. She knew how much JT loved his brother. "Don't. I'll . . . rally," she said, extracting pasta and canned tomatoes from her reusable bag. "There's just a lot to do now with them coming."

"Why don't we order a turkey? From the market."

"We'll figure it out," she said. "Look, I'm really happy you got the job. It's going to be great."

JT flashed his boyish smile. She poked him in the ribs. "What about your plans to go to chef's school?"

"That'll have to wait till the New Year," he said confidently. "Dave says this company is hot and has a ton of jobs coming up. If I get in with the producers, maybe there's more work in the future." He grabbed the box of spaghetti from the counter and waved her out of the kitchen. "I'm making dinner tonight. You go relax before work."

Vanessa dropped her shoulders. She couldn't stay mad at her husband. He was so sweet. Not a mean bone in his body. In her heart she knew that he really did want to help, no matter how unhelpful he was.

"You know," she said, running her forefinger down his supple spine. "There's nothing hotter than a man with a paycheck." With a thrust of her hip, she sashayed out the door and down the hall to the bedroom.

On Monday morning, Vanessa gave JT a quick kiss in the loading zone of Terminal 6.

"You are the best wife ever," he said, rolling his suitcase down the wide sidewalk to curbside check-in. "I'm going to miss you so much."

"Me you too," said Vanessa. Glancing back at the car, she checked the immediate area for LAX parking cops.

"V, don't forget to record the Holiday Sing."

"How do I charge the camera again?"

"Just ask Alex to help you. He knows how to work every-thing." JT handed his eticket to the skycap.

The blaring recorded announcement commanding her to unload and load only—no parking!—was making her ner-vous. With a quick wave good-bye, she leaped into the car and headed east towards Pasadena.

Breezing down the 105, she suddenly remembered that she was on the hook for three dozen cinnamon rolls.

Fuck, she thought. Fuck, fuck, fuck. I guess I'll buy those rolls in a can and bake them. She had a sudden image of Ms. Garcia looking horrified at her pop-and-bake rolls. "Yes, Ms. Garcia, they're not homemade," she imagined herself confiding to the bossy aide. "Because our cultural tradition is *store bought*."

ONCE A MONTH VANESSA AND THEA visited their mother at The Oaks, a small retirement community in the foothills of the San Gabriel mountains.

A circle of putty-colored apartment buildings surrounded a courtyard dotted with azaleas, oleander, and roses—no oaks in sight. As Vanessa strolled towards her mother's place in the back, she smiled and waved at a few Active Seniors who were sitting outside, enjoying the mild winter day.

She knocked at apartment 112. "Carol?"

Glancing through the window screen, she spied her mother seated at a small dining table, painting a hollow wooden bowl. An elderly gentleman in a bright bowling shirt sat beside her. Turning the doorknob, Vanessa let herself in.

"Oh, Vanessa." Carol smiled at her daughter. A very trim sixty-seven with ash-blond hair, she was dressed in billowy linen pants and a matching tunic. "Look at my decoupage. I think it's pretty good."

Vanessa kissed her mother and smiled at the balding, tanned, much older boyfriend. "Hello, Mr. Cassell."

Frank rose, extending a sun-spotted arm and a gentle hand. "Hello, young lady," he said clearly. "Your mother's a regular Georgia O'Keeffe."

Vanessa admired the bowl, appliquéd with cutouts of orange poppies. She assumed it would be wrapped and under her tree this Christmas.

"So, Carol, I have a favor to ask you. Do you think you could babysit tomorrow night? JT's taken a job out of town and—"

"Tomorrow?" Frank shook his head portentously.

Vanessa frowned at Frank and then continued. "As I was saying, I've got a job at the theater and my regular sitter is busy and I know the boys would love to see you."

"Well, now, let me check," her mother said, patting Frank on the shoulder. She stepped daintily over to a large calendar pinned to the fridge and scrolled across the week with her fingertip.

"We're singing Christmas carols at the Bel Rivage convalescent home in Sierra Madre," Frank recited.

"Oh, yes." Carol touched her hand to her chest. "I would love to help you Vanessa, but Bel Rivage has the housebound seniors."

"The inactives," said Frank.

"They look forward to our visit all year."

"The ones that are still alive," Frank added loudly.

Vanessa took a breath. "Then what about Wednesday? I'll be working that night too."

"That's the Holiday Social at the rec center," Frank said. "We're lighting the tree and the menorah."

Vanessa resisted a strong urge to shout out, *Who asked you, asshole?* "But, Carol"—she stepped between her mother and Frank, hoping to block him out of this conversation—"wouldn't you rather see your grandsons?"

"Your mother's the chair," Frank said, craning his neck around Vanessa to address his girlfriend. "How would it look if the chair wasn't at her own party?"

"I'm afraid he's right." Carol shrugged the shrug of the dutiful patron and then, gliding over to the aluminum sink, began to wash the sticky decoupage glue off her hands.

Trailing her mother into the galley-sized kitchen, Vanessa thought, Don't grandchildren trump senior center activities? "But you are coming to the Holiday Sing on Friday?" she said, tartly.

"Frank?" Carol twisted around to consult her social secretary. "Is it on the calendar?"

"It's up there," he nodded. "Right next to Saturday, when we're moving in together."

"What?" Vanessa's eyes widened.

The front door banged open and Thea hustled inside. Catching the horror on her sister's face, she muttered, "I just heard about this yesterday on the phone."

"Don't you girls spoil anything." Carol waggled a bright coral fingernail. Rosewood bracelets slid up and down her bony wrists and an enormous amethyst rode her right ring finger.

"When you're our age, if it moves, marry it." Frank wiggled his brows and Carol giggled coquettishly. Vanessa felt queasy.

"Why don't you two lovebirds find us a table in the courtyard," said Thea, "while we make lunch."

"All right," Frank agreed, leading his lady love out the door.

"Frank is kinda creepy," Vanessa said, squeezing past Thea into the kitchen.

"Yeah, he even talks for her—like a ventriloquist." Thea noticed the orange poppy bowl on the table. "I wonder if this will be joining the Kleenex box that she covered with buttons last year."

"Well, you're the one who encouraged her to explore her 'inner artist.'"

"I said 'artist' not 'inner tchotchke maker.'"

Opening the fridge, Vanessa stared dismally at their lunch choices. An assortment of deli meats and cartons of potato and macaroni salad that reminded her of funerals and dreary school meetings.

Deli was, however, Carol's favorite cuisine. Because it cooked itself and had a long shelf life.

Pushing aside the cans of Ensure, a bottle of white wine, and a few foil-wrapped Laughing Cow cheeses, Vanessa reached for the Best Foods. Then she opened a bag of rye bread and counted out eight slices. "Did you tell her maybe to wait a month or two before committing again?"

Thea snorted and yanked down four plastic plates from the cupboard. "Of course. And I wasn't tactful. I reminded her that Lou had helped himself to three thousand dollars in her savings account. I swear, these retirement joints are magnets for incontinent grifters."

Vanessa carefully aligned the meat over the bread. "Maybe she should go to some twelve-step program for love addicts."

"I think we've reached the point where one of us should cosign on her bank accounts," said Thea, filling up four glasses of water. "And we should go over her bills every month."

"Not me!" cried Vanessa. "I mean, not this month. I've got the kids and that job and JT's relatives are coming."

"Fine, I'll take December," said Thea, bussing the glasses out the door. "But this is your last my-family-life-trumps-your-single-life excuse till next year."

Outside, under a bright marigold umbrella, Frank was tucking into his macaroni. "Your mother is as pretty as a picture," he said, his mouth foamy from the excessive mayo in the salad.

Carol beamed and touched his hand. "We're like two crazy kids."

The sisters exchanged a quick glance.

"Frank is coming with me on Christmas." Carol turned to Vanessa. "I hope you don't mind."

"Uh, no, that's fine," said Vanessa stiffly. "Frank, what about your kids? Don't you normally see them at the holidays?"

"My daughter's in Manhattan," Frank said through a mouthful. "And I won't fly anymore. I'm not taking off my shoes. A man my age shouldn't have to take off his shoes."

"It isn't dignified," Carol clucked. "And what senior citizen is going to hijack a plane?"

"And my son's family goes skiing. But I don't like the cold so much. Besides"—he winked at Carol—"I wouldn't want to leave my Christmas Carol."

"And I wouldn't want to leave you." Carol looked sweetly at her daughters. "Do you remember how you girls used to let me sleep in on Christmas morning?"

Vanessa dropped her spoon. "That's not exactly how I remember it."

Carol forged on with her memory. "They were such dears. I was a hardworking mother and sleeping in was a luxury."

"I seem to recall more crying than sleeping," Thea said peevishly.

"And threats if we woke you," Vanessa added.

"My daughters are so dramatic." Carol waved them away like annoying gnats.

"But you know what I do remember?" said Thea. "I remember how Grandpa was always drunk and Dad never got you anything you liked."

WHEN LUNCH WAS FINISHED, FRANK BID good-bye to the three Claytons and shuffled across the courtyard to apartment 103.

"He has to nap," Carol informed her daughters. She was standing at the sink, washing the dishes by hand and placing them carefully in a powder-blue rack. At the counter, Vanessa and Thea swiveled, like small children, on tall bamboo bar stools.

"God, I'd like a nap," said Vanessa, suddenly feeling the late night hours of play rehearsal tugging at her eyelids.

"Vanessa, I want you to talk to your sister," said Carol. "She says Frank and I can't get married. She doesn't understand how important it is to make a commitment and say your vows."

"How important could they be," Thea mumbled, "if you've said them three times?"

"Frank isn't going to wait around," Carol continued, her brown eyes flashing. "If he doesn't marry me, he'll marry someone else. He likes having a wife."

"Do you even hear yourself?" The tendons in Thea's neck bulged. "What happened to the liberated woman? The mother who wanted to be called Carol and said she was 'equal partners' with her children?"

"That was the seventies," Carol shrugged. "Times have changed."

"If he really loves you," Vanessa broke in, "he'll understand. Because financially, you can't get married again."

"All those years I worked at the community center"— Carol rolled her shoulders defiantly—"to have a good retirement package."

"And Lou spent it on his construction business and Bob spent it at the track," said Thea. "Thank God for social security."

Carol thrust a dish into the drying rack. "But it's different with Frank."

"Wait awhile," said Vanessa, thinking she sounded like a high school counselor. "If it's true love it will . . . it will . . ."

"Stand the test of the other available widows," Thea finished.

Carol sprinkled cleanser into the sink and began to scrub. "I can't wait that long. Frank and I want to be intimate before then."

Thea jumped off her stool. "You don't need to be married to have sex. They're completely different."

"Not to a man like Frank." Carol gave the basin a final rinse. "If he thinks I'm easy, he'll lose interest."

"Okay, what decade are we in now?" said Thea.

"Don't you two have places to go?" Carol peeled off her pink rubber gloves with a resounding snap. "You must have more important things than sticking your nose in my love life."

But your love life always has a way of becoming our business, Vanessa thought unhappily. She sighed, wishing her father hadn't died, of a heart attack, at forty-five. Then at least she'd have the hope of another, possibly more involved, grandparent.

Walking out to their cars, the sisters wrapped their arms around each other for support.

"Okay, it's absolutely certain—she's not our mother," said Thea.

"Maybe that's the real reason she wanted us to call her Carol."

"That generation is so hypocritical," said Thea. "They wanted to be unconventional and then they moved to the suburbs."

"I guess she was liberated in work but not with men," said Vanessa.

"You know that was the theme for my series of Anne Arky."

"I loved those paintings," said Vanessa. "Especially the one of Anne in an apron on the kitchen table with the razor blades in her vagina."

"Yeah," Thea beamed. "That's in the permanent collection of the American Petroleum Foundation now."

"Why don't you paint anymore?"

"I don't know. I guess I wanted to create 'important installations'"—she laughed ruefully—"like everyone else."

They stood on the grass parkway and lingered. Thea noticed that all the streetlights on the block were twined with red and green tinsel. The afternoon sunlight bounced off the shiny streamers and cast streaks across Vanessa's car.

"It was funny how Carol remembered Christmas so differently," Thea said. "Something occurs every January, some kind of amnesia sets in and we erase everything that happened in December."

"Yeah," said Vanessa, noticing her windshield was impossibly dirty. "Sort of like ice skating. You think you liked it as a kid and then when you do it as an adult you remember it was horrible! Your hands get cold, your ankles cave in, and it hurts like hell when you fall on that ice."

"That disconnect between the memory and the reality fascinates me." Thea abruptly snapped her fingers. "I should record people talking about Christmas past . . . and Christmas present."

"What people?" Vanessa said warily. When they were teens, Thea had often employed her as the muse, posing Vanessa with fruit or cigarettes or fake blood.

"How about your family? I could come over Friday night."

"Can't you just do the holidays like the rest of us?" Vanessa said in exasperation. "Why does it have to be an art project?"

"It doesn't have to be . . . but I've been pretty dry lately—like two years lately—and this has inspired me. Why does that bother you?"

"It doesn't," Vanessa lied. "But can't we do some holiday activity just for fun?"

"Fine," Thea said tentatively. "Like what?"

Vanessa rocked back and forth on the uneven ground. There was the shopping, the relatives, the house, and the kids. Wasn't there something fun?

"Tomorrow night I'm working with Neil, but you could take the boys around the neighborhood to see the Christmas lights—that would be fun. Or on Thursday night, we're baking cinnamon rolls, that could be fun. And then Friday, there's the Holiday Sing at the school."

A shadow grazed Thea's eyes. Obviously she and Vanessa had very different definitions of *fun*. What was the path of least commitment? "Tell me the third thing again?"

"The Holiday Sing!" Vanessa opened the car door and tossed her purse onto the passenger seat.

"I'll do that one."

"Okay, but don't be late. Parking's a bitch on that morning."

"I'll be early," Thea grumbled. "But I think you should really work on your idea of fun. For next year."

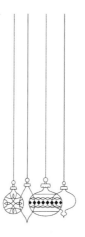

7

Patience was spending her afternoon wrapping presents at the dining room table.

She had sewn up twenty pale pink satin bags and was filling them with her own potpourri blend, a mixture of rose petals, orange peel, cloves, and bay leaves.

A portable CD player sat behind her on the sturdy buffet, and as she scooped up the flowers and spices, she hummed along with the *Bing Crosby Holiday Collection*. Periodically, she would glance out the bank of paned-glass windows and admire the twinkle lights she'd woven in the branches of the elm tree and the bright red bows she'd fixed to the boxwoods that flanked the front walk.

She tied up the pouches with gold braided cord and a handwritten tag that trumpeted *Peace on Earth* in her feminine, flowing script. Then she nestled the bags into forest-green boxes crowned with plastic holly berries.

For her nephews she had purchased two adventure books—one of pirates and one of knights—and two cashmere sweaters that she'd found in that children's shop in Boston. The blue for Alex and the brown for Ethan—to match their eyes. Then there was the chemistry set, the Lego kit of the Taj Mahal, and warm, flannel pajamas in surfing and skateboarding motifs. It was fun to shop for boys, she smiled, not like shopping for Libby.

What to do about her daughter? Libby had insisted her mother get her gift cards *(No more stuff I'll have to return!)* but gift cards chafed against every fiber of her being. She regarded them as uncaring and impersonal; tacky and unimaginative. One should take the time to pick out a thoughtful gift for one's daughter, one's friends, Patience believed strongly. What does a gift card really say? *I couldn't be bothered.*

However . . . However! She was also weary of returning all those expensive skirts and sweater sets, smart wool coats, and pearl earrings she'd carefully selected at stores like Jordan Marsh and Talbots and that Libby wouldn't dream of wearing.

So this year, in a calculated risk, she'd called up Libby's best friend, Sarah Metzger, and graciously invited the teen to accompany her on a trip to the Topsfield Mall. Standing helplessly in a store full of what she considered cheap, ill-fitting athletic wear, Patience watched Sarah gleefully fill her arms with fleece shorts, cropped sweaters, T-shirts with slogans such as FUTURE BABY MAMA, ripped jeans, and a tiger-striped bra.

"This stuff is awesome!" Sarah gushed.

Patience smiled grimly, suddenly astonished at what she was doing. Why on earth was she placing her faith in Sarah? Sarah, who was currently sporting sweatpants with a monkey-face appliqué on each buttock, a cropped hoodie, and sheep-skin bedroom slippers.

"Are you sure?" Patience felt dizzy.

"Mrs. P-C, I'm telling you, Libby's going to die, just die. I mean, I would be so stoked if my mom got me half of this! Not that I'm bagging on my mom, but with three sisters, it's like hand-me-down city."

Patience regarded this confession with admiration and a tinge of jealousy. Four girls! Imagine. It was straight out of *Little Women*.

"Sarah," she said, lugging the booty and her credit card over to an enormous slate counter littered with carousels of earrings, sunglasses, and cell phone jewelry. "As a thank-you from me, please pick out something nice for yourself."

With a sharp squeal, Sarah rushed to the rack of jeweled T-shirts.

As Patience waited on line, she imagined what it might be like to have four girls. In her fantasy, she was holding forth on a horsehair sofa, beside a crackling fire, her scrubbed, fresh-faced daughters assembled around her, knitting, drawing, and singing old English hymns. Each beguiling girl embodied a virtue such as kindness, faith, and generosity, those cherished ideals that seemed to fuel the myths of the holiday season.

Thinking of Louisa May Alcott, Patience cringed. Only last Saturday she'd made the unfortunate decision of forcing Libby to join her on a shopping expedition to Concord, the historic town just west of Wenham, which boasted, among many important sites, the Alcott family home.

"Can't you just go without me?" Libby had wailed. "I'm supposed to go to Sarah's for a sleepover!"

"You can spend two hours picking out a gift for your father," Patience said sharply. Then, feeling desperate, she ratcheted up the guilt. "Your father, who works so hard for us—for you! How is it that you cannot find a few hours on a Saturday to honor him?"

"I honor him all the time!"

Patience folded her arms across her navy blue blazer.

"Fine!" Libby's eyes narrowed. "But why do we have to drive to Concord? Why can't we just go to the mall?"

"I'm not setting foot in a mall on a Saturday. And you used to love Concord! There's that . . . men's shop with the ties and the shirts your father likes. And the tea room where we always have lunch. We could even take a walk down to Walden Pond."

Libby's eyes rolled so fiercely Patience was sure they'd pop out of her sockets.

"You said two hours," her daughter hissed. "And I have to be back by five."

SATURDAY MORNING WAS CRISP AND BRIGHT and Concord's main thoroughfare bustled with shoppers, strollers, and deliverymen. Fragrant wreaths of bayberry and pine hung on shop doors that tinkled merrily when opened and closed. The window displays brimmed with hand-knit sweaters and hats, tins of peppermint bark and tea, old-fashioned toy trains and dollhouses. Here, in this perfectly preserved Yankee village, there was an infectious feeling of holiday cheer in everyone.

Everyone except Liberty Polk-Channing.

She was slumped in her seat at the Sleepy Hollow Tea Room and spent the next forty minutes text-messaging *SOS! Mthr fing nsne thnks Im fing nfnt* to her wildly sympathetic friends.

Ignored by her daughter, Patience turned her attention to the adjacent table of two young mothers with their three little girls. The children had ordered trifle pudding and when the dazzling parfait glasses arrived, they swooned and gasped and scooped up the cream and raspberry filling with utter delight.

Every choice I've made as a mother has been wrong, Patience thought sorrowfully. I was foolish to insist on her coming, but I thought once we were here . . .

She paid the check.

At Hawthorne Haberdashery, Libby quickly snatched up a crimson tie for her father and, once it was wrapped and paid for, broke her vow of silence. "Can we go now?"

Driving out of town, past Louisa May Alcott's Orchard House and the ghostly fields of revolutionary war battles, Patience impulsively swerved right and headed over to Walden Pond.

"What are you doing?" Libby glanced up from her phone in alarm.

"It's such a beautiful day," said her mother, "let's just go look at the pond."

"Oh. My. God." Libby's contempt broke new ground.

They parked and hiked down the damp dirt path to the water's edge. Although it was too early in the winter for skating, Patience saw herself out on the pond in her red wool coat with ten-year-old Libby, gliding hand in hand across the heavy gray ice. Were they laughing back then? Were they joyful?

The daughter she'd longed for, the daughter she'd dressed and driven, kissed and cuddled, was now a sullen virago with a turned-down mouth and a permanent air of withering disdain.

Tears sprang into her eyes and she hid her face in her plaid muffler. "Let's go," she said huskily and, with a burning throat, marched back up the path to the parking lot with Libby trailing behind, chatting to one of her posse sisters on her cell phone.

A TEAR ROLLED DOWN PATIENCE'S CHEEK and fell upon the sachet she was wrapping for her sister, Hope.

She gently dabbed the watermark on the satin fabric and caressed the gift tag. *Peace on Earth*. With a tilt of her chin, she placed it in the pile of presents to mail to Florida. Then she made her way down to the cellar to rustle up a cardboard box for shipping.

It's all right, she reasoned, I'm sure Libby's just going through a phase. Things will be better when it's Christmas.

*   *   *

As LUCK WOULD HAVE IT, ON the morning Vanessa had designated as her Buy Every Christmas Present on My List Day, there was a holiday bazaar in the gym at the Jacaranda Elementary School.

Once Ethan and Alex and four cans of sweet potatoes for the homeless were delivered to Ms. Garcia, Vanessa was free to roam the banquet tables brimming with handmade crafts. At the Chic Sheep booth, she fingered a soft pashmina shawl embroidered with roses.

"This would be perfect for my sister-in-law," she remarked to a zaftig mom in the adjacent folding chair. "How much is it?"

"It's seventy-five." Chic Sheep Mom struggled to her feet and adjusted the oval mirror on her table. "But remember, twenty percent goes to the school!"

"I'll take it," said Vanessa. While the vendor ran her charge card and wrapped the pashmina in tissue, Vanessa pounced on a moss-green silk scarf. Tying it around her neck she turned this way and that before the mirror. It makes me look very sophisticated, she thought, pouting her lips like a chain-smoking European actress. She read the price tag and, reluctantly, returned it to the pile. Okay, she bargained, if there's money left over at the end of the day, I'm buying this for myself.

Her trip around the gym was fruitful. She snagged a charm bracelet for Libby and a pin fashioned from a brass key that was perfect for Thea.

This is great, she thought happily. I've contributed over thirty dollars to the school so now I don't have to feel guilty about that teacher's gift. I should really look at the scarf again.

She returned to the Sheep Chic and wound the scarf around her neck. Adjusting the mirror, she leaned back to get a better look and stepped on someone's toes.

"Owww!" Karen Maguire-Weinstock winced painfully. She had a baby strapped to her chest and Vanessa could see a thatch of dark hair peeking out from the leopard-print carrier seat.

"Oh, Karen, I'm so sorry! Ahh, you had your baby."

The infant mewed softly and Karen kissed its tiny head.

"He's beautiful," Vanessa said. "What's his name?"

"Chicahua." Karen beamed. "It's Aztec. It means 'strong.'"

Vanessa surged on, hoping Karen might have forgotten about . . . "Are you back at work already?"

"Yeah, back at work, back here at school. And of course we've got Hanukkah and Christmas!" Karen shook her head in amazement. "My parents are coming from Phoenix next week to see the baby. Indigo is so excited. She's practicing a Chopin étude to perform for all the relatives. She's just amazing."

Feeling like the top candidate for Slacker Mom, Vanessa reached into her purse. "I owe you . . ."

"Sixty-five dollars," said Karen firmly.

Handing over the money, Vanessa bid farewell to that chic green scarf. "Sorry it took so long," she said.

"Hmmm," said Karen. "See you tomorrow at the Holiday Sing."

"Yeah," said Vanessa, reminding herself for the tenth time to buy cinnamon rolls on her way home tonight.

*　　*　　*

A HALF HOUR LATER, IN THE center atrium of the Sherman Oaks Mall, Vanessa planted herself before the Store Directory and focused on Gifts. Alex, Ethan, JT, her mom, Richard. All in all, not too bad. If she got lucky, she'd be finished by school pickup.

I should get something for Frank too, she thought resentfully, adding him to the list. If this was truly the season of miracles, Carol and Frank would break up *before* Christmas and I wouldn't have to buy him anything.

In Macy's men's department, she found red plaid pajamas that were perfect for JT. This was too easy, she thought, scanning the floor for the cashier. The management had cleverly convened the checkout line past a row of tables laden with last-minute gift items. As she waited for deliverance, Vanessa was forced to consider polo shirts and bedroom slippers, travel gear and ties, and wallets and key chains.

As a hip-hop version of "Little Drummer Boy" blared overhead, a V-necked sweater in azure blue caught her eye. Should I get it for Richard? Ummm, she waffled, Patience usually buys his clothes. Better play it safe, she decided. Scotch or something golf-related.

But the sweater was really nice, and a great buy with her Special One-Day-Only store coupon. Neil flashed through her mind. God, should I get *him* something? She stroked the soft merino wool and then, as the line surged forward, she reached out and grabbed it.

For the next few minutes, while she witnessed one return, two byzantine sales involving credit vouchers and cash back, and then a coupon/exchange transaction that required the use of a key and a floor manager, she debated the sweater.

Stretching the sleeve along her arm, she pondered Neil's size. Would this fit? And was it the sort of style he would wear? Edging ever closer towards a clerk with pulsating candy cane earrings, Vanessa grew doubtful. Why was she even considering this? Last night, they'd finished their work together and wished each other happy holidays. If she bought the sweater now, she'd have to make another trip over to his house to deliver it.

Neil's not really a department store sort of person anyway, she concluded. Clothes and accessories just arrived in his closet in whimsical ways. Girlfriends probably buy him shirts and he finds cool scarves and shoes from street vendors like all New Yorkers do. In a vivid montage, she saw him roaming the city, on romantic, writerly walks, browsing in shop windows and carrying home classic jackets in tweed and suede.

"Next!" bellowed the cashier.

As if it were a hot potato, Vanessa volleyed the sweater back onto the table with relief.

Her own PJ purchase was relatively painless—just the one coupon—and so with a box, tissue, and ribbon tucked in her bag, she fled the department store and hustled down the concourse.

Now, on to the twins. Just past an enormous plywood gingerbread house and a gaggle of children and parents waiting for Santa, loomed the glass and chrome electronics store. The loudest and most annoying video games (Soccer Star, Destroy Like a Ninja) sailed into her cart along with the attendant plugs and pods that enabled kids to play them on everything from phones to foreheads.

At Kitchen Arts, she bought JT a flame-red stew pot for simmering and roasting. Standing glassy-eyed in the checkout line, she wondered if her husband was really serious about cooking school and, if he was, how much it would cost in both tuition and lost income. Moving up, she handed her credit card to the collegiate clerk. "Could you wrap it for me?"

"It's a twenty-minute wait," said Collegiate Clerk in the flat drone of the holiday sales force.

"That's okay, I'll come back," said Vanessa, whisking out into the crowded aisles of the mall to hunt down something for her mother.

Carol didn't read, didn't eat chocolate, and didn't want anyone to pick out her clothes. That left the scented soaps and lotions that everyone bought their older female relatives at the holidays. Ducking into a pink shop, Vanessa was knocked back by a gale-force wind of lavender and ylang-ylang. Rubbing her nose, she scooped up a boxed set of bath salts conveniently wrapped in silver and gold cellophane.

The Cash Only line was empty and she raced to the counter. Opening her wallet, Vanessa remembered that she had given the last of her money to Karen Maguire-Weinstock.

She gazed beseechingly at the clerk. "Oh, I thought I had cash. I'm sorry. Just this once, would you take the charge card?"

The tall woman behind Vanessa snarled, "I thought this was Cash Only!"

So, slinking over to the credit card line, Vanessa waited. All around her women were waiting. Waiting with body butter and revitalizing creams, milk pearls and sloughing scrubs. Waiting for gift wrap, waiting for help. Not for the first time, Vanessa imagined what it would be like if men did all the

Christmas shopping. Perhaps no one would get bath gel and scented soaps for Christmas.

And would anyone miss that?

She had just finished signing the sales slip when her phone began to sing. Grabbing her bags, she scrambled outside and leaned against the center railing.

"Hello?" Way down on Level One, Santa was arriving at the gingerbread house in a "green" sleigh powered by vegetable oil.

"It's Neil."

She thought guiltily of the sweater. "Oh, hi." Scooping up her parcels, she surfed the wave back to Kitchen Arts to pick up the stew pot.

"Can you meet me tonight?" he said. "I've rewritten the fishing scene."

Jeez, Vanessa sagged. Why can't this guy just drink some eggnog and buy useless gifts like the rest of us? "Tonight's not good," she said, counting the number of shopping bags in her hands. Where were those bath salts? Had she left them behind?

"I've changed my mind about Philip revealing the letters . . . you know I haven't been sure about it. So I reworked that scene."

Writers! Vanessa scowled. Just when you've convinced them to stop picking at their play they panic! "Can you email it?" she said. "I'll read it this weekend." Galloping back to the scented store, she cut to the front of the line and hurled herself onto the counter.

"Get back!" The startled clerk was poised to call security.

"But I was just here and I forgot my bath salts!"

The clerk eyed her warily.

"The prewrapped ones!" Vanessa pointed at the display then realized this wasn't her clerk.

"Look, I'm really stuck," Neil was saying. "I need you to look at it now. It won't take long."

"Uh, hold on." Vanessa scanned the cashiers until she spied her clerk, who was embroiled in some kind of heated exchange on the phone. Their eyes met briefly and then, with a swift dip of her silver-bangled wrist, her clerk pulled up a shopping bag and slid it across the counter.

"Thank you," mouthed Vanessa, grabbing her package and dashing out the door. She adjusted the phone to her ear. "Uh, Neil . . ."

The ambient noise was deafening and she really had no idea what he was saying. "Look, the play is great, it's solid, it's really, really tight," she shouted into the din, threading the throngs and dashing back to Kitchen Arts.

Whipping past the copper pots and cookie-decorating kits, she paused for his response but there was none.

"Neil?"

His silence set her babbling. "Look, I'm sure it's fine, but if you want, you could come to my house tonight and I'll take a quick look at it. But my kids will be there so we'll probably have . . . some interruptions so I hope that's okay."

"It's okay," he said, in that steadfast tone that was impossible to read. "I understand family life."

"You do?" She paused, hoping he'd elaborate. When he didn't, she surrendered.

"Come anytime after five." And, surging forward to claim her wrapped stew pot, she shouted out her address and then dropped her phone in one of her many glittering shopping bags.

She squeezed into the elevator with eight other patrons, rode down to Parking Level 2, and hiked a quarter mile to her car.

Oh, God, she shuddered, as she lifted up the hatchback and tossed her packages inside. Now that he's coming over, do I have to buy him a gift?

"So how did you become a dramaturge?" Neil asked. He had arrived at Vanessa's house, *sans* gift, and was sipping a pale ale at the kitchen counter and watching her unfurl Bake-It-Fresh rolls from a foil tube.

"Here," she said, handing him his own can of dough and a baking sheet, "help me out." This tactic covered the shock of his asking her a personal question. She'd almost been convinced that he didn't know her last name.

"I wrote a couple of bad plays in college—Cal State Northridge," she said, poking the spongy disks with her fingers. "It was clear I wasn't very good. But I loved the theater and worked a ton of shows. I was company manager at Back Alley, which sort of morphed into resident dramaturge—you know how small the budget is, everyone has to wear ten hats. And then after the twins were born I couldn't work full-time anymore so I started freelancing."

Shoving the cookie sheet into the oven, she sat down at the counter, facing him.

"Why?" she said.

"Why what?"

"Why do you ask?"

He shrugged, neatly lining up his cinnamon rolls. "Isn't this a cookie klatsch?"

She giggled and playfully swiped his arm. So he did have a sense of humor.

Ethan and Alex charged through the back door, dumping their skateboards on the linoleum.

"Boys. Halt."

They continued on to the fridge, hunting down some OJ.

Vanessa barricaded the refrigerator door with her body and swiveled their heads in Neil's direction.

"Alex and Ethan Channing, say hello to Neil Cohen."

"Hi" "Hey" they shouted. Vanessa retrieved the juice and handed the carton to Alex.

"Cookie dough!" Ethan reached out for a sample on Neil's baking sheet. Neil caught the boy's grubby fist before it made contact and then hoisted the pan high above his head, twirling it like a pizza.

The boys were momentarily derailed.

"No cinnamon buns till the potluck," Vanessa said.

"Will you do that again?" said Alex.

"Only if I can skate first," said Neil. "This your board?" He picked up the Alva Old School and headed out to the driveway with the twins on his heel.

Once the rolls were baked and they all devoured a pepperoni pizza, Neil and the twins played video games in the living room while Vanessa stacked the dishwasher.

She decided to stash the cinnamon rolls away from hungry nine-year-olds. She covered them with foil and set them on the washing machine in the service porch next to the kitchen. Then she wiped down the counters, and when they were marginally clean, joined the TV campfire. I wonder if Neil wants kids, she thought idly, watching him slay an animated purple dragon. He's probably the right age, around thirty-five, only a couple of years younger than me.

Why do I care? she scolded herself. He's charmed my brood and kept them occupied long enough to defrost and bake and I'm grateful for that.

"Ethan, Alex, last game," she said. "Then it's time to say good night."

After twenty minutes of "just one more time," she shooed the boys to the bathroom, watched them brush their teeth, and then tucked them into bed.

When she returned to the living room, Neil was sitting in JT's stuffed armchair, rereading his manuscript. Glancing up, he handed her the new scene.

"Here," he said.

She read the changes, a slight frown playing on her lips. When she finished, she dropped the pages on the battered coffee table and crossed her long legs.

"It was better before. Stop picking at it."

He waited a beat, then said, "I know, you're right."

"Let it go," she said softly. "Just . . . take a break, enjoy the holidays. When you come back in January, you'll have a fresh eye."

"Well, hey, thanks for reading it. I just . . . really needed a second opinion." He stood up and made a move towards the door.

"Oh, it was fun. You're great with the boys."

There was an awkward pause and she rushed to fill it.

"What are you doing for the holidays? Going back to New York?"

"No," he said, evasively.

"Oh, that's right. You grew up here. So I guess you'll be with your family?"

"I'm not sure what I'm doing."

"Oh." You should invite him over, a voice chirped inside her. It's the holidays! People shouldn't be alone.

"Why don't you come here on Christmas Eve?" she said, wishing instantly that she hadn't asked.

Neil looked slightly embarrassed. "But your family, your kids . . ." His voice trailed off.

"Yes," she said. "Unfortunately, my family and kids will be here. But they're not too terrible. And it seems you all like skateboarding."

Neil smiled. Vanessa was suddenly struck by how handsome he was.

"Sure," he said. "That'd be great. Just tell me what time."

She opened the front door and they lingered a moment and locked eyes.

His eyes! Pale and glassy, Neil's eyes were magical and seductive and for a second, a minute, she was pulled under. It was hard to think, hard to look away.

Women fall in love with those eyes, she thought, and she longed to float in that pacific realm to see what might happen.

"Mom!" A wail ricocheted down the hall. "I can't sleep!" Alex cried.

"What?" Vanessa snapped back. *I'm married.* She grasped the doorknob. "I'd better go see what he wants."

"Yeah, so, thanks for dinner," said Neil.

"Sure." She hesitated. "See you on Christmas Eve."

THE TWINS' ROOM WAS TINY, JUST like every other room in her twelve-hundred-square-foot house. Bunk beds, bookcases, and bureaus were stacked against the walls and the floor was littered with Legos, army men, and clothes. Vanessa stepped gingerly around the medieval fort and ducked down on Alex's lower bunk.

"What?" she said.

"I can't sleep," Alex moaned. "Please, please let me open my Christmas presents."

"What presents?" Vanessa feigned surprise. She thought she had done well to hide the loot in the garden shed behind the house.

"In the shed," Alex said.

"*He* found them!" Ethan shouted down from the upper bunk, careful to distance himself from the naughty brother.

"Alex, you'll just have to wait," Vanessa said sleepily. She was dead tired. And the thought of the next few days made her feel chilly. Or was she getting sick? She'd better find some echinacea and start downing it.

She kissed Alex's smooth cheek and tasted the slightly salty tears. She rubbed his arm. "It's hard for everyone to wait," she yawned. "Now get some sleep. We have the Holiday Sing tomorrow."

"I hate carols," Alex said defiantly. "They're stupid. I'm not singing. I'm just going to pretend."

"You can't do that," his mother said. "When you're part of a chorus, everyone needs to sing." Her voice sounded weak and unconvincing. Was that the extent of her argument? She racked her brain for something else.

"Okay, do whatever you want," she said lightly, and crossed to the door. "Just know I'll be really disappointed if you don't sing. And think about your dad! He can't be here and when he watches the tape he'll be so sad if he sees you just pretending."

"Okay, Mom." A sob caught in Alex's throat. "I promise I'll sing."

The guilt trip, Vanessa thought, quietly closing the bedroom door. I guess this is the time of year to employ it.

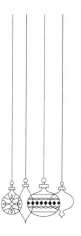

8

Thea hadn't been to AA in a couple of years—she'd lost both the desire for alcohol as well as the desire to talk about it. But she decided her old meeting at the Episcopal church on Venice Boulevard might be a good place to launch her new art project. So, in the hallway outside the church's community room, she set up two folding chairs and a tripod with her digital recorder. Then she sat down and waited for possible subjects.

She stared at a purple banner on the wall that she supposed marked some kind of ecclesiastical season—but which one? These AA meetings were the closest she'd ever been to religion. Periodically she heard the thunder of clapping, the roar of laughter, and the sobs of regret drift through the heavy mahogany doors. Tonight's meeting was packed, which didn't surprise her. The holiday season was a minefield of emotions and vivid childhood memories. Who didn't want a drink?

One smoker after another trickled out of the meeting, eager to join the after party on the steps outside the door. As recovering addicts fled past her, Thea smiled and lobbed a gentle pitch.

"Hi, there, I'm Thea Clayton, ten years sober," she'd say. "I'm creating an oral history project about the holidays. If you have a moment to record a memory about Christmas or Hanukkah or, well, any holiday you celebrate, I'd love to hear it."

It'd been an hour, and so far no takers.

But Thea was patient—art required her to dig in for the long run. This will lead me somewhere, she reminded herself, somewhere I've never been. And that wandering in the dark appealed to Thea. It was what thrilled and terrified her about art. She never knew what she was going to find, if she was brave enough to fly without a net. But as the minutes ticked by, she felt her determination, her drive to find something here, waning.

She'd never gone this long without a show. For years, she'd had work, she'd had press, she'd had admirers. But lately, it felt like her charmed well of inspiration was drying up. And what would she do if it never came back?

She tamped that horrible fantasy down firmly. That was exactly why she was here. She was exploring a new medium—and, with her solid background in painting, she'd bring something fresh, something new, to a filmed project. She just didn't know what it was yet. And that was okay, because, because . . . Oh fuck, maybe she couldn't pull it off. Maybe the well was dry after all.

At nine o'clock, the enormous doors flew open and about fifty twelve-steppers poured out, chatting and hugging, fumbling for cigarettes and gum.

"The Spoken Word Project," Thea said, tinkering with her pitch. "Take a moment to record your Christmas memories. Your story is powerful."

But the dry drunks ignored her and pushed past into the night, in search of strong coffee and more talk about working the program.

Until one man doubled back.

He was about thirty, with a shock of carrot orange hair and low-rider jeans. Thea didn't remember pitching to him, but he extended his hand, the three rubber bracelets on his wrist imploring him to *Live Strong* and *Never Forget* and *Be Here Now*.

"Dylan," he said in a nasal Jersey accent.

"Thea Clayton."

"Hi, Thea. So, you making movies?"

"Digital journals. I'm archiving stories about Christmas."

"Got a lot?"

"No, actually, I'm waiting for someone to break the ice."

"Cool! I love being first." He bobbed his head.

"I'll need you to sign this release, which says I can include your story as part of my installation and that I'm not going to pay you." She handed him a form, which he nervously folded and refolded.

"If you'd like, Dylan, you can make the tape, and then decide if you want to sign the form. No questions asked."

"All right," he said, relaxing into the folding chair facing her. "Let's do it. So what, I just talk about Christmas?"

"Yeah," Thea said, straddling the camera. "Any holiday memory, it doesn't matter if it's good or bad, the best or the worst. I'm not interested in quantifying anything. I'm just curious about people's . . . perceptions about Christmas. Their hopes and fears, their relationship to it."

Dylan wet his lips nervously. "Wow! I never thought I had a relationship with it!"

You gotta bring this way down, girl, Thea thought. "Where'd you grow up?" she said, switching gears.

"In Jersey, an hour from the city."

"What did your dad do?"

"He sold insurance."

"Did you celebrate Christmas?"

"Sure, man, what kid doesn't?" Dylan thought a moment. "We'd always go to Macy's and visit Santa."

"Do you remember asking for anything special?"

"Fuck, I hated Santa. Sitting on some dude's lap, fuck."

Thea felt nervous—this wasn't as easy as she'd hoped. "Did you ever make a Christmas list?"

Dylan suddenly brightened. "One year I asked for a mountain bike—they were totally new back then. Man, that thing was rad. The one with the fat tires. Fuck!" He smiled at the memory and shook his head.

"But I didn't get it. My dad got me a basketball hoop instead."

Thea let that sink in for a moment. Then she spoke gently. "Do you think your dad knew you were disappointed?"

"Nah, I doubt it. But you know, my old man was like that. He'd give me something he wanted. Like jigsaw puzzles, baseballs . . . he never bought me anything I was interested in. Like I loved those Hardy Boy mysteries, but he gave me a book on World War Two, you know?"

Thea nodded. Her chest felt tight. Dylan's face was suddenly so childlike.

"I think Christmas is sort of a letdown," he said quietly. "After a while I figured I was never going to get what I wanted, so I just didn't care. And that's how my dad was . . . you know he never really saw me for myself, he wanted me to be like him."

Dylan's eyes watered and he turned his head away from the camera. "I can't believe I thought of that," he said. "I haven't thought of that in a long time."

His cell buzzed and he checked the ID. "Hey, I gotta go. I'm meeting people."

"Thanks," said Thea. "I appreciate your candor."

"Sure." Then, signing the release form he said, "Am I going to be on HBO or anything?"

NEIL PREFERRED WORKING AT NIGHT. THE low hum of the dark city was soothing. The drone of passing cars on the freeway. The occasional howl of coyotes. The neighbors who played Mahler's mournful adagio at two A.M.

He liked being alone; he had always been a loner. But there was something about this night, leaving Vanessa's house—he didn't feel like going home. He strolled down Laurel Canyon to Ventura Boulevard and caught a cab there on the corner in front of the newsstand.

About two miles west, the taxi dropped him off at La Sombrero, a squat Mission-style stucco restaurant with a neon sign of a cactus wearing a large Mexican hat. He crossed the parking lot and used the pay phone against the wall to call Ashley, the actress in his show. They'd had a couple of late-night drinks after rehearsals and he thought she was hot.

Inside, the restaurant was packed with a jovial mixture of families, divorced blonds of both sexes, and tattooed barflies. He took a seat in a corner booth and ordered a beer. Red chili pepper lights were hanging above the bar and a Mylar banner declaring *¡FELIZ NAVIDAD!* was strung across the bottles of tequila and vodka. The whole room was crimson and green, from the rolling Naugahyde chairs to the flickering webbed candles. Somehow he didn't think the color scheme was just for the holidays.

He watched the bartender coat the rim of a glass with salt and wondered why he'd told Vanessa that he had no plans for the holidays. In fact, on Christmas day he'd be seeing his dad and stepmom and his two stepbrothers at their house in Calabasas. They'd eat turkey (a nod to Cheryl) and latkes (a nod to Dad), and if the afternoon was sunny, Dad would suggest they hike up Old Topanga Road and take in the view of the valley. Dad would ask him about the Jets, a team and a sport he didn't follow, Cheryl would ask him if he'd met someone special, and it'd be boring. But most holidays had been boring since his mom died, of breast cancer, five years ago.

Ashley arrived wearing knee-high black leather boots, a flirty rayon skirt, and a distressed corduroy jacket. Over margaritas and guacamole, they rehashed the play (Ashley was amazing and the writing was brilliant), and then she drove them back over the hill to his house, where they had pretty good sex aided slightly by the lingering buzz of tequila and the general despair of the season.

In the morning when they woke up, Neil suggested the Farmers Market for breakfast.

Ashley frowned, her pouty mouth kissed clean of last night's frosted mocha lipstick. "I don't really like it there . . . and isn't it kinda cold to sit outside? I know an organic place over on Third with awesome cinnamon rolls."

Cinnamon rolls, thought Neil. Seems to be a theme.

The inside tables at Pure Food were full so one of the jaundiced waiters seated them out on the sidewalk, under a heat lamp, and handed them menus.

"Can I get you anything to start?" he recited dolefully.

Neil glanced at Ashley. "Two cinnamon rolls?"

The waiter fondled his silver ear cuff. "Do you mean our yeast-free rice-flour muffin?"

"Does it have cinnamon topping?" said Ashley.

"Cinnamon, oats, and raisin juice," said the waiter.

"Yeah, that's it." Ashley smiled and rubbed Neil's thigh.

How could anything like that be considered a cinnamon roll? wondered Neil. He thought about Vanessa's kitchen counter and for a moment he wished he were there.

"Oh, are you okay with this?" Ashley quivered nervously. "I mean, it's really important for me not to eat gluten but I don't judge anyone else."

Her eyes were soft and pretty. "It's fine," he grinned, returning the thigh rub. Then, glancing over at the waiter, he cocked his eyebrows. "But you do have real coffee?"

"Sustainable organic, single origin, or micro-lot?"

LIBBY LOVED TO SPEND THE NIGHT at Sarah's house. Not because it was over on the dodgy end of town, or that it was built in 1771 by a distant relative of John Adams. But because the peeling clapboard, with doll-sized eighteenth-century rooms, was superclose to the convenience mart and was stuffed with the detritus of four sisters: clothes, shoes, makeup, and sparkles.

Sitting side by side on the bathroom counter, Libby and Sarah were sharing a joint and blowing the smoke out the open window into the frosty Wenham night.

They huddled under a pink crocheted blanket for warmth, and periodically Sarah would spritz Lysol into the air to mask any lingering scent of pot.

"So," said Libby on the exhale, "what did my mom get me for Christmas?"

"Those awesome shorts you wanted and a cropped sweater and low-rider jeans."

"Sarah!" There was a fierce pounding on the door and Libby flinched.

"Hurry up! I need to pee," wailed a frantic little sister.

"Ten minutes," Sarah called out.

Libby's eyes grew wide. "Are we going to get busted?"

"No." Sarah frowned. "My mom won't be back for at least an hour. She's at yoga."

Libby relaxed and peered through the window screen. She could see Sarah's neighbors watching TV in their living room. "Wow! I can see the people next door," she said, fascinated. "The only thing outside my house is trees."

"Sometimes, when the dad's alone he turns on porn," said Sarah.

"Eeewww." The girls were grossed out.

There was another rap at the door.

Tamping out the stub, Sarah stashed the joint in an Altoids box and heaved her shoulders dramatically. "You are so lucky that you don't have sisters!"

"But my mother's such a cop."

"Your mother's nice, she bought me this." Sarah pulled up her gray sweatshirt and modeled the jeweled T-shirt.

"She's nice to people who don't know her," said Libby, suddenly feeling dizzy. Lying down on the cold tile floor, she closed her eyes. "She never leaves me alone, she treats me like a baby, she doesn't want me to go to school in California."

"She gave you a car," said Sarah, who was now plucking her eyebrows with the aid of a magnifying mirror.

"It's my dad's old one."

"Well, I have three sisters and no one's getting a car so shut up you bitch."

"Okay, sorry," Libby said. "It's just . . . I wish she'd get a life. All she has is her stupid committees and her stupid horse."

"I'd love to have a horse. You are totally spoiled."

Libby shifted uncomfortably. "Fine, you live in my house and I'll stay here."

"Deal." Sarah tweezed a wiry hair and winced. "Ouch! Why do we do this?"

"If I go to Santa Cruz I probably won't have to shave," Libby giggled.

"If I didn't shave I'd look like Chewbacca," Sarah said.

The fervent knocking resumed. "I am so going to tell Mom you're smoking weed!"

Dropping the tweezers with a clatter, Sarah threw open the door and faced down her younger, blonder sister. "Go ahead. And I'll tell her about that fake B in Spanish and then we'll be even."

"I'm never telling you anything ever again!" Younger Sister's cheeks flamed. "And you can't take my silver flats."

"You're such a mofo," Sarah said indignantly. "I hate you."

"I hate you." Younger Sister spun on her heel and retreated.

Withdrawing into their opium den, Sarah slammed the door.

"So what should we do now, Libs? Walk to the Super-Go?"

On Friday morning, Ethan stood solemnly next to his parents' bed and poked at the sleeping carcass of his mother.

"Mom?"

Vanessa declined to join the living. "Just ten more minutes."

She clung to her soft, cushiony world. With the late rehearsals at the theater, she hadn't banked more than five hours of sleep a night, and she couldn't bear to leave this wonderful, blissful state.

"Mom!" Alex's voice penetrated nirvana. "Is this what we wear to the Holiday Sing?" He waved a plastic package containing a folded dress shirt and clip-on tie in front of her face.

"Uh-huh." She glanced groggily at the clock.

It was eight fifteen. They were supposed to leave in fifteen minutes. "Oh, no! We're late! Hurry, hurry, go put on your navy blue pants."

Vanessa threw back the duvet and felt a worrisome tickle in her throat. Oh, my God! She squelched a growing panic. I cannot get sick!

Hitting the bathroom, she knocked back a dropperful of echinacea and goldenseal. She applied a slash of rouge and a zip of lipstick before clanging down the hallway to assess the boys. Thankfully, they were wearing the right pants, but they were also engaged in a game of Frisbee, zinging the shirt packages around the room.

"Stop!" Intercepting the pass, she freed the shirts from their cardboard sleeves and tossed each boy his formal wear.

"Clip the tie at the collar," she said, miming the motion.

"I'm not wearing that," said Alex, reaching for a grimy blue T-shirt on the floor. Vanessa stepped firmly on the sleeve.

"This is not a choice," she said sternly and returned to her bedroom to finish dressing.

Unused to dress clothes, the twins buttoned their shirts haphazardly and then began to snap each other with the ties until the doorbell rang.

"Get the door." Vanessa's voice reverberated down the hallway. "It's Grandma."

Carol stepped inside, wearing a loose, gray satin jacket. "You're both so handsome," she said, beaming at the boys. "Look what I brought." She pulled two enormous candy canes from her purse.

"Wow!"

"Can we eat them now?"

"Of course." Carol smiled beatifically. "It's Christmas."

The boys ripped off the wrappers and jammed the peppery, sweet suckers in their mouths.

What am I forgetting? Vanessa wondered, dashing into the living room. She glanced at her mother. "Don't you look nice." Then she spied the candy. "Carol!"

"Oops." Her mother shrugged guiltily.

Vanessa snatched the canes and stowed them on top of the home entertainment unit. "You know my rule about sugar in the morning."

"We'll get them down later," Carol whispered to the boys.

"I heard that," said Vanessa, wrinkling her forehead. Now, what was she looking for? Oh, yes!

"Carol," she said, gently pushing the twins towards their grandmother, "please help the boys with their ties, and then everyone, get in the car. I have to find the camera."

Darting into the bedroom, she ransacked JT's side of the closet. Nothing. Was it in the dining room?

In the top drawer of the china hutch, she struck gold.

Tucking the small, sleek camera into her purse, she hurried out to the car, checked that everyone was buckled in, and drove off towards school, wishing she had time for a triple latte.

Just as they reached the parking lot, Vanessa remembered her traditional potluck dish back at home on top of the washing machine.

"Fuck!" she said, causing the twins to scream and Carol to frown. "Fuck! Fuck! Fuck! I forgot the cinnamon rolls."

"Mom said 'fuck'!" Ethan kicked the seat with glee.

"Four times!" Alex clapped his brother with a high five.

The last available parking space was within her reach and she snagged it. Sighing, she turned around and faced the twins. "Boys, please help your grandmother out of the car."

While the twins jostled Carol to the pavement, Vanessa bowed her head on the steering wheel and weighed her options:

1. Stay here, enjoy the Holiday Sing, and let go of the rolls.
2. Leave, go home, pick up the rolls, forfeit her parking space, drive around looking for another one, and risk missing the entire show.

With a deep, cleansing breath she chose number 1. It really doesn't matter in the scheme of things, she decided. No one will notice and there'll be a ton of other food.

The auditorium was ablaze in stage lights and humming with the nervous shouts of children and their equally vibrating parents. The twins ran off to join their class and Carol and Vanessa found choice spots in the tenth row on the aisle.

"Is Thea coming?" said Carol, looking around at the chatting relatives.

"Who knows?" said Vanessa, perusing the Xeroxed program. "She's the worst aunt ever."

"She just doesn't understand," murmured Carol. "She's a working girl."

"And I'm not?" Vanessa squirmed. Carol always defended her oldest daughter, when, in Vanessa's opinion, Thea didn't have a leg to stand on. "Look at this place," Vanessa hissed. "Chock-full of aunts and uncles. I'm sure most of them have real jobs and yet they're here!"

Carol patted Vanessa's knee. "Don't be unhappy on such a nice day."

Vanessa felt her blood churning. This was her mother's answer for everything: smile and repeat bland bromides. Ignore that people treat you like crap and do nothing.

But she held her tongue and instead marked two Xs against both Carol and Thea on her internal scorecard.

Her phone rang. She checked the ID: It was JT. Sticking a finger in her right ear and the phone on her left, she scrunched down and answered. "Hi, honey!"

"Hello, sweetheart! Are the boys there? I want to wish them good luck."

"They're with the class, getting ready to sing," she said, feeling a wave of sadness. "I wish you were here."

"I wish I was too. I miss you and I can't wait to come home. It's ten degrees in Chicago and everyone's got some kind of flu. We've been shooting the same penguins for three days and the crew is over it. Everyone wants to be home with their families."

Vanessa said nothing. The sound of JT so far away made her lonely.

"Did you remember to charge the camera?" he said.

Tears filled her eyes. "Oh, no, I forgot. And I forgot the cinnamon rolls, too," a little sob burped in her chest.

"V, it doesn't matter. Just call me later and tell me all about it. Maybe they can sing when I get back."

"I'm lost here without you," she said, feeling desperate, like a woman awaiting her husband back from the front. Or a job in the Midwest.

"Lost? But you're my capable girl."

Capable of what? she thought. Capable of . . .

"I'll be home in four days," JT was saying merrily. "Then you can take a break and I'll wait on you hand and foot."

Vanessa wiped her eyes and smiled. Of course, that wouldn't happen, but still, his sweetness made her feel lighter.

The lamps dimmed and parents in the aisles scurried to their seats. "I've got to go," she whispered. "It's starting."

"Love you."

"Love you."

She set her phone to All Off and sat back in her chair. The couple directly in front of her were cuddled up, watching their digital camera screen. Everyone's husband is here, she thought wistfully. Except mine.

The program began. The fourth grade aced the dreidel song in Russian and the sixth grade upped the ante with a Gregorian chant. Vanessa couldn't help wondering if the parents of these linguistic children had been required to coach them in Russian and Latin on top of the rest of their homework. She uttered a silent prayer that when her twins were in fourth grade, American pop songs were in vogue again.

A guitar soloist in kente cloth plucked a tune commemorating Kwanzaa, and then the kindergartners, always the real stars of any school show, belted out "All I Want for Christmas Is My Two Front Teeth." A swarm of paparazzi kindergarten parents stormed the proscenium while the seated parents smiled, remembering their own first Holiday Sing.

Finally, it was time for the third grade. They tackled Joni Mitchell's "River," a song that, even in the summertime in ninety-degree heat, made Vanessa swoon with melancholy. She gazed at the children performing this wrenching poem about the bleakness of winter and her chest tightened.

What is it about this time of year that makes us want to flee down a frozen river? All around her, mothers were reaching into their purses for Kleenex and she joined them as they dabbed at their eyes and mouthed the tender lyrics.

She stared mistily at her boys. Ethan's hair was neatly combed and he was intently following the beat of his teacher's arm signals. Down the row to the left was Alex, who appeared to be pinned there, against his will, but was singing nonetheless.

My dear sweet Alex who hates to sing is singing! She clutched her tissue and quivered under a bank of emotion. My children are so precious, my husband is so precious. It's all over too soon. I cannot waste a moment!

When the last note faded away she applauded mightily and turned to Carol. "Wasn't that beautiful?"

Carol nodded. "I loved that they sang in different languages. I think the boys should take Chinese. That's where the world's headed, you know."

Afterward, when she and her mother had made their way up the aisle and out into soft December sunshine, Thea appeared, dressed up in a black leather blazer and jeans, holding her digital camera.

"Wow," she said, "they were amazing."

"You came." Vanessa felt her heart fill with gratitude. "You came! I . . . didn't think you would."

"I was way back, but I got great shots of Alex and Ethan. Although I don't think Alex was really singing. But he's a good lip syncher."

Vanessa smiled. She felt buoyed by her sister's presence. "We're going back to the classroom for the potluck," she said, touching Thea's arm. "All the relatives are invited."

"This should be part of my installation." Thea was glued to the camera screen, rewinding and replaying her shots.

Vanessa's happiness teetered. "So the only reason you came was to scam footage for your project?"

"Of course not," said Thea, hitting the Pause button. "But there's something in their singing, something about the children that's universal. Maybe this is what we long for. Not the presents and the crap—but the humanity that ties us all together."

"Oh," said Vanessa meekly. She knew it was true, what Thea said was true. But she didn't want it to be universal. She didn't want it in an installation. She wanted it to be their own home movie.

"Vanessa." Thea searched her sister's face. "If I used the footage, would it really upset you? There's more to all of this than I can process. I mean, you're in it, all of you." She extended her arms to include the circles of beaming, proud parents chatting around them. "I'm watching on the outside. And maybe as a voyeur, I can see things in a fresh light. It's, well, interesting to me."

Vanessa was confused . . . why was she being so petty? Wasn't it enough her sister was here, no matter the reason? She was pulling back from the emotional edge when she felt a tap on her arm.

It was Karen and Scott Maguire-Weinstock. She was cradling their baby and he was filming their daughter, Indigo, who was skipping around the courtyard in a cherry-red velvet dress.

"Wasn't that beautiful?" said Karen.

"Beautiful," Vanessa echoed.

"And now the potluck," said Karen. "I just love seeing what everyone brought, all the different foods, the different cultures. It's so festive. My sisters came over yesterday and we spent the whole afternoon baking cookies with the kids. We had so much fun! It's been a tradition in the Maguire home for three generations."

Vanessa froze, imagining the glittering Maguire-Weinstock house filled with warm, loving relatives and delicious, traditional food.

"Anyway, what did you bring?" Karen was asking.

Vanessa faltered. What had she brought? And, more important, what did she ever bring to this holiday? Peering jealously at Karen, who seemed to have miraculously dropped her pregnancy pounds in a mere two weeks, Vanessa realized she would never best this woman. In fact, when you got right down to it, she would never best anyone.

So she coughed. And then coughed again.

"Are you all right?" said Karen.

Vanessa patted her chest. "Sorry. I think I'm coming down with something. Maybe the flu? I feel a little congested."

Karen took a worried step back, her hand covering Chicahua's mouth. "You should go home and get into bed."

"You're right." Vanessa held her wrist to her forehead. "I'm feverish. I don't want to give this to anyone!"

Karen slipped her hand into Scott's and they hurried away from this pestilence and plague towards grade three.

Vanessa whirled around and clutched her sister's arm. "Will you bring the boys home when they're done with the party?"

Thea's smile faded. "What?"

"Please, I need some time to myself." She kissed her mother on the cheek. "Thea will bring you back, too," she said, challenging her sister to a duel. "I'm going home to bed."

"Do you think it's okay for me to film the other kids?" Thea added quickly.

"Okay?" said Vanessa. "Yours will just be one of twenty-five digital cameras."

Back home, she knew she should be cleaning the house and wrapping presents, but she sat on the couch and cried instead. When she felt better, she brewed some French roast, took two vitamin Cs, and climbed into bed with the morning paper. I'm not really sick, she told herself, I just need two hours.

Two hours alone.

Then she remembered the cinnamon rolls.

Padding into the service porch, she plucked the nicest two buns from the baking sheet and warmed them in the microwave.

Once she was snuggled against her pillows with her potluck dish, she felt delirious with pleasure. Dunking the sweet sticky pastry into her dark rich coffee, Vanessa decided that cinnamon rolls in bed would be *her* holiday tradition.

And, to make it even more delicious, she'd be sure to make them store-bought.

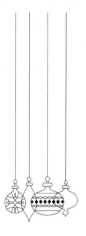

9

Patience, Richard, and Libby were booked at the Holiday Inn in Studio City, about a mile from Vanessa's house.

The rental car rolled up a circular drive lined with king palms, flowering hibiscus, and bougainvillea. Inside, the lobby was painted a tropical green and the couches and chairs were covered in bamboo print fabric. In the corner stood a small Christmas tree with blinking lights and a cottony blanket wrapped around its base to look like snow. A long, white Formica counter served as a buffet table for the daily continental breakfast, a repast of stale, waxen pastries and syrupy coffee in florid flavors like raspberry crème.

While Richard checked in, Patience addressed her surroundings and wondered about the sort of people who visited hotels during Christmas week—a time she felt one should be at home among relatives and one's own special holiday decorations and traditions.

She noticed a retired couple, in khakis and visors, holding a map to the Getty Center, and a gay couple in tank tops and swim trunks strolling leisurely out the double glass doors that led to the pool.

"Oooh, let's go swimming!" Libby said to her mother, following the men outside.

"Don't you think we should call Vanessa and head over there first?" said Patience, ever the mistress of propriety.

"Mom, we've spent hours in a plane and we just got here . . . and they don't have a pool and it's summer."

"It's not summer."

Patience trailed her daughter and peeked at the terrace. Mesh lounge chairs and thatched umbrellas flanked a rectangular pool with a frothing Jacuzzi and cascading lava-rock fountain. It reminded Patience of a high school gym decorated in an island theme for prom night.

All that's missing are the silly drinks, she thought, and then noticed a woman clutching a coconut shell festooned with a jaunty candy cane.

Richard charged up, waving two plastic key cards. "Adjoining rooms facing the mountains," he said pointedly to his wife. "Away from the pool and any possible noise from wild drunken revelers."

Up on the fourth floor, their rooms were clean and aqua and did, indeed, feature views of a hillside jammed with bulky homes, three gigantic radio towers, and a few hearty oak trees.

Richard and Libby changed into swimsuits and hurried to the pool while Patience dropped down on the king-sized bed for a nap.

Lying on her side, she gazed out the window at the hazy Los Angeles afternoon and counted back all her forty-eight Christmases. How many had she had away from home?

Two.

One year, when Libby was a baby, they had joined her parents in Florida. Libby had had colic and Patience's father had suggested they give her a dropper of scotch to calm her down.

And now they were here, in Los Angeles, on a cloudless, seventy-two-degree December afternoon.

She felt extremely out of sorts, and not because of the jet lag.

She pushed her face down into the polyester pillow but the tears remained locked inside her. If you cry, you'll ruin everyone's holiday, she admonished herself. Don't be selfish. You're here, make the best of it.

So, fortifying herself with good manners, she donned a slimming black tank suit and a matching short robe and padded down the ghostly hallway to the elevator.

Down at the pool, Richard had commandeered a raft and was bobbing gently in the water while Libby swam a few lazy laps.

Patience stood on the first step in the shallow end and

quickly abandoned her stance against swimming; the water was warm and inviting. Plunging in, she glided over to her husband and kissed him on the cheek.

His arm shot out and scooped her up beside him on the air mattress. Buoyed by the water and the *slap, slap* sound it made as it hit the sides of the pool, Patience relaxed and nestled her head in his shoulder.

"P, this is the life," said Richard, hooking her trim waist. "I think we should move out west and retire the snowblower."

"Richard!" Patience frowned. "Isn't it enough that we're here at Christmas?"

He kissed the top of her wet head. "Patience, you're my hope and joy," he said.

"And you're my love and happiness."

In their charmed life raft they failed to spot Brian Kim, the willowy waiter who had just served Libby an iced mocha and had a perfectly heart-stopping sort of smile.

"That'll be five-fifty," he said, tapping his pen nervously on his thigh.

"Can I charge it to the room?" Libby giggled.

"If you show me your key." Brian had a dimple on his left cheek.

Libby placed the plastic card on his tray. Clicking his pen, Brian wrote the room number on her bill.

He gently handed back the key. He had slender arms that were almost hairless, which Libby found intoxicating.

"So where're you from?" he asked.

"Massachusetts," said Libby, stroking her wet hair. "We're visiting my aunt and uncle for the holidays."

"That's cool," said Brian.

"Do you have to work on Christmas?" Libby thought she had never seen such velvety brown eyes.

"No, my parents would kill me if I didn't come over to open presents," he laughed. "Plus I have younger cousins."

"So you're from here?"

"Yeah, Los Feliz. I'm majoring in film at UCLA."

"Wow! It's so hard to get in there."

"Yeah, but you know what grinds Asians are."

Libby knew that that dimple was pretty adorable, grind or no grind. "I just applied to Santa Cruz," she said. "We're going to visit there after Christmas."

"You know it's not as radical as it used to be—they even give grades now."

"Yeah, that's a good thing," Libby sighed. "Otherwise my parents definitely wouldn't let me go."

"Libby!" Patience had suddenly switched on her radar.

Libby ignored her. "So, are there any cool places around here?"

"Do you like sushi?" Brian said hopefully.

"Sure," said Libby, feeling that any food with Brian would be fantastic.

"There's a place just down Ventura. They make this amazing roll with salmon, tuna, and cream cheese. And there's this awesome movie theater in Hollywood. Lots of foreign films."

Libby saw her mother heading towards them. "I have to go do relative stuff, but I'll be back later," she said urgently.

Brian whipped out his cell. "Give me your number. I'll call you. I'm off tomorrow."

"Libby . . ." The *slush, slush* of Patience's sandals was drawing closer.

Libby fired off her number and Brian escaped before Patience pierced the atmosphere.

"Who was that?" she said. Brian's backside zipped through the service door into the hotel kitchen.

A date! Libby thought. A date with a boy in California.

"Room service," was all Libby said. "You can order drinks by the pool."

"Well, he was very cute," said her mother.

"Oh," said Libby, "I didn't notice."

"It's so good to see you!" Vanessa cried, as she ushered her in-laws into the house.

Patience, her hair slicked back from her swim, extended a cheek for a quick kiss. Richard enveloped Vanessa in a warm hug, and the twins bypassed the adults completely to swarm Libby.

"I can't believe this weather," said Patience. "It's so warm!" She shrugged out of her tailored blue jacket and hung it on a peg next to the front door.

Throwing a quick glance around the room, Patience noticed two cardboard boxes marked XMAS STUFF next to the fireplace. Other than that, there were no decorations to speak of.

"What's going on?" boomed Richard. He lifted Alex up and spun him around like a whirligig. "Where's the tree? Don't tell me they don't have Christmas trees in California!"

"My turn!" Ethan tugged his uncle's arm, ready for a chance at spinning.

Vanessa followed her sister-in-law's glance around the room. "We're a little behind in our holiday decorating. I've been so busy, I haven't had time to get the tree."

"Well then," said Richard, exchanging Alex for Ethan in the spin cycle. "I guess I'll have to help you get this Christmas up and running."

Patience raised her brows in surprise. When was the last time Richard had helped with anything other than knee surgery?

"I appreciate that," Vanessa was saying, as she led Patience and Richard back to her kitchen. "Would you like some wine? I thought we'd go out to dinner tonight. . . . I didn't feel like cooking."

Patience looked at a dismal platter of a dozen wheat thins and a dry wedge of cheddar cheese sitting on the counter.

"Good idea," she said.

Libby and the boys raced past them dribbling a basketball.

"She loves those boys," said Patience. "Remember how she used to have dance parties with them, all in pajamas?"

"They adore her," said Vanessa. "She's their only cousin and all."

"Your sister never had children?"

"And the future's not promising," said Vanessa, pouring three glasses of California chardonnay. "Shall we sit outside?"

Off the kitchen was a small deck facing a neglected lawn and a gnarled oak tree. To the right were a low wooden fence, the garage, and a basketball hoop. For a few awkward moments, they watched the kids shoot baskets and chase the ball down the driveway.

"How was your flight?" said Vanessa, noticing the redwood table was spotted with sticky black goop from last month's barbequed chicken.

"Fine. And we've already been swimming," said Richard. "You know, I think I'll show them a few pointers." Ditching the cocktail hour, he hurried across the lawn, peeled off his navy blazer, and hung it up in the oak tree.

Patience and Vanessa exchanged polite smiles.

"How's your horse?" Vanessa took a grateful sip of wine.

"Oh, Beau hurt his front leg, so there won't be any hacking for us for a bit."

"Hacking?" Vanessa knew nothing about equines—hadn't even gone through a horse phase when she was a girl—so she had nothing to add besides insincere concern.

"Riding. That's what we say in New England . . . Now, Vanessa," Patience's voice assumed the directness of a Scout leader. "Richard has a golf date in Palos Verdes tomorrow—you know his college roommate lives down there. Endocrinologist."

"I can never remember, is that the glands or the gums?" Vanessa chuckled.

"Glands. Anyway, Vanessa, I can see that you've been really busy with work and the kids." Patience gave her head a little shake. "So, please, let me help you shop and prepare. I really have nothing else planned and I'd be happy to."

"Oh, okay," said Vanessa, growing uncomfortable about the prospects of a home-ec class with Patience.

"And while we're at it, we could get a tree."

"Sure," said Vanessa. "We'll get one tomorrow. There's a lot just down the street."

Patience whispered conspiratorially, "It's not that *we* need a tree—ours has been up for weeks. I just thought your boys would miss it. You know how kids are."

"Oh, they'll be fine." Vanessa bristled slightly. "Everyone has to learn to wait for things sometimes, life isn't always perfect." She hoped she sounded convincing, like a wise parent who understood the importance of the Teachable Moment. But underneath, she worried that Patience judged her as some kind of slacker mom.

She took another sip from her wineglass and wondered how she was going to get through dinner.

AFTER COFFEE AND DANISH IN THE hotel lobby the next morning, Patience and Richard drove over to Vanessa's house. The front door was wide open and Alex and Ethan were running around the lawn, shooting each other with the spray from their water bottles. Patience hopped out of the car and waved at the boys. "Hold your fire!"

"Hey, Aunt P," Ethan yelled, before being zapped by a squirt from his brother. "We're going on a hike!"

Vanessa appeared in the doorway wearing a hat and smearing her face with sunscreen. Noticing her sister-in-law approaching, she looked surprised. "Uh, hi."

"Have fun, you two!" There was a toot from the white rental sedan and Richard drove away.

"He's off to his golf game," Patience said. "And Libby's jet-lagged and wanted to sleep, so I left her at the hotel."

Vanessa's heart sank. She had secretly hoped Libby might

stay here and babysit the twins while she did her errands. She turned to Patience. "I didn't know you were coming so early. . . . Why didn't you call me?"

"But I did. I spoke to Alex."

Vanessa eyed her boys, who were now pelting each other with shriveled pomegranates they'd plucked from the neighbor's tree. "Alex, why didn't you tell me your aunt—"

"Oh, it doesn't matter," Patience interrupted. "I'm here and I'm ready to help. What shall we do first? Bake our pies? I was thinking apple, of course, and I also have a wonderful recipe for a cranberry caramel tart."

Vanessa plunked down on a low bench next to the front door and laced up her running shoes. Of course Patience could go on and on about dessert and decorating. She'd only known life with Libby. A lovely, compliant girl who probably offered to help her bake and decorate wreaths and God knows what else. Romantic, sepia-toned images of holidays at the Wenham home scrolled through her mind—the twinkling lights on the house, the welcoming fire, the magnificent tree, the homemade eggnog—till Vanessa shut them down.

"Oh, you don't have to make anything. Thea is bringing dessert," she said, sounding like a rude teenager. "And right now, I promised the boys we'd go on a short hike."

That's madness, Patience thought. If we wait much longer the crowds will be impossible and the stores will be bedlam.

"Don't you think we should shop early in the day?" she said tentatively.

"Probably," Vanessa said. "But I have boys, Patience. Nine-year-old boys. They are just not into crafts. Or cooking. If you haven't noticed, they spend their time beating the crap out of each other. So, if I want to have even the smallest chance of a sane day, I have to wear them out first."

Or discipline them, thought Patience.

Vanessa jumped to her feet and strapped on a water bottle. "You're welcome to join us." She looked slyly at her in-law's immaculate designer loafers. "But the path is slippery and kind of steep."

"Oh," said Patience in a tiny voice. "Well maybe I should stay here and wait for you. I haven't read the paper yet."

ANY RELIEF VANESSA FELT FROM DITCHING Patience was soon vanquished by guilt and remorse. I could have loaned her some sneakers, she admitted silently, as she led the twins up a rutted, sandy road. She'd probably like to see something besides the hotel and my living room.

The hike up Fryman Canyon had breathtaking views across the San Fernando Valley to the Santa Susana mountains on the north. The sky was clear and the air smelled both clean and slightly smoky. Lavender and toyon berry bushes tangled against the hillside, and there were acres of weeds that, although dry and dangerously flammable, looked like golden cotton candy in the soft winter light.

We should make a Winter Solstice Altar! Vanessa realized, remembering her former vow to inject meaning into their lives.

"Alex, Ethan!" she cried, steering them towards a single track that veered from the main road. "I have an idea. Let's collect some leaves and branches and make a solstice altar."

"A what?" Ethan wrinkled his forehead.

"It's an altar that honors . . ." What did it honor, again? Winter? Death? Druids? That magazine article from *Living Simply* had explained it so beautifully. She remembered that the arrangements in the photo spread were gorgeous—twigs and candles and holly berries, like something out of a fancy store window.

"It honors light." Alex pointed dramatically to the sun. "We did one in kindergarten."

"You did?" Vanessa felt slightly dim-witted. "Oh, yeah. Good, then you know what I'm talking about. So let's collect things that remind us nature doesn't die during winter . . . life is hibernating until spring."

"But I want a Christmas tree." Alex charged gleefully towards a suspicious, fly-ridden brown pile.

"Winter dies?" Ethan looked dubious.

"That's not what Ms. Nichols said," Alex called back to his mother. "She said the soul's lips is about light. All the holidays are about light."

Vanessa paused. Why am I always surprised when my kids remember anything they learn in school—isn't that what they're there for? "Yes, you're right, it's about light. And death," she couldn't help adding. "So let's find some leaves and branches. And we'll add candles when we get home."

"Okay," agreed Ethan. He grabbed a fistful of dried white sage and thrust it under Vanessa's nose. "This looks really dead."

"How about dog doo?" Alex poked his toe at the mound of fresh, moist Labrador shit. "It's got dead stuff in it."

"Alex, get away from that poop, it'll smell up your shoe." Vanessa bent down to examine a shiny caramel-colored acorn. "Look, Ethan," she said softly, "an acorn. Isn't it beautiful?"

Ethan poked the smooth seed with a jaunty cap. "It looks like it's wearing one of those hats the artists wear."

"It looks like a penis," said Alex.

Vanessa stuck the acorn in the pocket of her yoga pants. "We have the acorn and the sage. What are you putting on the altar, Alex?"

"Nothing! I want a tree," he said.

"We'll get a tree. And we'll have the altar too."

Ethan shaded his eyes from the sun. "What are we, Mom? Are we Christian or Jewish?"

What should I say? Vanessa worried. I want to keep their minds open to the . . . beauty and value of all religions. "Well, we're not a member of any church or temple, but we believe in God, or a . . . higher spirit," she finished beatifically. "You could say we're very, very spiritual."

"Spiritual?" Alex gagged. "Who wants to be that?"

"I LIKE THIS ONE," SAID VANESSA, scrutinizing the price tag on a five-foot Scotch pine. It was sixty dollars, twenty more than she wanted to spend, but it wasn't too scrawny and there was only a slight bald patch on one side. She'd turn that place to the wall.

She was wandering around Mr. Delaney's Christmas Trees with Patience and the boys. She hadn't seen anyone who resembled the Dickensian gentleman featured on all the painted signs, but Ricky and Juan knew their firs and pines and were experts at attaching those confounding tree stands.

"Hmm," said Patience, her gaze turning from Vanessa's humble tree. "Let's keep looking. Just for fun." She cocked her head thoughtfully. "I had no idea California grew such lovely full trees."

Why does she act like California is a frontier outpost? Vanessa wrinkled her nose. My God, there're four million people in this city alone.

The boys had raced ahead to what their mother thought of as the Beverly Hills section of towering, fragrant firs and spruces.

Alex seized a nine-footer with glorious foliage and a price tag of $120. "Let's get this one!"

"Yeah," echoed his brother. "Can we get this one, Mom?"

"That is a beauty," their aunt agreed.

Vanessa squirmed. This was just like Patience, who, being a surgeon's wife, really had no idea what it was like to live on a budget. "The other one will fit in our house better. We have low ceilings."

"Why don't I put in half?" Patience snapped open the gold clasp of her black handbag.

"No!" said Vanessa. "I mean, you're our guests, you've already paid for airfare and a hotel." She flashed on the beautiful guest room in Wenham that overlooked a forest of maples and pines. This was where she and JT always slept. They had never had to book a hotel in Wenham. Visiting Patience and Richard was sort of like a vacation at a country inn. A country inn with a very controlling innkeeper.

"But Mom, this one is better," said Alex.

"Please!" Ethan was circling the tree like a dog.

Great, Vanessa thought, now I look cheap. She shook her head. "Boys, it's just a tree—and spending more money doesn't make our Christmas happier."

Disappointed, Alex and Ethan dragged their rubber soles back to the scrawny tree while Vanessa peered around for the salesmen.

"You stay here with the boys, I'll find some help," said Patience.

A few minutes later, she returned with Juan, a squat bulky man in a plaid flannel shirt. They breezed right past Vanessa's sad sack tree and over to the magnificent noble fir with the swell price tag.

Before Vanessa could speak, Patience tapped her on the arm. "It's all taken care of. Just show Juan where to put it on the car."

"Yeah, yeah!" cried the twins, scampering and crashing into every tree on their path. "Thanks, Aunt P!"

Vanessa looked down at her clogs. "That was nice of you, Patience." It was all she could do to keep the anger out of her voice.

As the day progressed, Vanessa felt as if she were losing control of her holiday. Patience had winced at the turkey selection in the discount market *(They look like they've been frozen since last December! A few dollars more will make all the difference in taste),* and then begged Vanessa to drive two miles farther down Ventura Boulevard to the new Organic Living grocery store.

This upscale market also featured a long line of upscale cars waiting for parking spaces. It took fifteen minutes before Vanessa secured a spot. Once inside, they faced down half of the valley competing for the best possible ingredients for their holiday meals too.

"Oh, my God." Vanessa looked stricken. They weren't even past the cache of shopping carts and Alex and Ethan were already punching each other.

"Boys," Patience said and led the twins over to the magazine racks adjoining the flower/espresso bar/concierge corner of the store. Fishing a pen and a small spiral notebook from her purse, she opened to a fresh page and wrote down *red hat, frog, corn, basketball player, lipstick, surfboard, vice president.* "While your mother and I shop, I want you to find these photos in the magazines and then bring them back to me. Winner gets five dollars!"

"Cool!" said Ethan, grabbing the list.

"What an interesting idea," said Vanessa, "but they'll probably be back in two minutes."

"My mother always used that trick on my sister and me," said Patience. "Sometimes her list was a mile long."

Nabbing a cart, Patience rolled towards Produce. "Now how many of us will there be?"

Vanessa trailed behind like the help. "Let's see . . . Thea and Marcus, my mother and Frank, you three, and . . . Neil, the playwright."

"The playwright?"

"The writer I've been working with. He lives in New York and isn't going back for the holidays." Vanessa realized she knew very little about his personal life. "I mean, he's originally from here but for some reason he wasn't seeing his family and I didn't want him to be alone on Christmas."

Patience nodded absently. "Twelve," she counted out loud. "A nice round number."

As she surveyed displays of prebaked pie shells, parbaked sourdough, and overbaked canned yams, Patience ruminated on Christmas dinner.

"I think the stuffing really anchors a meal, don't you agree? Richard prefers oyster—but perhaps that's too East Coast. Do you have something regional, something more Californian? I saw a recipe for a corn bread dressing with pumpkin seeds in *Food & Wine*. And there was a yummy-looking Southwestern spread in this month's *Gourmet*."

"A lot of people out here in the West like Mrs. Cubbison's," Vanessa said sarcastically.

"Oh, they do? Would you prefer that?" Patience parked herself before a pyramid of Yukon Gold potatoes. Tearing a plastic bag from the dispenser, she began to fill it. "I think Yukon Gold make the best mashed potatoes. Do you like to add anything, like garlic or chives?"

"I don't think so. The boys won't eat anything green," Vanessa cocked her hip petulantly.

"So no chives. Just butter and cream?"

"JT usually does the potatoes."

"Should we call him?" Patience looked sincere.

"Call him? No, he's probably on the plane right now. I'm sure we can buy potatoes without his input, jeez." Vanessa hoped she could manage this errand without a catfight, but it seemed entirely possible that store security would soon be charging her with disorderly conduct. *The judge would be on my side,* she concluded defensively, *if he met Patience.*

Confronting the meat aisle, Patience bypassed a watershed of turkeys in every size and permutation and gazed excitedly at the standing rib roasts.

"A roast beef really says 'Christmas' to me. And what about Yorkshire pudding instead of stuffing? I think everyone tires of turkey by Thanksgiving, don't you?"

That was the only turkey we've had all year, Vanessa thought. Her heart hammered when she caught the price of the beef: $150! "The turkey is bigger," she said quickly, laying a proprietary hand on the bird. "Nineteen pounds."

"But the roast will easily serve twelve," Patience explained, placing her hand on the beef. "And there'll be leftovers. Don't you love a roast beef sandwich the next day?"

Vanessa wrestled her bird from its refrigerated roost. "The turkey's on special. It'll feed everyone for forty dollars."

"Well, I could—" Patience began.

"No!" Vanessa dropped the tom into the basket. There was no way she would allow Patience to pay again. "No, I think we should get turkey."

"Of course," said Patience, taken aback. "It was only a suggestion."

Claiming the cart, Vanessa pulled out into traffic, leaving Patience to flounder in her wake.

"If Thea handles dessert, I'll have my mother bring the crudités . . . she doesn't really cook so she can pick up one of those vegetable platters. I'll make the turkey and stuffing." She spied an enormous tower of Mrs. Cubbison's, and pulled two bags into her cart. "Then JT can mash potatoes, we'll pick up some frozen peas and cranberries." She yanked four cans off another display and smiled triumphantly at Patience. "I think our work here is done."

"But frozen peas." Her sister-in-law looked horrified. "Don't you think they're more of an everyday sort of food? I mean, don't you want something special for Christmas?"

Vanessa's withering glance sent Patience scurrying to the frozen foods aisle.

Once the lowly peas were secure in the cart, the two Channings headed to the front of the store.

"Well, I think we have everything," Patience said. "But now that everyone's bringing something, there's nothing for me to make."

"We could really use a couple of bottles of wine," said Vanessa, mentally checking items off her list.

"Oh, all right," said Patience dejectedly. *I don't really know anything about wine and I make a wonderful apple pie* but, "whatever you'd like," was all she said, then she bobbed her head in the direction of the magazine rack. "Shall I check on the boys?"

"Good idea," said Vanessa, searching through her purse for any forgotten coupons.

"Funny, they're still at that game," Patience added pointedly. Then, smoothing her feathers, she abandoned Vanessa and her spoils to the snaking line ahead at the checkout stand.

*   *   *

BACK AT THE CAR, THEY LOADED up the groceries and gave the twins their five-dollar prize money.

Patience rode up front in the passenger seat, a stack of magazines on her lap. When she'd discovered the boys had ripped out the photos from half a dozen issues, she'd felt obligated to buy them all.

She glanced at her watch, then over at Vanessa. "What are the plans when we get home?"

"How about a massage, a cocktail, and room service?" Vanessa giggled, then smacked her forehead. "Oh, you mean my real-life plans?"

Patience stared at the passing scenery with fascination. Festive silver banners spanned the wide boulevard: HAPPY HOLIDAYS! and SEASON'S GREETINGS FROM YOUR STUDIO CITY MERCHANTS! Colored lights wound up the skinny, skyscraper palm trees. The shops had scenes of winter painted on their windows and fake snow strewn around the displays.

How weird, she was poised to say, scenes of winter wonderland in this balmy climate! Then she snapped her jaw shut. These poor souls! Clearly, there were people out here who missed the *real* holidays and they were trying to re-create it as best they could.

She swiveled around and smiled at the twins. "Should we decorate the tree when we get back?"

"Yeah!" "Yeah!"

Vanessa licked the corner of her mouth. "Patience, I'd like to wait till JT gets home later tonight to trim the tree. It's really the only time we'll have together, just the four of us."

"No," said Alex, "I'm sick of waiting!"

"Dad doesn't care," his brother insisted.

Patience remembered back when Libby was small and the three of them would make hot cocoa and decorate the tree together. Richard always put out a jigger of scotch for Santa, and Libby always put out protein bars for the reindeer—they had so far to fly.

Sometime in the velvet hours of the night, Libby would climb into their bed, insisting she was too excited to sleep alone. Patience would be giddy too, from the presence of her warm, sweet daughter beside her and the anticipation of the morning yet to come.

Now those days were gone, leaving her with a longing she couldn't fathom and a heartache so sharp she wasn't sure she could breathe.

"Of course I understand," she whispered hoarsely. Then turning to the boys she said, "Your mother's right. Your daddy would be heartbroken if you trimmed the tree without him."

"Uhhhh." Alex gave a boisterous groan.

Patience dug into her purse and checked her cell phone: The message box was empty. "You know, Vanessa, I still feel a little jet lag. Would you drop me at the hotel before you go home? Libby's probably awake by now and maybe she wants a late lunch. At the very least"—she held up the stack of magazines—"I have plenty of reading material."

"Oh, God, I feel so bad that you had to buy all those magazines."

"It doesn't matter." Patience flipped through a copy of *Animal Planet*. "I'm really very interested in the survival of the red-legged frog."

The two women laughed. Their private world inside the car suddenly felt gentle and forgiving.

Vanessa rolled up the hotel driveway and parked beside the lobby entrance. "See you tomorrow night."

"Do you want me to come early and help?"

"No, JT and I are going to do it together," Vanessa said. "So just relax, sit by the pool. Or maybe you guys could go up to the Getty Museum. Thea said there's an amazing photo show about world poverty and the Great Depression."

"Hmmm," said Patience, feeling little desire to consider the bleakest of images at this time of year. She rested her hand on the latch. "You know, Vanessa, I am a little concerned about dessert."

The seed of goodwill that Vanessa had planted shriveled up and died. "We're fine," she said curtly. "Thea's bringing pies."

"Well, if anything happens, I'd be happy to come over and bake my cranberry tart. It's guaranteed to turn perfectly intelligent people into slobbering idiots."

"Look, Patience!" Vanessa burst out. "Every year for the past six years, we've gone to *your* house. Just once, let's do it my way." She glanced in the rearview mirror at the boys and lowered her voice to a hiss. "I know I don't have a cranberry tart, but I'm sure Thea will bring something nice."

"Oh, of course she will . . . I'm sorry if you thought . . . uh, and I'm sure everything will be . . . okay, I'll see you tomorrow." Hastily, Patience reached back and squeezed the knees of each boy. "Love you two," then sprang herself from the car.

As Vanessa circled back to Laurel Canyon, she exhaled deeply. Okay, maybe I could have been more diplomatic, she admitted. Okay but maybe not! Stretching her back against the seat she reminded herself to stay calm, and that in just a few hours JT would be home and their real holiday would begin.

Zooming along on autopilot, she imagined tomorrow's holiday meal, glossy and garnished, all laid out on her dining room table. As she swung into her driveway, she realized with horror that what she'd been envisioning was a standing rib roast, a golden Yorkshire pudding, and a crimson cranberry tart.

Oh, my God, she gasped, what if Patience is right? What if people are tired of turkey after all?

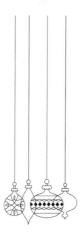

10

J ust as Libby climbed into Brian Kim's silver hybrid, she felt a gnawing fear. She had been so preoccupied fussing with her hair—up with clips or wild and loose?—and changing her clothes—cropped jacket with T or silk cami?—she had sort of accidentallyonpurpose forgotten about her parents.

Years of her mother's anguished warnings clanged inside her head. "Never get in a car with a stranger!" "Always let us know where you are!" "Don't ever, ever make a date with a man on the Internet!"

With rising panic, Libby shot a furtive look over at the would-be abductor in the driver's seat. Brian was wearing skate shoes, an anime imprint T-shirt, and cargo pants. If outward appearance was an indicator, he looked like a nice college guy.

Whipping out her cell, she called her father.

"What's up, Lib?" Just the sound of his deep, unflappable voice soothed her nerves.

"I just wanted to let you know that I'm going to the movies with Brian Kim."

"Who?" Richard put down his driver. He was standing on the fairway at the Palos Verdes Golf Course, gazing towards the clubhouse in anticipation of postgame beers and burgers.

"He works at the hotel. Remember? I met him yesterday at the pool." With utter certainty, Libby knew her father wouldn't remember anything but would pretend he did.

"Oh, yes, of course. Did you clear this with your mother?"

"I think she's still out with Aunt V," Libby sidestepped. "Anyway, we're going to the . . ." she tapped Brian's shoulder. "Where're we going, again?"

"The ArcLight. It's a theater complex in Hollywood. Do you want to give them my cell just in case?"

Libby relaxed. What kind of serial killer would give her parents his phone number?

"Yeah, that'd be great. You know how *they* are." She rolled her eyes emphatically. Returning to her dad, she repeated Brian's name and his cell and the name of the theater. "I'll be back by dinner! Love you!"

"Love you, too," said Richard, setting up the next shot.

*   *   *

JUST BELOW THE BUSTLE OF SUNSET Boulevard, and hidden behind a restaurant, a culinary academy, and a cascading water curtain were the ArcLight Theaters. The lobby doors were flanked by Christmas trees, and silver stars that mimicked the Hollywood Walk of Fame were suspended overhead. As Brian and Libby strolled up to the entrance, the familiar strains of "White Christmas" drifted through the air.

"It's so weird to hear Christmas carols when there's no snow and it feels like summer," she giggled.

"Not when you grow up in L.A." Brian opened the door and they entered a soaring lobby with a dozen ticket agents and an electronic signboard that flashed the titles of the films.

"This is going to blow you away," he said. "Fujiyama totally rocks. Have you ever seen anime before?"

"No," Libby admitted shyly. At home in Massachusetts, she would never have picked a cartoon in Japanese, but here in Los Angeles it felt both natural and exotic.

The film was colorful but oddly stilted and Libby didn't think it was all that great. But afterward, as they sipped chai lattes in the lobby café, she listened intently to Brian's critique and enjoyed the crowd of young film buffs in leather jackets and slouchy jeans lounging on the banquettes and playing with their cutting-edge phone gear.

Brian reached over and placed his hands over hers. "I'm sorry. I'm talking too much about film."

"No, you're not," she smiled. "It's your passion."

"Yeah," he said, embarrassed. "But everyone tells me to shut up already."

"It's good to have a passion," Libby said.

"So, what's yours?"

Libby thought for a moment. "I don't have one big thing in my life. Like film for you or horses for my mom or golf like my dad. I'm just . . . I guess I'm an ordinary girl."

"You're not ordinary." Brian openly admired her heart-shaped face and wavy brown hair, her blue eyes with long, fringed lashes. "You're really beautiful," he added sincerely.

Libby swooned. She wondered if this was what it was like to have a real connection with someone. To meet a man whom you knew, instinctively, was going to be the great love of your life! The soul mate who was going to change everything!

"I hope I didn't offend you or anything." Brian seemed worried.

"No, no . . . I . . ." she trailed off, unable to think of anything to say.

Jumping up, Brian self-consciously reached for her hand. "Come on, I'm going to give you the tour."

As he led her around the streets of Hollywood—the Chinese Theatre, the Kodak, the embedded stars on the sidewalk—Libby hardly heard a word he said. She was acutely aware of her hand in his and how much she wanted to text Sarah that she was falling madly in love with a guy in L.A. who was going to make amazing films.

Later, after weird orange-speckled rolls at his favorite sushi bar, they returned to the hotel and he walked her back up to her room.

She stood awkwardly at the door. "I had a really good time," she said, looking down at his shoes.

"Libby . . ." Brian leaned over and kissed her gently on the lips. He tasted like nutty rice and mint gum and tea. When he started to pull away she tugged him back against her.

Pressed against her door, they had a hot three-minute make-out session before breaking for air. Libby was shocked by her desire—she had never really wanted a boy like she wanted Brian. Was this passion? Like Romeo and Juliet? Like Leonardo DiCaprio and Kate Winslet? Suddenly, she understood how girls could just forget about waiting and condoms and limits and tear off their clothes with abandon.

"God," she panted.

"Fuck," he echoed. Then, "Sorry. I didn't mean to swear or anything."

But the sensible part of Libby stirred inside. The Patience Polk-Channing imprint that insisted she consider the moment and all its consequences. "I should probably . . . go," she said reluctantly.

"Can I see you again?" His eyes were pleading.

"Yes!" She kissed him harder this time and with her hips. "How about later tonight, after dinner?"

AFTER MONTHS OF FEELING LIKE SHE was circling lost around the same two blocks, Thea had suddenly discovered the on-ramp to inspiration.

She had spent the morning at her desk, reviewing her

interview tapes and drinking French-press coffee—the addict's approved contraband.

She had recorded a dozen subjects of various ages reminiscing about Christmas and, generally speaking, she'd hit pay dirt. Yes, there was the usual, "I never got the doll/bicycle/PlayStation I wanted" sort of stuff.

But there was also something deeper, more complex. In fact, it seemed to Thea that with the entire country suffering from some kind of holiday stress syndrome, HSS would soon be listed in the *DSM*.

At the moment, she was fixated on Katie, twenty-eight, a cousin of Angela, her Pilates teacher. A recent transplant from Omaha, Katie had replied to Thea's email, *Seeking Holiday Memories for Art Series*, only because she needed material for her own blog, hick2hip.com.

"The holidays were awful," Katie was confessing, zipping and unzipping her pink cotton sweatshirt. "My dad—he's a minister—was always stressed. People get crazy this time of year so he'd have to do a lot of extra counseling. And then, of course, there's the pressure of coming up with the sermon. I mean, it had to be good. Better than last year's."

Katie looked beseechingly at Thea. "Oh, boy, I really shouldn't tell anyone! What if his congregation found out?"

"I won't tell anyone," Thea had promised. "This is just for my own personal research. But I am wondering . . . well, after the holiday services were over, didn't he feel good about being there for so many unhappy people?"

Katie had seemed dubious. "I don't think so. He always spent the week after Christmas alone on the couch, drinking tons of Coke and watching reruns of *MASH*."

Her voice grew thin. "My mother wouldn't let us speak to him until January second."

"Wow, that must have been hard." Thea stroked her braids thoughtfully. "But aside from all the difficulties, did you feel like you had a overall religious connection to Christmas?"

Katie guffawed. "A minister's daughter is the last person to ask about religion!"

Closing the lid of her laptop, Thea stared out the window at a lone biker, tootling along on the path next to the canal. I've got to find someone, anyone, who can give me a joyful, even spiritual, take on the holidays, she vowed.

There was a knock at her front door. "I'm here!"

"Coming," Thea called. Scooping up her cell and house keys, she opened the door and greeted a small, thin Latina with sculpted biceps and a prominent angel tattoo over her left breast.

"Hey girl," said Tina Rodriguez, giving Thea a hug. "Ready to stuff tamales?"

"This had better be fun," said Thea. "Everyone is so god-damned depressed this time of year."

"Tamale making is really fun. It was always what I liked best about Christmas. That and the toys. My parents always went crazy with the toys."

The two friends drove east to Highland Park, to a street jammed with old compact cars, boxy apartment buildings, and sagging stucco bungalows. Tina angled her red pickup on the cement lawn of a tidy turquoise cottage. Flipping down the sunshade, she glanced into the mirror and applied a bloodred lipstick to her still-girlish mouth. "Okay, don't talk about Mel. It will upset my mother."

"What? She doesn't know you're gay?"

"She doesn't *know* know and she insists it's a phase." Tina lined her lips with a darker red pencil.

"A phase? But you're thirty-five."

"Denial is stronger than Kryptonite. Look, my mother grew up in a very traditional Catholic family. Her parents were from Mexico. They still think God will punish you if you're gay. And don't bring up the church. We'll just steer clear of that too."

"I thought you said this was fun." Thea looked doubtful.

"It is . . . within very tight parameters."

Tina slithered up the walk in skinny jeans, a floral-print silk top, and ropes of glittering jet beads, her signature medium. In the past ten years, she had made a mark in the art world with a series of beaded objects. Her midcentury kitchen constructed entirely of crystal bugle beads had been bought by MoMA, and her rhinestone-encrusted Pinto was on permanent display in the center of a fountain of a Las Vegas casino.

Lupe Rodriguez, Tina's mother, welcomed the girls with a broad grin. She was an older version of her daughter plus fifty pounds. Her jeans were stretched over cascading hips and her cleavage was fighting to escape its fuchsia spandex container. Sparkling earrings dangled from her lobes.

"Tina, mia!" She swept up her daughter and kissed her on both cheeks.

"Mom, this is Thea. I think you met her at my show at Bergamot Station."

"Of course, come in! How are you?" Lupe squeezed Thea's hands.

She led them through a house crammed with a stunning variety of furniture: leather armchairs, a velvet sofa, a green plastic patio set. The Christmas tree was smothered with ornaments and there was a TV tray with a dozen glowing candles featuring the Virgin of Guadalupe, Baby Jesus, and seasonal bayberry.

Lupe clapped her hands and a Santa doll on the coffee table began to sing "Jingle Bell Rock." "I got it at Costco! Don't you love it?"

"Hmmm," said Tina thoughtfully. "Maybe I should do a beaded Santa?"

"I don't know," said Thea, just as thoughtfully. "It feels like Christmas is already sort of beaded."

"You're right. I should go with something more obscure . . . like a groundhog or a leprechaun."

The kitchen was in the back and overlooked a concrete patio with an ancient swing set. The jade-green linoleum was scratched and the cabinets needed a fresh coat of paint, but otherwise the room was spotless.

"Thea knows nothing about tamales," Tina said teasingly. She plucked two colorful aprons from a hook in the walk-in pantry. "And I don't know how much help she'll be. I've never actually seen her prepare food."

"I can cook." Thea squinted uncertainly at the table against the wall. Cornhusks were soaking in a Tupperware container next to a bag of masa, a huge stainless bowl, ears of corn, and a cutting board.

"We can always use an extra pair of hands," said Lupe, dumping the cornmeal into the bowl. "Your sisters . . ." her eyes narrowed. "They say they're too busy to come today. Can you believe it? Too busy for family. It's not right."

"Mama, come on. Monica's studying for the bar and Jennifer works retail," said Tina. "You want them to what, lose their jobs over tamales?"

Lupe dropped her jaw. "Family, tradition. In the end, that is more important than a job."

"Okay, then let's get this tradition going." Tina seized the chef's knife and an ear of corn. "Thea's searching for the meaning of Christmas," she said, slicing cleanly through the kernels. "For an art series."

Lupe stood in front of a clay-colored range stirring minced onion and poblano chili in a large sauté pan. Airily, she swirled her wooden spoon. "Your life. That's your real art." She snapped on the clock radio next to the sink and tuned in the AM big-band station. For the next hour, as they wrapped up the corn mush into neat golden packages, Tina and her mother gossiped about family and stacked their tamales in large aluminum pans.

"So why haven't I seen you at church?" Lupe frowned at her daughter.

"I'm busy! I'm beading a herd of buffalo. Anyway, I am very close to God," her daughter said steadily, "but I choose to worship Her in my own way."

"God is not a woman, quick! Say a Hail Mary." Lupe crossed herself, then looked at Thea. "You go to church?"

Thea shrugged guiltily. "Sorry."

"Mother! Thea's spiritual life is none of your business."

Lupe waved her palm. "Okay." She zeroed in on Thea's left hand. "You're not married either?"

Tina let out a long sigh of exasperation. "Not your business."

Thea grinned. "No, I'm not married, Lupe."

"Only one of my daughters is married. What's wrong with you girls? You'll end up old maids, no one will want you."

"Mom, not that shit again." Tina's cool was cracking.

"Christina Heather Rodriguez, don't you talk to me that way!"

"Sorry," Tina said and dropped her head meekly. "Why can't you be happy for me? I'm a successful artist. I'm in MoMA! Do you understand how hard, how incredibly . . . big that is?"

"Of course I'm proud of you, my love." Lupe hugged Tina fiercely, planting a trail of cornmeal across her daughter's back. "But a mother wants to see her children happily married. It's natural."

The two friends exchanged a warning look.

"I was engaged once," said Thea quickly.

Lupe briefly abandoned her daughter to flash her glittering eyes at Thea. "Really? What happened?"

Thank God, Tina exhaled in relief. Let it be her and not me.

LIKE MANY ARTISTS IN THE EARLY '90s, Thea and Cal had each found day jobs at a large graphic arts company in Hollywood. From nine to five they worked in a converted warehouse, bent over drafting tables, pasting up ads for toothpaste and bubble gum and shampoo. At home at night, they pursued their real art: Cal was painting a series of portraits in red while Thea was assembling verse, lace, and cocktail napkins on canvases with ornate gold frames.

For several weeks, they had been circling each other around the communal light box at Angel City Graphics. Thea had admired his supple fingers, stained with ink, and the tautness of his spiny frame. Cal was intensely quiet. He hadn't said anything more personal to her than, "Are you finished with that loupe?"

But now it was Halloween, the one holiday that seemed to turn jaded, blasé artists into twittering schoolgirls. The illustrator in the cubicle next to Thea had come to work dressed as Vegas Elvis and the meek storyboard artist had come as RuPaul. No one was working now that the camera department was mixing up a lethal brew of cranberry juice, vodka, and Galliano.

Thea had donned her favorite costume: spell-casting witch. In a long black wig and flowing gown, she felt magical and mysterious. Even Cal, whose daily uniform was rumpled jeans and black T-shirts, had embellished his look with a trashy blond Andy Warhol wig and thick black-framed glasses.

While airbrushing a photograph at her station, Thea felt a warm heat at her back.

"What are you doing tonight?" Cal was asking.

"Haunting," she'd replied, her voice muffled beneath her painter's mask.

He swiveled her taboret table. "I'm going up to the CalArts party. Have you ever been?"

Her eyes blinked wide and sultry above the white paper shield. "I went to Santa Cruz."

"Okay, fewer pot-smoking dreamers, more manic-depressives. Wanna come?"

In the arid hills just north of Los Angeles, the California Arts campus was teeming with students and alums in a rainbow of styles. Vampires and ghouls, party girls and schlubby guys were all packed in the cavernous breezeways tipping beers and plastic cups of Coke and vodka. A Devo cover band droned in the courtyard.

There were an impressive number of costumes featuring bare breasts. Full and ample, small and petite, breasts were hanging out on Renaissance portrait girls, Greek goddesses, Barbarellas, and Helmut Newton Night Porters in black leather shorts and shiny policeman caps.

After they'd passed their tenth or eleventh set of tits, Cal turned to Thea and grinned. "You might be overdressed."

She fluffed her glam wig. "I'm an artist, not an artist's model."

Cal moved in closer. He smelled faintly of varnish and tobacco. "But I want you to be my model."

She cocked her head dismissively, but he caught her chin and tipped her mouth up to meet his. The kiss was sharp and numbing.

Too strong.

"I'm bored of this shit," he said. Grabbing her hand, he threaded a path through the mob, nearly colliding with Mona Lisa and Ziggy Stardust.

He whisked her to a cowboy bar in Valencia that served greasy barbeque. Nestled in the corner booth, they drank beer and chomped on sticky baby back ribs.

The crowd was boisterous, the Oak Ridge Boys twanged from the jukebox, and Cal relaxed over dinner.

"I used to come here all the time when I was a student, to get away from those pseudoart types."

"So you're not a pseudoart type?" Thea arched back against the leather banquette.

"Maybe. But not forever." Cal tugged her back. "Don't pull away from me," he begged.

This sudden vulnerability surprised her. "Okay," she said, pressing her shoulder against him.

His studio apartment, on the top floor of a gray art deco building, overlooked Hollywood Boulevard. He'd lit candles and then undressed her on his futon, the only furniture in a room strewn with canvases and paint.

His work was romantic and figurative, unusual for the era, for unlike most of his contemporaries, he could really draw. He didn't need to assemble things or be overly clever or ironic. He conjured flesh and desire in the curve of a mouth, in the slant of the eyes . . . or the tensed backbone of his mostly female subjects.

As she fell back into his arms, back into his world, Thea felt herself losing control.

Too strong.

GAZING UP FROM THE BOWL OF corn mush, Thea realized Lupe and Tina were gaping at her.

"So what happened?" Lupe repeated. "What happened to your engagement?"

"Oh, that," said Thea. "We broke up."

"Was he bad? Unfaithful?" Lupe's pupils grew large and curious.

"It was . . . he was . . . well . . ." her voice faded away, searching for the short answer.

"Mom! Stop snooping, jeez." Tina tied up a tamale with a thin strip of husk. "She's our guest."

"Maybe now it'd be different," said Thea. "But fifteen years ago art was all I could manage. You have to give so much to a husband, to a family. I just . . . I was afraid of losing myself to that. I couldn't figure out how to do it all."

Lupe started to speak, but Tina cut her off. "Mama, we should really get these into the steamer."

Lupe carefully set aside a dozen tamales and then dropped them into two plastic bags. "Here, both of you, bring some back to your houses."

"Oh, that's okay," said Thea. "I don't want to take anything away from your Christmas meal."

"You need them more," Lupe clucked her tongue. "I know how you girls live. There's probably nothing in your freezer."

"It was fun being with your mom, talking and cooking," said Thea on the drive back to Venice.

"Maybe for you," Tina said. "For me it was a land mine—all those fucking marriage questions."

"Well why don't you tell—"

"Just stop," Tina cut her off. She straightened her back. "So who were you engaged to?"

"Cal Hawkins."

Tina whistled. "I remember that guy. He was hot in the nineties. I think we slept together."

"Really?"

"Nah, just kidding. But there were some embarrassing moments from my straight period. So what ever happened to him?" Tina was bordering on giddy. "All those red portraits of women."

Thea wondered what he looked like now, if he was still as intense as he'd been when he was twenty-five.

Oh, why do you care? She scolded herself. He hasn't called you. You haven't called him.

But she mentally traced his profile and his hands, the expert way he held an X-Acto knife. The T-shirts with obscure slogans in Japanese or Italian. That tangled thatch of curly dark brown hair.

Fuck, she thought. I must be bored with Marcus. Why else would I be writing this pathetic romance novel in my head?

"I don't know," Thea said breezily, gazing out at the clutter and diaspora on Venice Boulevard. "Vanessa said he moved up north to Point Reyes."

"If he was smart, he married one of those Marin County trust fund babes," said Tina.

"You're so cynical," Thea laughed.

"If I was going to get married, that would be a good reason." She pulled up to Thea's condo. "Well, here you are, back on the canal."

"Thanks," said Thea. "Tamale making is good for the soul."

"Or what's left of our souls."

Thea reached over and kissed her friend on the cheek. "Going to the gym tomorrow?"

Tina gripped the steering wheel. "Listen, I'm going to tell my mom, but not now, not during the holidays. If I say something now, then Christmas Day she'll be weeping, my sisters will take sides, Jen will be pissed at me for telling, Monica will stand up for my rights . . . This is not the time to do it. It's hard enough for me to get through this season without that. It just makes everything loaded. Anyway, I'm sure you don't tell your mother everything."

I don't tell my mother anything, Thea thought.

Standing at the curb, watching the pickup rattle away, she felt let down. It had been festive in Lupe's kitchen, her hands in cornmeal, the creamy scent of sweetness and a pine tree. The closest she'd been to holiday cheer.

But it's a borrowed cheer, she corrected herself. Borrowed from another family. People with secrets and hidden sorrows just like everyone's family.

What was it with this season that made people postpone the inevitable? Why do we pretend things are different than they really are?

Jangling her keys, she trudged up the stairs to her quiet, undecorated house and a fridge that held coffee and yogurt. She smiled, thinking of Lupe, and tucked her tamales in the freezer.

The holidays are set up for families, she decided. I'm always on the outside looking in.

And yet. What am I looking at?

Carol and Vanessa were her only family and she often felt separate from them. *We don't really connect at this time of year,* she frowned. And Carol was never especially *merry* at Christmas.

With any of her husbands.

Thea's father, Bill, had loved Christmas. He always mixed up a special batch of gingerbread pancakes, scenting the house with cinnamon and nutmeg. He acted like a child himself, eagerly assembling the dollhouse and the track for the Hot Wheels, stringing plastic pearls from the jewelry-making kit, and beating them at Clue.

But Carol hadn't liked Bill's family; she always pouted on the drive up to Bakersfield Christmas afternoon. And there'd be a tense argument in the car that would cloud the happiness of their merry morning with hurt, wounded feelings.

After their parents divorced, when Thea was seven, there was David, her Jewish stepfather, who lit candles for Hanukkah and served them latkes and crisp twenty-dollar bills. He didn't celebrate Christmas, and Carol, always deferential to her men, hadn't made it an issue.

Their last stepfather, Robert, had a knack for finding "bargain getaways" the week of December 24 and would coax Carol away to Big Sur or La Jolla, places you didn't really visit with stepdaughters. Thea and Vanessa were in their early twenties then and would assure their mother that "it didn't matter" and they were "too old for all that stuff," so she should "go and enjoy herself." Then the sisters would fend for themselves, joining a college friend or a coworker for potluck dinners that usually involved guacamole, chips, and a turkey from the deli. Thea vividly remembered Robert's paranoid political views and obsession with mutual funds. In a way he did us a favor, she concluded. I didn't really want to spend the holidays with him either.

In her studio, Thea dawdled for a few minutes at the window seat, staring down at the canal. The fog had crept in, and the late afternoon was dark and moody. There was a trio of joggers crossing the bridge and several seagulls gliding overhead. Meandering over to her laptop, she grew restless and dissatisfied. She wasn't interested in talking heads anymore. There's a universality to everyone's holiday, she decided. She would mine her own images. Sliding a sketchbook from the shelf above her desk, she flipped to a fresh page. With a gray Prismacolor pen, she played around with some holiday icons: a trio of carolers, a sleigh filled with presents, an angel and a star. Then she drew a window trimmed with boughs of pine and holly. Tipping back in her office chair, she imagined the people behind the paned glass.

They seemed Victorian, dressed in fur-trimmed cloaks and muffs. In their hands were small cups of something. Wassail, eggnog, poison?

She glimpsed loneliness and forced frivolity in their faces. We can't mandate happiness on the calendar, she thought, and yet, every year, we try to do it anyway. We strive to be merry and joyful.

She thought again of her dad and felt a tenderness inside her. He made Christmas special and she wondered if everyone

was chasing that same long-ago moment. Then she remembered the Barbie dream house that Carol had bought for her
and Vanessa, and she smiled. Okay, so maybe it's only about
gingerbread pancakes and a doll's hot pink crash pad. Maybe
that's all there is to it and maybe that's enough.

Flushed with excitement, she sketched another window
and searched for the images on the other side of the glass.

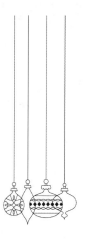

11

On the morning of the 24th, JT was lying in bed, his cheeks flushed, a thermometer protruding from under his tongue.

"I'm just tired from the show," he said weakly, as Vanessa checked the display.

The numbers had fixed at 101.2 This definitely wasn't fatigue.

She refilled the glass of water on his bedside table and pulled down the shades. Just last night, when she'd met him at the airport, he'd looked ashen. So she'd immediately scuttled their tree-trimming plans and told the boys they'd hang the ornaments this morning, just the four of them, before the guests arrived.

Now, once again, she yanked that fantasy off the stage and struggled not to shout, *I told you I didn't want your relatives to come out here and now you're sick and I have to entertain them by myself!*

Slipping quietly out the door, she pasted a creaky smile on her face and then corralled Ethan and Alex in the living room, where they opened the XMAS STUFF boxes.

"Daddy's sick, so the three of us are going to decorate the tree," she said, noticing this month's copy of *Living Simply* in a pile of bills and Christmas cards on the coffee table.

"Is he going to miss the presents?" said Ethan.

"No, I'm sure he'll be fine by tomorrow."

"Dad always puts the lights on first." Alex pawed though a box of ornaments and seized a tangled web of pine-green cords. "I know how to do it."

"I know how to do it, too." Ethan grabbed the plug on the end.

"You can both untangle the lights and then take turns winding them around the branches," said Vanessa. She had opened the magazine and was earnestly absorbing bullet points from an article titled "The Winter Solstice: Creating a Meaningful Dialogue."

"Guys, listen to this. 'The solstice reminds us that at the end of the long winter nights and cold barren days there will be spring, a time of abundance.'" Glancing out the window at the bright green orange trees and the flowering hibiscus, Vanessa squinted. She tried to imagine a world where people were hunkered around their cast-iron stoves, praying for deliverance from the bleak, colorless landscape that surrounded them.

"We already did that," said Alex, pointing to the dusty clutter of sage branches and acorns they had dumped on the mantelpiece after their hike in Fryman. Vanessa frowned. She'd forgotten to add candles and design and the necessary verve to her solstice altar.

"This is the best ornament!" Ethan dangled a snowboarding polar bear with a muffler that shouted, "Happy Holidays, Dude!"

"Ooooh, I remember buying that," his mother cooed. She had found Ethan's bear, and a dolphin for Alex, when the boys were just five. Returning her magazine to the pile of bills, she dug through the packing peanuts and extracted a shoe box marked FAVORITES. She carefully lifted out two egg-carton-and-pipe-cleaner ornaments the boys had made in preschool. "And remember these?" Her throat tightened.

But the boys were moving swiftly through another box: the brass toy soldiers, the reindeer figurines, and the trumpeting angels fashioned out of tin.

"Can we play *The Chipmunks Sing Christmas*?" said Ethan, rummaging through a pile of CDs next to the entertainment cabinet. "They're animals, so that's nature."

He popped in the disc and they all chirped along to "The Twelve Days of Christmas."

Vanessa sat on the floor, leaning against the couch, and watched the boys hook most of the ornaments on branches four feet off the ground, just about their shoulder height.

Our tree sort of resembles a hula dancer with a bare torso

and glittering skirt, she thought wryly. Declaring it awesome, she forced her sons to stand still for a photo and then shoved the remaining boxes of glittering gewgaws into the corner.

She had a turkey to roast.

Joy of Cooking instructed eighteen minutes per pound for a stuffed turkey or fifteen minutes per pound unstuffed. Quickly putting pen to paper, she realized her nineteen-pound tom would need 342 minutes divided by 60, which was more than five and a half hours.

Glancing at the clock, she saw it was already eleven thirty and her guests were slated to arrive at five.

Best not to stuff the bird.

Ethan clambered beside her. "I want to help!"

Oh, no, Vanessa worried. With Ethan's help this could take forever.

Immediately, she felt like a horrible mother. Buck up! She told herself, you want him to *participate* in holiday preparations.

"Okay, dial the oven up to 350," she said, placing a saucepan with a stick of butter on a low flame.

After carefully setting the oven temperature, Ethan dragged a stool next to his mother at the counter. Climbing up, he loomed over the moist carcass nesting in a rack in a disposable tray.

"Now," instructed Vanessa, reading from her book, "reach inside the cavity and remove the neck and giblets."

Ethan shot his slender fist into the bowels and gleefully extracted a leaky sack of slimy organs. "Yuck!" He flung them into the sink, sending a shower of pink, watery poultry blood across the counter and down to the floor.

"Oh, my God, Ethan!" his mother shouted. "Turkeys are teeming with fatal bacteria." Miserably, she revisited the wisdom of a standing rib roast—a slab of meat that didn't require any trussing—and decided that Patience was right.

"Come on, we have to clean this up." They wiped the floor and the counters until she felt they'd be cleared by the health department.

"Can we stick it in the oven now?" said Ethan.

"After we season it." She whisked the saucepan off the stove.

"Aunt P always puts stuff in the butt," said Ethan.

"I know, but we're going to do it differently." Carefully, she brushed some melted butter over the breast and then let Ethan sprinkle the bird with kosher salt and dried thyme and sage.

"Now let's say a prayer for the bird, to thank him for giving up his life to nourish us."

Ethan looked dubious. "Aunt P never does that."

"Well, don't you think we should?"

"No, he can't hear anything."

Vanessa smoothed his hair. "I want us to be grateful. That's what we remember this time of year. To be grateful."

"I thought we were grateful at Thanksgiving."

"Well, we can be grateful for two days. Okay, help me get it in the oven."

He lowered the door and Vanessa pushed the roasting pan inside. She set the timer for four hours and placed the melted butter and the basting brush beside the stove.

Standing at the sink, she scrubbed her hands with fragrant honeysuckle soap. The smell of raw meat had made her slightly nauseous.

"Vanessa . . ." JT's voice dribbled pathetically down the hallway.

"I'll be right there."

She reached the bedroom just as her husband vomited all over the freshly laundered comforter.

"I'm going to throw up again," he moaned.

Grasping his arm, she steered him into the bathroom, where he hunched over the porcelain bowl.

"Should I call Dr. Gold?" Vanessa charged back to the bed and quickly unbuttoned the duvet cover. She prayed the bile hadn't soaked through onto the comforter.

It had.

Dumping the whole lot into the bathtub, she plucked a washcloth from the cabinet next to the sink, ran it under the tap, and applied it to the back of her husband's neck.

"I feel like shit." He laid his cheek on the toilet seat.

Dear God, please don't let me get it, she prayed.

After a final round of dry heaves, JT declared he was finished and crawled back into bed.

"Don't sip any water for a half hour," Vanessa said, a little too harshly. Opening the closet, she reached for a wool blanket and then smoothed it over the sheet.

JT would not be mashing the potatoes.

Her head throbbed, but she told herself it wasn't from his virus or fatal turkey bacteria. Just mounting anxiety at the thought of twelve for dinner in . . . she glanced at the clock. Four hours and forty minutes.

Closing the bedroom door, she padded to the kitchen and snatched up the cordless phone.

First she dialed Carol.

"I'm sorry dear," her mother said, "but Frank and I are organizing dinner today at the Pasadena Shelter."

"But *Mother*," Vanessa emphasized their genetic relationship, "I need help."

"Vanessa, these people are *homeless*. And at this time of year, the need is critical."

"I know," Vanessa said in a little mouse voice. The mere mention of impoverished families made her own problems seem petty. And, as a former director of a perpetually under-funded nonprofit, it was Carol's job to exploit people's guilt.

"I'm sure Thea can help you," her mother was saying. "Why don't you give her a call? And don't worry—I've got the veggie platter."

Vanessa groaned and dialed her sister's cell phone. She heard shouting and screaming on the line.

"I'm at Marcus's mom's house and I can't talk," Thea whispered. "She just found out that his brother Kingston sold the car. It's complicated. But don't worry—I've got dessert."

Vanessa balled up her fists. Why do I even bother with those two? she thought angrily. Then another voice inside her took charge. Call Patience! it ordered. She can do this with one arm tied behind her back.

But a stubborn streak had erected a wall where her sister-in-law was concerned. I don't want Patience, she thought childishly. She'll want to do everything her way and we'll have to chitchat and it'll be worse than being alone.

Vanessa decided to make herself a cup of coffee. As she waited for the water to boil, she remembered the kitchen in Wenham and the first time she met Patience at Christmas.

She'd only known JT a few months, and, unaware of the local dress code, had worn a too-short skirt and too-saucy pumps. Sexy, but totally impractical in snowy, not showy Massachusetts.

When Patience had opened the front door, her studied glance at Vanessa's outfit had telegraphed BIG MISTAKE.

Patience was the epitome of good taste in cashmere, cashmere, and classic patent loafers. A tidy string of pearls tickled her neckline, and her skin was fair and dewy—the complexion of one who had never battled the ravages of a California sun.

Vanessa felt judged and unwelcome, and as the evening progressed, she hewed to this initial impression. Neither chatty nor warm, Patience had given her a perfunctory greeting and a limp handshake and then proceeded to discuss, at length, friends and family that she and JT and Richard all had in common, having grown up and gone to college in New England.

The final blow came while Vanessa was quietly peeing in the guest bathroom right next to the kitchen.

"I can't believe he broke up with Amanda for *her*," she'd heard Patience say to her sister, Hope.

"Well, she is pretty, and you know, men go for that tacky California look," Hope had sighed. "Where'd she go to college?"

"I think it was a state school." Patience had sounded so smug, so . . . superior. "Not that that's something to be ashamed of . . ." her voice had trailed away, ripe with innuendo.

Afterwards, upstairs in the guest bedroom, Vanessa had cried the pitiful tears of the odd girl out. "What a bitch!" she wailed to JT. "So Cal State Northridge isn't . . . Middlebury!

But so what! I mean, what difference does it make? I'm a smart person with an interesting job."

"Oh, honey, Patience is just . . . She's just . . . I don't know, when you get to know her, she's different," JT had said lamely. "I think she's acting this way because she was best friends with Amanda, but she'll just have to accept that I've moved on."

The name Amanda electrified the air. JT and Amanda Barlow had been engaged . . . until he'd moved to L.A. and met Vanessa Clayton. Before that, the Channings had assumed JT would live in Wenham and take over the family business. But he'd stayed in California, Richard Channing Sr. had passed on, and forty years of Channing's General Store had morphed into a new seafood restaurant on Main Street.

Vanessa bristled. "I asked her a million questions. She hardly said a thing. And she didn't seem interested in the Left Coast Ensemble or that cop show you just finished."

JT sat on the bed and laughed. "V, people in Wenham have no idea about life outside of Wenham. And they certainly don't know what a gaffer does. My brother is clueless about film and sets and lighting."

"But why isn't he interested in your work?"

"It's not that he isn't interested. We're just two different species. He understands medicine and I understand the importance of making a box of cereal look good. Now, let me give you some advice on topics of conversation here in small-town Massachusetts." He took her hand and pulled her onto the bed. "Weather, the Big Dig, the possibility of a new traffic light downtown. You could coast for a year straight just on those subjects alone."

Vanessa giggled. "Or die of boredom."

"Well, before you die of boredom"—he kissed her neck—"we could talk about . . . the best clamming on the North Shore or taxes for the new high school."

"You really know how to talk dirty," she said.

"Traffic on Main Street," he murmured, unbuttoning his shirt.

THE CORDLESS PHONE IN HER HAND jingled, breaking the reverie. "Hello?"

"Hey, it's Neil."

Neil? Why was he . . . Oh, my God, she realized. *Neil's coming tonight.* She steadied herself against the kitchen counter.

"You were supposed to call and tell me what to bring," he was saying.

An unexpected groan escaped from her throat. "Uhhh . . ."

"Are you all right?"

"Well, JT is sick and I'm sort of . . . doing this alone and I guess I'm freaking out." *Freaking out?* What was she, a Disney Channel tween?

"Well, I could come over and help," he said simply.

"Really?" Vanessa felt a warm wave of relief. At the very least Neil could occupy the twins. "Do you know anything about cooking a turkey?"

"I'll see you in an hour," he said, hanging up the phone.

Vanessa rushed to the bathroom, where she brushed her

teeth and applied a thin coat of mascara. Spying the soiled comforter in the bathtub, she dragged the shower curtain across the rod to conceal it.

She felt a guilty pang. Why am I letting Neil help me but not my sister-in-law?

Then, as she twisted her hair into one of those casually-not-casual chignons, she rationalized. Patience and Neil are both annoying, she concluded. But Neil is just everyday annoying whereas with Patience, there's annoying plus a decade on top.

Tiptoeing into the bedroom, she peeked at JT, then striped off her sweatpants and changed into slim cropped pants and a white boyfriend shirt. What she didn't admit to herself as she zoomed back to the kitchen was that Neil was a whole lot sexier than her sister-in-law.

NEIL ARRIVED WEARING WRITER BLACK TIE: black jeans, untucked midnight-blue shirt, and dark wool blazer. He was carrying two bottles of white wine and two narrow cardboard boxes, which he presented to Ethan and Alex.

Tearing open the end flaps, each boy removed a five-foot-long skateboard rail. The perfect metal bar for grinding.

"Cool!"

"Sweet!"

Neil smiled. "You gotta expand your skatepark."

He helped the boys set up the rails in the driveway and then watched as they rode their skateboards and slid across the tops. After a few grinds of his own, he wandered back to the kitchen and retrieved a bottle of wine. "Shall we get this party started?"

Vanessa, who was peeling potatoes, grinned nervously. "Okay, but just half a glass for me. I have to stay focused."

"Corkscrew is . . ."

Waving the peeler, she indicated a drawer on his left. "And the glasses are just above you."

Cupping two glasses, he said, "How many wine drinkers tonight?"

"Eight."

He lined up eight wineglasses on the counter. "Why don't I go ahead and set the table?"

She hesitated. "Uh, sure."

"You think I can't do it?" He grinned. "I have been to a dinner party before."

"No, I mean yes, thank you. The plates are over there." She bobbed her head to the right. "The silverware is in the drawer next to the corkscrew and the linens are in the dining room buffet."

"Any Christmas tablecloths?"

Vanessa bit her lip. "No. Just use whatever's clean."

"Okay," he said, expertly carrying four goblets to the dining room. "I think snowflakes and sleighs look weird in California anyway."

While Vanessa scraped away at the tuber skin, Neil ferried place settings to the table, extracted her best white lace tablecloth and napkins from the bowels of the dusty china hutch, and unearthed silver candlesticks that she'd forgotten she owned.

"So," he said, fifteen minutes later, "what next?"

"Could you help me do the stuffing?"

AS THEY SIPPED THEIR CHARDONNAY AT the butcher-block counter, Vanessa marveled at how relaxing it was having someone to share the cooking. She and JT mostly divided up the chores separately - rarely did they actually perform domestic duties in tandem. Stealing a glance at Neil, she admired his clean look and his competence, even the way he chopped onions on the cutting board. She let herself fantasize about being married to a sophisticated New York writer . . . the dinner parties they'd give and the vacations they'd take in the Hamptons and Europe with all their New York friends. "New York" friends sounded funnier, livelier, more fascinating somehow. They'd own a rambling farmhouse—make that a recently restored farmhouse—and they'd collect something. What? Tin toys? Salt and pepper shakers? Milking stools?

"You'll be happy to know that I haven't looked at the play," Neil interrupted her fantasy on the farm. "I decided you were right. I had to let it go."

"That's great. So what have you been doing instead?" Vanessa cut the potatoes into chunks and dropped them into a large stockpot.

"Mostly seeing friends . . . and some of the cast. Gary and his boyfriend had me over for dinner. I think I was the only straight guy there. But everyone was very *courteous,*" he emphasized the word. "I felt like the prom queen."

Vanessa pouted a little. "He didn't invite me!"

"Well, you couldn't have brought the twins. The house is filled with breakable things. Plus there's nowhere to skate-board."

Vanessa shrugged. One less present to buy anyway.

"Married people always feel sorry for us singles at the holidays," Neil opined as he read the instructions on the package of Mrs. Cubbison's. "I get a lot of invitations this time of year."

"Like mine?" Vanessa said impishly.

"Like yours."

"Jeez, how come no one feels sorry for married people?"

A tense current shot between them. Vanessa hefted her potatoes to the sink and filled the pot with water. "What I mean," she said hastily, "is that no one worries about us because they assume that we're busy with our own families."

"Aren't you?"

Vanessa hesitated. "Yes. No. Well, yes I'm busy, but no, I often feel alone this time of year."

"Everyone's a little bit lonely this time of year," Neil said quietly.

Opening the fridge, he reached for a stick of butter. Then he lifted a sauté pan from the rack next to the stove and turned on the flame. In short order, he was sweating the minced vegetables.

"Uh, do you need anything else?" Vanessa glanced at his workstation.

"No, I'm good."

They chopped and stirred in companionable silence. Vanessa scooped out cranberry sauce and measured cream and butter for the mashed potatoes until the arrival of nine-year-olds broke the culinary spell.

"Neil," Alex tugged on the writer's shirtsleeve. "Can you take us down to the alley? Mom won't let us go alone."

"I have to finish the stuffing," Neil said.

"We'll help you!" Alex jumped up and down in excitement. Vanessa raised an eyebrow.

Neil consulted the directions on the bag. "Okay, we need some cans of chicken broth and a large covered casserole."

"I know where the cans are." Ethan dashed to the cupboard flanking the window.

Alex scrunched up his forehead. "What's a casserole?"

Vanessa wiped her starchy hands on her pants and opened the cabinet doors beside the oven. "They're all in here." She chose three white Corning dishes in various sizes. "Which one will fit?"

Neil lowered the bowl of stuffing down to kid level and Alex appraised it thoughtfully. "That one," he said, pointing to the largest rectangle.

The twins took turns spooning the bread cubes into the dish and then Neil covered it with a lid.

"Should we check the bird?" Vanessa said nervously.

"Turkey blood is toxic," Ethan announced.

"Oh, really?" Neil opened the oven door and easily lifted the roasting pan onto the stovetop. Picking up the pastry brush, he basted the crisping skin with the melted butter and then returned the bird to the oven.

Dusting off his hands, he grinned at Vanessa. "I think we're okay here. Mind if we check out the alley?"

"All right, but"—she wagged a spoon at her crew—"back in an hour to wash up before the guests arrive."

Standing at the kitchen sink, she watched them race across the yard. As she slit open the pouch of frozen peas and dumped them into a large saucepan, she thought about how great Neil was with kids.

Perfect husband material.

And then, as she washed and dried the knives and cutting board, she speculated about Neil's future wife.

And wondered what life would be like . . . if it were her.

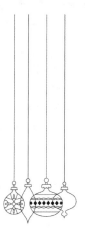

12

The last thing Thea expected to find in Vanessa's kitchen was a handsome stranger.

French kissing her sister.

Vanessa heard the footsteps and, horrified, flung herself from Neil's embrace.

"Hi," Thea said, plunking down a stack of white pastry boxes. "I'm Vanessa's sister. But you're not my brother-in-law."

Neil shrugged gamely and Vanessa gagged. "Oh! Thea—"

Her sister interrupted. "Richard just parked the car, so they'll be here any—"

"Hello!" The front door banged open and they heard the clatter of shoes and the rustle of packages.

"Merry Christmas!" Richard's voice ricocheted through the house.

"This is a moment," Neil said under his breath.

"You haven't introduced me to your *guest*." Thea nudged Vanessa into consciousness.

"Uh, this is Neil Cohen."

Richard, Patience, and Libby burst into the room and Vanessa cranked into fourth gear, babbling through a list of introductions.

Once everyone was properly known to one another, they decamped to the living room and showered the twins with presents.

Patience, who was sitting next to Vanessa on the couch, turned to her sister-in-law with concern. "How is JT doing?"

"Still in bed. He won't be joining us for dinner," she said. Looking up, she noticed that Neil was watching her from across the room.

She returned his gaze for a moment, then shook him off. But she kept repeating the scene, over and over again, in her mind.

With dinner under way, she'd gone back to the bedroom to check on JT, who was sleeping soundly. After a quick shower, she'd changed into a scarlet dress with a fitted bodice and sheer sleeves. With black sling backs and fresh lip gloss, she'd returned to the kitchen and found Neil back from skating and basting the turkey.

"You don't have to do that," she'd said, grinning.

"No. But there is something I have to do," he'd said.

Then he'd just . . . kissed her.

He'd slammed the oven shut, strode across the floor, circled his arms around her, and in an instant, they were lip-locked.

"What are you doing?" Vanessa swirled in a cyclone of shock, desire, and the fear of being caught.

"I want you," Neil said. "I'm in love with you."

"You are not," Vanessa whispered urgently. "Stop saying that! I have a husband . . . children . . ."

"It doesn't change anything," Neil said and kissed her again.

And then, in complete surprise to herself, she had kissed him back. She had opened her mouth, opened her heart, pressed herself against his chest and . . .

And her sister had showed up.

Damn it, Thea! Vanessa thought. Now I don't know what possessed him! What he meant . . . what happened.

But she did, sort of.

And she couldn't think about it anymore because Carol and Frank were smiling at her and holding out the veggie platter. "Carrots, dear? Ranch dip?"

And the family was gathering around the tree and someone—Richard?—was serving wine.

The boys were staring blankly at the new sweaters from their aunt and uncle.

Patience was hugging Alex.

Ethan was jumping on Libby.

All she could think about was how desperately she wanted Neil to disappear. But there he remained, stationed firmly by the fireplace—in JT's reading chair!—deep in conversation with Marcus about surfing in Australia.

And now Patience was heading her way with a cherry-red gift box from Talbots.

"But I have to get your gift," Vanessa felt flustered. "And Libby's. Where are they? Maybe in the back of the tree?" The memory of her scandalous kiss superseded a shawl and a charm bracelet.

"Well, open this first," her Cheshire-in-law beamed.

It was a matching sweater set in persimmon cashmere, the sort of expensive apparel that Patience liked for herself.

"Everyone always needs a sweater set," she said with authority.

Even fallen women who cheat on their husbands? Vanessa wondered.

"That color is perfect on you," Patience nestled the cashmere against Vanessa's chest. "Are you all right? You look a little flushed."

"I'm fine," Vanessa said. "It's . . . the kitchen was very hot."

She blushed again.

Then Frank was arm wrestling Alex and Thea and Marcus were smooching in the hallway, but Vanessa remained in a trance.

A trance that kept her from interrogating Neil.

And leaving the house.

With him or without him—she couldn't decide.

But the turkey needed carving and the potatoes needed mashing.

People needed more wine.

I can't be alone in the kitchen with him, Vanessa realized.

Shakily, she rose and tapped Richard's arm. "Will you make sure everyone has another drink?" Then she turned to Patience. "Will you help me with dinner?"

"Of course," said Patience, pleased to be asked.

With her sister-in-law at the helm, the meat was sliced, the sides were garnished, and all was whisked to the dining room.

As they prepared to quit the kitchen for the meal, Patience laid a gentle hand on Vanessa's arm.

"You're sure you're all right?"

Oh, my God! Vanessa freaked. She knows about the kiss! "I'm fine," she said, imploring herself to remain calm. "Just a little frazzled . . . from all the prep."

"Of course!" Patience nodded sympathetically. "A meal like this takes so much out of you. But it's just beautiful. You were right to insist on turkey."

Okay, she's being too nice to me, Vanessa exhaled with relief. So clearly she *doesn't* know.

At dinner, there was talk about the New England Patriots, the skyrocketing cost of surfboard foam, and the shrinking lobster population in Essex.

"We're driving up to UC Santa Cruz after Christmas," announced Libby, steering them towards an interesting topic.

"Can we go?" Ethan bounced in his chair.

"Oh, Eth, you'd be totally bored," his cousin soothed. "It'll be . . . just old people talking and stuff."

"That's my alma mater," said Thea.

Libby's eyes flashed. "When were you there?"

"A million years ago when they didn't have grades," Thea said dryly. "Perfect for art majors."

"It's one of several colleges we're considering," said Patience.

"*I'm* considering." Libby dropped her fork with a clatter.

"Well, I loved it," Thea smiled. "It's a beautiful place to be."

"When was the last time you were there?" said Libby.

"It's been a few years."

"It would be so cool to go to school in California." Libby heaved her shoulders emphatically.

Thea winked. "More than cool."

Patience turned to Neil on her right. "I understand that Vanessa is helping you with your play."

Neil directed his reply to Vanessa, who was seated at the head of the table. "Yeah, I'm really lucky to have her."

The way he phrased it, caressed it, caused the entire group to grind to a halt.

Everyone glanced at Vanessa.

"He's a brilliant playwright I had nothing to do with it *hee hee hee,*" she said breathlessly.

"Is it your first play?" Patience reached for another piece of turkey breast from the platter.

"No, but fortunately, I was able to dine out on that one for years," Neil shook his head ruefully. "My last show bombed."

"Been there," said Thea. "Every show is your first show."

"We saw *Mamma Mia!* in Boston," said Patience. "Don't you just love Abba? What's your play about?"

"Two brothers confronting their father's suicide."

"What's sue's inside?" Alex interrupted.

"Suicide is when someone takes his own life," said Neil.

"Takes it where?" said Ethan.

"Boys!" Patience abruptly picked up the bowl of mashed potatoes. "Would you like more potatoes? Your mother did an excellent job. They're very creamy." She turned to Vanessa. "Did you do something special?"

Vanessa looked puzzled. "Mashed them?"

Thea resumed her common ground with Libby. "Have you picked a major?"

"No, but I think I want to do something for the environment. Or maybe international studies. And I really want to travel."

"Who's going to take over my practice?" said Richard.

"Dad, please, I'm not going to be a doctor."

"I'm going to be a doctor," said Alex, "and cut people up like Uncle Richard.

"That's the spirit," said Richard, reaching across the table and giving his nephew a high five. Everyone laughed and the mood grew lighter.

Vanessa scraped back her chair and darted towards the bedroom. "Excuse me. I think I'll check on JT."

She found her husband awake and curled on his side. She sat next to him on the bed and gently smoothed his damp forehead.

"How're you doing?"

"Fine," he whispered.

"I think your fever's down."

He stared glassy-eyed into space.

"I'm sorry you're here alone, I'm sorry you're sick," Vanessa said. Tears shimmered in her lashes.

"It sounds like everyone's having a good time," JT said hoarsely.

She threw her arms around him dramatically. "No! It's terrible without you!"

"Oh, honey," he frowned. "I'll make it up somehow, I promise."

Vanessa kissed the top of his greasy head, not even caring that he smelled rank and moldy. She reached for the glass of water and helped him take a sip. "Do you need anything else?"

"No." He closed his eyes. "Just sleep."

She pulled the blanket up around his shoulder and then, fortified in marriage, she slipped away and returned to her guests.

WHEN DESSERT WAS OVER AND COFFEE was served, Richard hugged his nephews close and made his annual announcement.

"Time for football!" he boomed. "I'll be one team captain and Neil, you can lead the opposing team."

"Sorry, but I'm more of an individual sports guy," said Neil.

"Aw, come on. Where's the fun in that?"

"I'll be team captain," said Marcus.

"You will?" Thea looked at him with surprise.

"Hey, I was a receiver in high school," Marcus grinned sheepishly.

"Isn't it kind of late for a game?" Patience glanced out at the dark winter evening. "You won't be able to see where you're going."

"I'm sure V has lights outside," said Richard.

Vanessa seemed doubtful. "There's one over the garage."

Frank rose slowly to his feet and beat his chest. "Go Trojans!"

Patience and Vanessa exchanged worried looks.

"And I'll be cheerleader," said Carol, giving a little shimmy.

"It's not the same without JT," said Patience sadly. "You know how he and Richard love to pretend they're Kennedys."

WHILE THE REST OF THE PARTY battled for scrimmage, Vanessa wrapped up leftovers, Neil loaded the dishwasher, and Patience wiped down the kitchen counters.

"Are you enjoying it out here in California?" Patience asked Neil.

"Yeah," Neil said, jamming dirty forks into a packed cutlery basket. "I'm remembering the things I liked about it. The Farmers Market, the view of the hills, American Girl Place." He glanced slyly at Vanessa.

"The weather is nice, but I would miss the seasons." Patience diligently scrubbed the turkey grease and crusted grime on the stovetop.

Vanessa scooped cranberry sauce into a plastic container and listened to Patience and Neil chat amiably about hiking in Vermont, New York theater, and the summers he spent on the Cape working for a boat rental.

Why is he talking to her! Vanessa bridled. He kissed me and said he loved me and now suddenly he's, he's, he's flirting with my sister-in-law? Angrily, she snapped the lid down on her Tupperware.

The burping noise made Patience glance over. "Vanessa, do you want to go outside and watch the game? We'll finish up in here."

"Fine," said Vanessa, slamming the leftovers into the fridge. She opened the back door and nearly collided with Richard.

"Frank's down!" Richard said. "V, have you got a cold pack?"

"Is he all right?" said Vanessa.

"He's fine, it's just a minor contusion," barked Richard. "I think he didn't see the boys coming."

"Because it's dark outside!" Patience said indignantly.

Vanessa extracted a gel pack from the freezer and Patience snatched it away.

"Someone always gets hurt in these games. I knew it was a bad idea." Following Richard outside, she left the guilty couple alone in the kitchen.

"Why did you do that?" Vanessa pounced on Neil with a fervent whisper.

Before he could answer, Thea and Marcus burst in.

"Well, this game's over," said Thea. "So we're going to head home. It was nice meeting you, Neil." She smiled, a little too catlike.

"Listen, man," Marcus said and cocked his thumb and forefinger. "If you want to check out the waves this week, I've got a board you could ride."

"Call me later?" Thea shot a pointed look at her sister.

Realizing she couldn't have this conversation with Neil—not now, not ever—Vanessa tagged after them.

"I'll see you out."

Then, while she kissed her guests and fussed over Frank's swelling knee, Vanessa rehearsed her good-bye speech. *It was a wonderful moment,* she'd say to him. Or, *I don't know what came over me—it must be the holidays.* Or maybe, *regardless of our feelings, this can never happen again.*

God! She thought, I hope I don't sound totally pathetic. Closing the door behind the last of her relatives, she screwed up her courage and blazed back into the kitchen.

Neil was gone. There would be no tragic farewell.

So he didn't really love her after all!

REELING FROM THE DRAMA AND ATTENDANT fantasies, Vanessa pried her boys from the new video game and swept them into the bathroom where they all three brushed their teeth.

"There're still presents under the tree," said Ethan.

"Those are from me and Daddy," said Vanessa.

"Can we open them now?" said Alex.

"No. Tomorrow morning. And you have to wait for the sun to come up." Vanessa wished she had checked the time for sunrise in the weather section of the paper. Hopefully it was past six-thirty. "That way you'll have something to open on Christmas day."

"I can't wait," said Alex, clutching his middle.

"We didn't put out cookies for Santa!" Ethan dribbled toothpaste on the floor.

"I never believed in Santa," said Alex with a superior air.

"Yes, you did," Ethan shot back.

"You both did," said their mother. Sniffing, she thought she detected a faint whiff of bile from the comforter.

She groaned. Who could have an affair with the lingering scent of vomit in the house?

She snapped off the light.

Retreating to bed, she had just closed her eyes when the phone rang. *Neil!* Her heart did another flip-flop as she snatched the handset.

"Vanessa?" said Thea. "Why haven't you called me?"

Her spirits fell. "Hold on." She took the phone into the living room, settled on the couch, and stared out the window at her quiet street. "Okay, what?"

"Okay, what the fuck was that? Are you guys having an affair?" Thea's voice trilled with both horror and fascination.

"No, of course not! It was just . . . it was just . . . a momentary lapse of judgment."

"It didn't look momentary. It looked hot."

"It's the holidays," Vanessa insisted, thinking, God, it was hot! "People go crazy. I don't know what happened."

"Yes, you do," her sister prompted.

Vanessa watched as, across the street, a front door flew open and a merry band of revelers spilled out. *I kissed a handsome man who says he loves me.*

"I'd tell you if there was something going on."

Would she? Thea wondered. "I don't want you and JT getting divorced over some pretentious writer."

"He's not pretentious!"

"Yeah, right. What was with that help in the kitchen routine?"

"He's a single guy in his thirties. I'm sure he goes to a million dinner parties. And anyway, *my sister* didn't come over and help me!"

"Because I promised Marcus I'd go to his mother's house first."

"Let's not argue about this. It was stupid and it won't happen again. And since when are you the patron saint of monogamy?"

"Since I see that your marriage works. And I love JT. I need to know there are couples like you out there."

"Oh, Thea," Vanessa laughed. "You're like the Japanese who pay their monks to pray so that they don't have to pray themselves."

"Okay, kinda," Thea said. "But yes . . . I want you to stay married and keep hope alive."

"I can't believe I'm hearing this from a person who sleeps with a new guy every, I don't know, two years."

"I'm different. I'm not you."

Vanessa didn't have the strength to pursue this. "Look, I'm exhausted, and the kids will be up at dawn. Can you just believe me and let it go? I have to get some sleep."

"Fine, but don't cheat."

"Fine, good night."

Vanessa signed off but continued to watch her neighbors. They were lingering on the sidewalk, bidding good night to their guests. Someone was singing "Let It Snow! Let It Snow! Let It Snow!"

Glancing at her fireplace, she longed to put out cookies and milk for Santa. The boys are nine, she told herself sadly; they don't believe in that anymore. She tried to remember if they'd left out cookies last year at Patience's house. Yes, of course they had. Even though Alex had proudly announced that he "never" believed in Santa, Patience had cheerfully laid out homemade gingersnaps. Plus a bowl of carrots for the reindeer. And then later that night, she and Richard and JT had finished up the cookies with small glasses of port.

All those Christmases they'd spent in Wenham with her in-laws. Sometimes it had snowed and sometimes the ground was bare. But it was always dark and crisp outside and Patience made it snug and cozy inside with a fire and homemade eggnog and spice cake. Now that she thought about it, it had been nice and special and sort of relaxing.

Fuck, Vanessa thought. I am a total failure at Christmas.

Squinting her eyes, she looked out the window and pretended that lacy white flakes were falling and sleigh bells were ringing.

Christmas Eve is over and I didn't do anything with JT, she realized. We didn't bake cookies. We didn't wrap presents together. It didn't feel particularly merry.

But her body thrilled at the memory of Neil's mouth on hers. His breath. His cheek. The passion it evoked. There were no cookies, but there had been a kiss. A spine-tingling, glowing, glittering sort of kiss.

An unexpected Christmas present.

But in keeping with holiday traditions, tomorrow morning she would have to take this present back.

She hugged herself tightly. But not tonight. Tonight, she'd keep it tucked inside her. A shimmering, secret Santa gift.

Merry Christmas, Vanessa.

Have you been naughty or nice?

*   *   *

EVEN THOUGH IT WAS JUST PAST ten, Patience and Richard were exhausted, and, after kissing Libby good night, they retired to their room.

Libby sprawled on her bed and read text messages. Four were from Sarah, and one, the very, very best one, was from Brian. She skimmed through Sarah's missives first (Sarah was, after all, her best friend), the last of which said, *gt ttly lme gfts m n bthrm smkng hw yr xmas c brn?*

Satisfied that Sarah had nothing urgent going on, Libby read Brian's post: C U 2nte?

She texted back: Hme nw.

Two minutes later, her cell rang.

"Can I come over?"

"Now?" she giggled.

"It's not that late."

"Okay. But knock softly! My parents are sleeping next door."

She swapped her holiday-with-the-relatives V-neck sweater and black skirt for low-rise jeans and a new lacy tank. Then she layered her lashes with 24/7 longestloveliestluscious mascara.

Nervously, she bounced up and down on the bed and texted Sarah again.

Finally, there was a knock.

When she opened the door, Brian kissed her.

"I couldn't wait to see you," he said.

Libby churned in turmoil. She wanted to invite him in, but she knew what would happen if she did.

They'd have sex.

Lots of it.

They'd do *everything*.

And she wasn't prepared.

She didn't have condoms, didn't know if he did, didn't want to tell him she was a virgin, didn't know how to deal.

She'd had some sex with two other boys but that was so *completely* different. In tenth grade she'd gone to a couple of parties with Shane O'Connor and they'd gotten drunk and made out in his parents' gazebo. Then last spring, she and Corey Larsen had had a thing for a few weeks. She'd let him feel her breasts and she'd even given him a blow job in his mom's Volvo, but it had felt very clinical. Like a cultural fact-finding mission in a National Geographic TV show.

With Brian it was pure lust. She wanted him to touch her; in fact, her desire was overwhelming.

"Let's go downstairs," she said, "and hang out at the pool."

"It's kinda cold outside," he said, a hint of disappointment in his tone.

"My parents . . ."

"Okay, no worries." He smiled and touched her hair. "But you'd better get a jacket."

Hurrying over to the closet, Libby plucked her cropped jacket from a wooden hanger and then noticed a folded blanket on the shelf above. Impulsively, she grabbed that too.

Outside, they were alone with the still, illuminated water, the rustling palm fronds, and the inky sky. Brian pushed two lounge chairs together and they snuggled under the warmth of the wool cover. Their kisses grew longer and more urgent.

He reached under her shirt, so she pulled it off.

He unclasped her bra, so she set it free.

He touched her breasts and she gasped.

"Libby, I want you so much," he said, softly panting. "Ever since we met, I've wanted you."

The idea crackled in the air above them.

"I haven't done . . . everything," she said finally.

"We'll be safe," he said. "I have protection."

So it could happen.

If she wanted.

Suddenly, a security guard strolled towards them, flashing his beam across their laps.

Brian ducked down under the blanket. "I don't want my uncle to know I'm out here," he whispered.

Libby shaded her eyes against the light. "Oh hi, I'm a guest here. Room four twelve."

"Sorry to disturb you," he mumbled, hastily retreating to the opposite side of the pool.

"We can't stay out here," Libby giggled softly. "I think we should go upstairs."

"Are you sure?" Brian eagerly searched her face.

She kissed him and, adjusting her bra back in place, led him from their public boudoir into her private one.

IN THE END, SHE DECIDED TO wait.

For everything.

And Brian was okay with that.

They touched each other with their mouths and tongues and fingertips.

She discovered the pleasure of making him come, of hearing him call out her name, of feeling him shiver. For the first time, she let a man caress her to climax, and it was thrilling, maybe more thrilling than if they'd gone all the way and she'd been nervous with worry and fear.

After they'd explored a myriad of options except for *that one,* they fell asleep, cradled in each other's arms, the gentle hum of the Ventura Freeway a distant lullaby.

A MILE AWAY, AT FOUR A.M. on that same Christmas morning, Alex stood next to his parents' bed.

"Mom," he stuck his nose in her face. "Mom, is it time to get up?"

Vanessa heard an echo at the end of a dark, dark tunnel. What was it?

"Mom!"

Her eyes flew open but her body felt heavy and drugged. Why was Alex here in the middle of the night? "Are you sick?" she mumbled.

Crumpling onto the bed, he began to weep. "I can't take it anymore! I can't, I can't!"

"Honey, what's wrong?" Worried, Vanessa gathered him into her arms and felt his forehead.

"I can't wait any longer," he sobbed. "I have to open my presents."

JT groaned slightly and rolled over. Vanessa felt a jolt of anger at both of them. Really! Why couldn't Alex let her get some sleep? And how long was JT going to be sick? She needed him RIGHT NOW.

"Mom, please get up." A small, quivering mass of nerves, Alex melted against her body, his hot tears streaming down her neck.

Squinting at the clock, Vanessa registered the time. Unbelievable! She'd been asleep only three hours! Why the hell didn't I let them open EVERYTHING last night and get it over with? I am an idiot! She was on the verge of screaming GETTHEFUCKBACKTOBED when something about his misery made her pause.

He was just a boy. An anxious nine-year-old boy. And unfortunately, she was his mother.

So she kissed him and walked him to the hallway. "I have to discuss this with Daddy. Go back to your room and I'll see you in ten."

"Okay," Alex scampered. "Please, please hurry!"

"And don't wake your brother!"

Vanessa returned to her sweaty, unhelpful husband. How could he sleep through this? He was probably faking it. Suddenly, she didn't care if he had *pneumonia*; he wasn't going to make her do all the heavy lifting anymore.

Leaning over his ear, she hissed, "Honey, we have to talk RIGHT NOW."

"Okay," JT murmured.

"Alex wants to open presents."

"Okay, open presents."

"But it's four A.M."

"Okay, wait."

"JT! This is important." *Is it important?* she silently asked herself. *Is it really?*

JT flopped against the pillow and picked up the glass of water on the nightstand. "I back you up completely."

"But I haven't decided on anything," said Vanessa. "What are we telling him if we let him open his presents?"

"Merry Christmas?" said JT.

"I mean, should he wait until morning, like all good children everywhere? And is it important to wait? Is this a Teachable Moment?" The more she thought about it the less certain she was that they were teaching him anything.

"He's nine, he can wait."

"He said he can't. He's weeping. He's weeping because of stuff. Materialistic stuff. But I told him to wait till the sun comes up. Should I be firm? Did I draw a line in the sand?"

JT yawned. "When you put it like that, it does sound stupid." Slowly and carefully, he creaked out of bed, crossed to the bureau, and rustled through his bottom drawer.

"What are you doing?"

He pulled on a gray sweater. "Going to open presents."

"But you're sick!" Vanessa suddenly felt awfully guilty for dragging him into this.

"I'll lie on the couch," he said, shuffling into the twins' room.

"Do you have a fever?" Running after him, she stuck her wrist on his forehead. He did feel warm.

"I can have a fever and open presents. Multitasking."

Vanessa caught her breath. JT was so sweet. He didn't mean to be sick, he didn't mean to make things difficult.

"I love you, honey." She began to cry.

"Dad's up! Dad's up!" Ethan and Alex jumped up and down like trained circus dogs when their father entered their bedroom.

"Here's the deal," he said gruffly. "We'll open presents, but then you have to let Mom and me go back to bed. And you can't wake us until we say so."

The boys nodded obediently.

"Okay, then." He turned to Vanessa. "Don't forget the camera," he said, leading the troops into the living room.

And then, remembering that she'd be featured in these photos for years to come, she brushed her hair before joining them.

The boys gleefully ripped through the final installment of Christmas: video games, knee pads, battery-operated simulated automatic weapons. In twenty minutes it was over and the twins swore a solemn oath not to disturb their parents until further notice and Vanessa and JT were back in bed.

As Vanessa snuggled up against the backside of her damp, snoring husband, she felt a wave of tenderness. JT was such a good man, he hardly ever complained. He was a wonderful father and an all-around great guy. They had so much together—how could she have even considered putting everything at risk?

Rolling onto her back, she relaxed her spine. So I went a little crazy, she thought dismissively. Every girl goes crazy sometimes, but the healthy woman doesn't act on those impulses. If Neil calls, I'll be polite but firm with him. I mean, really, we have nothing in common.

Nothing in common at all.

LIBBY WAS SHOCKED AWAKE FROM HER sensual cocoon by the shrill clanging of a phone.

What phone?

A sturdy landline on the bedside table next to Brian.

Climbing over his spent figure, she picked it up. "Hello?"

"Liberty? I tried your cell but all I got was voice mail. Anyway, Merry Christmas, dear!"

"Mom," Libby mumbled. "Can we talk later?"

"But it's Christmas! And wouldn't you know it? Your father's pulled his back out—didn't I say that football game would end badly?—and he's staying in bed. So it's just you and me for breakfast. Unless, do you think we should order room service? No, that doesn't seem very Christmassy. The restaurant downstairs says they have a special blueberry French toast this morning. I mean, it won't be like home, but if we're together, we'll make it Christmassy. So why don't I come over now—"

"What?" Libby panicked. "I mean, no, don't come over now! I just got up."

"Is everything okay?" Brian woke with a start.

Libby covered the mouthpiece. There was a beat while her mother read between the lines.

"Liberty, what's going on?"

"Nothing."

"I heard someone."

Riding a high-speed search through her options, Libby knew if she lied and her mother found out, they wouldn't let her see Brian again.

"Yes," she said, choosing an offensive play. "Brian Kim came over. We're going out to breakfast."

"On Christmas morning?"

"Well, today's his day off."

"And you said yes without discussing this with me?"

"I knew if I asked you you'd say no."

Patience fell silent. Of course she'd say no.

"Mom, can you just try to understand? He's really nice. He's showing me L.A. You can't expect me to spend my whole vacation with relatives!" Libby bit her lip. That last remark could weaken her position.

"Libby, I'm not comfortable with you seeing so much of this boy. We don't know anything about him."

"Mom, his uncle owns the hotel, he's from L.A., he's a junior in college! Dad has his cell phone number."

"I'm coming over."

There was a click and Libby shoved her lover out of bed. "Get dressed!"

"RICHARD! RICHARD, DO SOMETHING!" DROPPING THE receiver with a clatter, Patience pinched the shoulder of her dozing husband. "Libby and that boy are going out for breakfast."

Richard winced. "P! My back is killing me."

"There are more important things than your back, Richard," said Patience, snatching a plush white guest robe from the bathroom hook. "You need to put a stop to this."

Through dry sockets, Richard contemplated his wife as she whirled in a fury. "You go," he said gruffly. "You're armed and dangerous."

"You're her father! You need to lay down the law. I mean, what do we really know about Brian Kim?" she said, shrugging into her loafers.

"We know that he had a five point oh to get into UCLA," Richard muttered.

"Everyone out here is so casual! You meet a pool boy and suddenly you're driving around eating sushi." She checked her appearance in the mirror above the writing desk.

"That's how young people meet," Richard sighed. "As I recall we met in a bar in Middlebury."

"We did not." Patience was incensed. "It was that Indian restaurant by the river."

"Which served Indian beer to minors." Richard smiled fondly at the memory.

"Really, Richard, that was completely different."

"She's almost eighteen, P, you've got to learn to trust her."

"This isn't about me." Patience rimmed her mouth with rosy lipstick.

"I think you're overreacting," Richard said firmly. "What are you going to do next year when she's in college? Tag along?"

*   *   *

BRIAN CHARGED OUT OF BED AND searched through the tangle of clothes and covers for his boxers and pants.

Libby slipped on a T-shirt and jeans, and then together they made up the bed.

"Libby," Patience called and knocked on the door.

Brian looked worried. "Your parents aren't . . . gun owners or anything?"

"You came over to take me to breakfast," Libby repeated. Then, taking one last look at the room, she calmly opened the door.

"Hi, Mom, this is Brian Kim."

"It's nice to meet you," Brian said, extending his hand.

"Yes, it's nice to meet you." Patience knew she looked ridiculous in her robe but she pressed on, scouring the room for signs of illicit activity.

"He just came over." Libby fired her opening statement.

"He just came over." Patience drew out each syllable.

"And I was going to call but I didn't want to wake you up."

Patience lowered her voice. "Liberty, I need to speak to you privately."

"Mom, can it wait till I get back?"

Facing down her youthful opponents, Patience felt outmatched and adrift in shark-infested waters. The possibility of her daughter and this boy—a college boy!—having sex. In a hotel room . . .

Slamming the brakes on the sordid images in her imagination, she cleaved to the idea that everything was perfectly innocent, that it was . . . well, it was California! Where people met at the pool and went out for raw tuna and, and, her knees were buckling.

"Mrs. Channing." Brian flashed a polite smile. "Is it okay if I take Libby to breakfast?"

Focusing on Brian she was further derailed. He doesn't look all that different from Richard, she realized. Khaki pants, polo shirt, merino wool sweater. The only variation was the skate shoes with no socks.

Although Richard never wears socks with his Top-Siders. She frowned.

What am I doing? She checked herself. I've got to put a stop to this, this, unseemly situation!

"Mrs. Channing, would you like to come with us? There's a great place down the street with awesome pancakes," Brian was selling her. "And amazing coffee. Organic free trade. I think you guys would like it."

Patience rolled up her collar. This Brian person was creeping under her radar in a very wholesome way.

"Come on, Mom . . . we'll let Dad sleep. He won't mind." Libby was acting so normal. Considerate, even.

"Well, I don't know." Patience was rapidly losing ground. "I mean it's Christmas. Don't you think they'll be closed?"

"No," Brian said and grinned. "This is L.A. A lot of people don't even celebrate Christmas."

Patience raised her eyebrows. Who was he talking about?

"Mom." Libby took her mother's arm and whispered in her ear, "I really like Brian. I want you to get to know him."

Patience glanced furtively over at this Romeo with the spiky black hair and burnished skin. There was nothing she wanted so much as to quash all these . . . unsavory thoughts from her mind.

Shouldn't she at least go out for pancakes and talk to him?

"Oh, all right. As long as we're not gone too long. I don't want your father to think we've deserted him on Christmas morning."

"Great," Libby said smoothly. "So you go get dressed while I brush my teeth. And then we'll meet downstairs in fifteen minutes."

In the hallway, while she fit her key card in the slot, Patience followed Brian's receding figure as he strolled towards the bank of elevators.

Like a detective at a lineup, she shuffled through the faces of the boys Libby had dated. That Shane O'Connor whose parents were divorced and whose father was surely an alcoholic. And there was someone named Corey who smelled like poisonous aftershave and never looked her in the eye.

Patience shivered. She hoped that Libby would tell her when she lost her virginity, but she couldn't be sure.

Even in the age of cell phones and text messaging, it was impossible to know what her daughter was doing. And with Libby acting so secretive lately, Patience felt cut out of the loop.

But deep down inside she knew that Richard was right. Liberty was old enough to make her own choices, and there was nothing she could do to stop her. Oh, I pray some of what I've taught her has sunk in! And that she doesn't get drunk and drive or take drugs or go out with deviant, creepy, menacing . . .

Brian stepped into the elevator and, turning back, gave Patience a friendly wave. She smiled awkwardly and stumbled into her hotel room.

Choosing a crisp white shirt and blue corduroys, she began

to dress. At least Brian has manners, she noted with a slight nod of approval. You can tell he comes from a good family. Of course Libby's too young to get serious with anyone, but for goodness' sake, we're only here a week, it's just a holiday romance. I shouldn't make too much of it.

The realization that it was temporary soothed her frazzled nerves. We'll go back to Massachusetts and that will be the end of it, she thought happily.

She brushed her hair and fit gold earrings into her delicate lobes. When Libby's off at college she'll be old enough for more serious relationships, she thought rationally. And then, when she's old enough *for that*. Patience shut her eyes tightly. Well, I hope she finds a boy as sweet as Brian for her first time.

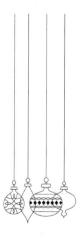

13

Christmas was over till next year, leaving Vanessa with a filthy house, a headache, and a secret, blissful sense of relief.

Padding into the kitchen, she joined JT and the twins, who were seated at the island slurping cereal.

"Hi, honey, you look better this morning."

"I'm fine," he said. "I woke up feeling pretty good."

"Well, don't eat too much." She winced, remembering the comforter she'd had to wash. "You should probably go easy on your stomach."

"I thought I'd take the boys to the park this morning, play some ball."

"Okay," she poured herself a bowl of bran flakes. "If you think you're up to it."

"And maybe later we could see a movie with Richard and P."

"I think they're driving to Santa Cruz today."

"Yeah? I didn't know that. I'll give him a call."

Adding milk to her cereal, she buried herself in the paper. She felt strangely detached from everything.

After all the boys left, Vanessa wandered from room to room unable to commit to anything—not cleaning, not reading, not even a shower.

She made herself a cup of coffee and was just about to settle down on the couch when her cell rang.

"Hello?"

"Vanessa, it's Neil."

"Neil!"

"Look, I think we should talk. Do you think you could come over here?"

"Neil . . ." Stalling, she attempted to conjure up the right tone. Caring but firm. Warm but professional. "I don't think that's a good idea. We have a good working relationship, we're colleagues. That night was a . . . slight transgression, but it's behind us, so let's just keep it in the past." There! She'd said it, and she'd sounded like a woman in control of her destiny.

"But I can't stop thinking about you. I left without saying good-bye because I was afraid I'd kiss you again."

Her heart melted. He wanted to kiss her again! This man was passionately in love with her!

"Look," he was saying, "I'm going to stay home all day and wait for you. Please think about it."

There was a click.

And he was gone.

This is . . . ridiculous, she thought. It's so . . . adulterous! People don't act this way in real life. Come on! This isn't Tolstoy. It's not a telenovela! Of course I'm not jumping in my car and racing off to some . . . tryst.

But, God, I want to!

Shot up with wild adrenaline, she spun herself into shampooing and moisturizing and all the while imagined what he'd look like naked, next to her in bed.

And what it'd be like to sleep with another man.

And while she would never, ever dream of cheating on JT, she dug through her lingerie drawer for her sexy push-up bra and suggestive lace panties.

Then she ransacked her wardrobe for her best-fitting jeans and a low-cut black ruffled blouse.

She was on the cusp of satin kitten heels when the phone rang.

"Hello?" She took pains to sound seductive.

"Vanessa? It's Patience. Listen, I have an enormous favor to ask you . . ."

"What?" Vanessa said, admiring her long legs in the full-length mirror on the closet door.

"You know Richard's hurt his back. He says it's a lumbar sprain. Anyway, he was in agony all day yesterday and while it's better, he still can't sit for long periods of time . . ."

Reaching inside her shirt, Vanessa scooped up her breasts and adjusted the bra cups for a fuller cleavage.

". . . and I'm on the way to the pharmacy to pick up a prescription. But we have these reservations in Santa Cruz tonight. And Libby has a campus tour tomorrow and . . ."

"No!" Vanessa suddenly realized what Patience was saying. "I can't come over and take care of Richard—" *Because I'm on my way to fuck a gorgeous writer!*

"Vanessa," Patience interrupted, "I'll take care of Richard . . . and I'd be happy to make dinner for the boys tonight."

Vanessa frowned. Had she missed something?

"Hello?"

"Yeah, I'm here."

"I know it's a lot to ask, but I was hoping that you or JT might actually enjoy the trip up the coast—"

"You want *me* to drive to Santa Cruz?" The nerve of this woman! Why couldn't Richard, the doctor, just medicate himself for the day?

Vanessa clamped her left hand on her hip. "Really, Patience, isn't there anything else you could do? I'm exhausted from the holidays."

"I know, I feel terrible. But Libby can't legally drive the rental, and I didn't feel it was appropriate to ask to borrow your car." She waited a beat and then, with no response from Vanessa added, "Oh, it doesn't matter because I wouldn't feel comfortable letting Libby go up there alone."

"Can't you just cancel?" Vanessa tossed her robe and nightgown into the closet and slammed the door.

"Normally I would, but they don't usually give tours this week. I had to make special arrangements with the admissions office and I can't back out now."

The front door slammed, and a moment later the twins and JT invaded the bedroom with their sweat and grime and bats and balls.

"Mommy, you look pretty," said Alex, jumping on the freshly laundered comforter with his muddy cleats.

"Honey, you look hot." JT was admiring her. "Are we going somewhere?"

"Can't I just try on some clothes and makeup without the third degree?" Vanessa covered her embarrassment with self-righteous indignation.

JT threw up his hands in surrender. "Whoa, you win."

"I have to call you back," she barked into the phone. Then, kicking off her heels, she faced her domestic buzz kill. "Patience wants us to drive Libby to Santa Cruz."

"Can we go too?" said Alex.

"Richard's back is still out and he can't make the trip."

JT looked wan. "I guess we could go." Then he mouthed, "With the twins?"

Vanessa shook her head. "It's a college tour, it's not really a family vacation."

Like magic fairy dust, the murmurs of a serious parental discussion caused the boys to vanish instantly.

"You're right," he said. "She wouldn't want her little cousins hanging around with her."

"Well, we both can't go. Someone has to stay behind with them."

"You decide." JT wrapped his arms around her. "You've had to carry the load lately. Whatever you want to do . . ."

Have sex with Neil, she thought.

"It might be fun, a little road trip. Get out of the city."

The phone rang and he picked it up. "Hey, Thea," he said. "Yeah, I'm back in the world of the upright."

Vanessa looked over at her very sharp, very intoxicating black shoes and felt afraid. I can't believe I even considered going over to Neil's, she thought. I am behaving like a lunatic. Or one of those cheating women in a country-western song.

She grabbed the phone from JT. "Thea? Please, please, please will you come with me to Santa Cruz?"

"I TRIED," VANESSA HEARD LIBBY MOANING in the backseat. "I tried and tried, but she just wouldn't listen. My mother is a total psycho bitch."

In the front seats of the green wagon, Vanessa and Thea exchanged amused, titillated looks.

"Why is she mad at Patience?" Thea whispered.

Vanessa stared straight ahead at the scant traffic wending north on the 101. They were just passing the turnoff to Malibu Canyon. Another four hours and they'd be in Santa Cruz.

"I don't know, does it matter? She's seventeen, she hates her mother," Vanessa giggled.

"It's good you have boys," Thea said. She glanced at her watch. "We probably won't see the campus before dark."

"Brian? Brian?" There was a scream from the backseat. "Aunt V! My cell's dead!"

"The reception's iffy through these hills," said Vanessa.

The sound of weeping threatened to implode the car. Thea glanced anxiously at Libby, who was now sprawled across the seat, clutching her phone to her chest.

"I think we should pull over," she said to her sister.

Vanessa zoomed up the Chesebro off-ramp, cleared the intersection, and parked on the dirt shoulder across the road.

"Libby, are you all right? Should I call your mom?"

"No!" Libby cried harder. "I'm never speaking to her again! She's ruined my life."

Thea looked helpless. "What should we do?"

Vanessa climbed out of the car and eased herself into the backseat. With gentle motions, she lifted Libby into a sitting position and draped her arm around the girl's shoulders. "Why don't we talk about it?"

"It's Brian. She hates him!"

"Oh, I don't think she hates him. She's just—"

"He offered to drive me to Santa Cruz," Libby interrupted. "And she wouldn't let him! He even called his work and got time off. She said it was 'inappropriate'! She's inappropriate! Now we have two less days to be together." Libby unleashed her waterworks onto Vanessa's right breast.

Thea grimaced. "Should we turn around?" she mouthed at her sister. Vanessa shook her head "No."

For a few minutes, Vanessa stroked Libby's hair and let her cry. She remembered how clingy her niece had been as a little girl, always hiding behind her mother's back. She recalled Libby as being rather shy. They'd all heaved a collective sigh of relief when she finally came out of her shell. When was that? Somewhere around thirteen, when she'd grown so pretty and gone off to that summer camp, where they card their own wool and weave their own cloth.

"Libs, what was the name of that place in Vermont? Where you churned your own butter?"

Libby sniffled. "Canterbury."

"If we ever have enough money, I want to send the twins there. Do you think they'd like it?"

"It's really great. We got to feed the animals and swim in the river."

"I remember you were so grown-up when you came back."

"It was started by Shakers and they're kind of weird but they're cool, too. Their respect for the land and nature and stuff."

With a small smile, Libby lifted her head and looked into Vanessa's eyes. "I'm sorry, Aunt V, I didn't mean to go insane."

"I know. You're just . . . sad. You miss him."

Libby nodded. "I wish you were my mom. I know you'd let me go."

"Let's not go that far," Vanessa groaned. "Anyway, we'll try to do our best to keep you company the next, what, twenty-four hours? We'll race back the minute you've seen the campus, how's that?"

"I can show you the highlights in forty minutes." Thea snapped her fingers.

"Okay," Libby exhaled deeply.

Vanessa resumed her place in the driver's seat and switched on the ignition.

"Why don't you tell us all about Brian," said Thea. "I mean, until we pick up cell service again?"

"He's a filmmaker. But he's an artist, really. He has made the most amazing animated short. Anime." Libby wiped away her tears and searched for a stick of gum in her purse.

"An artist," said Thea. "That's a heartbreaker."

Vanessa glanced in the rearview mirror. "When Thea was around your age, she had a very passionate affair too."

"What happened?" said Libby.

"Let's not drag up my past."

"What else have we got to do for three hundred miles?" said Vanessa.

"Did you love him?" Libby gazed out at the pink and gray Agoura hills.

"I think obsessed is the right word."

"You should call him when we get up there tonight," Vanessa said suddenly. "He's not that far away."

"Hello? Point Reyes is way north of Santa Cruz." Thea rolled her eyes. Everyone in Southern California is geographically challenged, she mused. They all think Northern California is one small town with San Francisco serving as its main street.

"If you loved him, and he was *the one*, you should definitely call him," agreed Libby. Glancing at her phone, she emitted an ear-shattering squeal. "I've got four bars!"

Punching Redial, she listened eagerly for the connection. "Brian?" she said. "Sorry. We were somewhere with *no service* . . ."

Thea glanced at Vanessa. "Did we ever act that way?"

Vanessa shook her head sternly. "Never. We were always grown-up women with perfect control."

So why am I thinking about Cal Hawkins? Thea thought.

So why am I thinking about Neil Cohen? thought her sister.

PATIENCE DECIDED THAT THEY WERE ALL sick of turkey and that she should make a meaty ragu sauce and serve it over spaghetti with a crisp green salad.

Standing at Vanessa's counter, she minced three garlic cloves on a wooden cutting board and then gazed out at the backyard. She marveled at how bright a winter's afternoon was in Los Angeles and at the novelty of oranges hanging in a tree in the adjacent yard.

She felt comfortable in the kitchen and was amused by the banter drifting in from the living room. The guys were hunkered down around the television watching football. Over the course of the last two hours, she had proffered an endless stream of snacks—cheese, crackers, crudités, sliced apples—and JT and the boys had thanked her profusely.

Poor dears, she thought, it appears that Vanessa never feeds them. But the jab at her sister-in-law pricked her guilt. Vanessa had, after all, stepped in to help with Libby, allowing Patience this unexpected retreat in a den of men. And, she admitted, it was a nice change from life with a sullen, distant daughter.

She added the garlic along with ground beef and veal to a sauté pan moist with soft onions. Breaking up the meat with a wooden spoon, she examined why she and Vanessa had never really hit it off.

The first time they'd met, it had been at her house in Wenham. Vanessa had arrived in a cloud of rose oil and a garish spray of glitter across her eyelids. And she didn't bring a gift. Somehow, this had rankled. Patience, who was brought up to shop for hostess presents and offer help in the kitchen, had been shocked at this brazen lack of etiquette. And furthermore, Vanessa and JT had spent hours alone in their room—presumably having sex—and then hours away from the house sightseeing around town. As Patience recalled, the couple had taken the train to Boston, on Christmas Eve, to tour the Museum of Fine Arts. That day I was expecting fifty for my Open House, she frowned. And I could have used an extra pair of hands.

After Christmas, Vanessa had insisted that the four of them go down to New York and see a show. They'd stayed in a hotel in Times Square—noisy and expensive—and watched an unpleasant drama with a cast of coarse, oily men, all swearing and sweating.

Patience would have preferred a musical—wasn't *Cats* playing back then?—something uplifting. But Vanessa and JT subscribed to "cutting-edge work," and Patience, unsure of herself in the dazzling world of Manhattan, had remained quiet and accommodating.

When JT and Amanda were together, things had been different. They'd all gone skiing in the winter and sailing in the summer. But Vanessa didn't like the snow and she and JT couldn't afford the seasonal rentals on Nantucket or Martha's Vineyard. Patience knew it was expensive for her in-laws to travel, but somehow she suspected it really wasn't about the money.

There isn't a bond between the women, she thought sadly. And I suppose that's what you need to keep the family together.

After Vanessa and JT had departed for Logan Airport, Patience had climbed the stairs to the guest bedroom. It reeked of a cloying perfume and some smoky substance—incense? pot?—and there was glitter all over the sheets. How could anyone sleep in a bed with all those sandy particles? Patience wondered.

A crashing noise from the living room shook her from the memory.

JT rushed in and snatched the dish towel hanging on the oven door handle. "It smells great in here, P," he said, giving her a quick peck on the cheek before sprinting out again.

Would he have been happier with Amanda? she thought idly. But after JT, Amanda had met a stockbroker and moved to New York. For a couple of years, the two girlfriends had called each other every week and sent cards and letters. Patience had even visited a few times with Libby.

But Amanda had two girls and a boy and was heavily booked with school activities, sports schedules, and family vacations. Patience and Amanda had lost touch, and now, except for the yearly Christmas card, never spoke at all.

Vanessa makes JT happy, Patience admitted grudgingly. She understands his freelance life and they have that show business world in common. I don't suppose JT would have made enough money for Amanda, she conceded, visualizing the posh apartment on the Upper East Side and the exclusive schools the children attended.

It had been a magical time, those college years in Vermont. Biking along Lake Champlain, hiking in the forests around Middlebury. It was a land of Robert Frost, autumn leaves, and flowing rivers.

Perhaps if she and Vanessa had something, anything, that they could do together.

I have so few friends, Patience thought with a pang. I always thought maybe she and I would . . .

Her eyes blurred as she stirred the ragu.

Resting the wooden spoon on a plate next to the stove, she ran to the sink and tore off a paper towel from the dispenser.

This never happens at home, she thought, dabbing gently at her eyes. Were the onions stronger out here in California?

LIBBY, THEA, AND AUNT VANESSA ARRIVED in Santa Cruz at dusk, when the sun had just slipped into the gray Pacific Ocean.

They were booked at the Dolphin Inn, which featured free Internet and a spectacular view of the California coastline. After check-in, they dumped their bags in two adjoining rooms and then buzzed down to the boardwalk for dinner.

"A beach town is a beach town," Thea said, strolling past T-shirt shops, a storm of skateboarders, and a seedy convenience mart on the main drag.

A chilly sea breeze toyed with Vanessa's hair and she shivered underneath her tapestry coat and jeans. She noticed that many of the locals were clad in sandals and shorts. How was it that beach people never felt the cold?

"Aunt V, I'm starving." Liberty was eyeing Sharky's Grill. The name was splashed across a surfboard suspended above heavy wooden doors. It was one of those oceanfront restaurants with an open floor plan, a noisy clientele, and baskets of greasy corn chips on the tables.

"I think it used to be called the Lusty Lobster, but it looks the same," said Thea.

It was early—or maybe it was just the holidays—and the crowd was thin. A rowdy pack of unwashed surfers was knocking back microbrews and watching a big wave competition on the plasma screen over the bar.

A ruddy blonde in a polar fleece vest and sheepskin boots led them to a wobbly table alongside a bank of windows.

"Can I start you off with drinks, ladies?" She handed them enormous menus. A florid tattoo of a rock-climbing angel scaled her left biceps.

"I'll have a margarita," said Vanessa.

"Me too," Libby said casually.

"Make mine a virgin," said Thea, and then, glancing over at Libby, added, "Two virgins."

The waitress departed and Libby frowned. "My dad lets me have wine with dinner. Sometimes."

"That's very European," said Vanessa. "Too bad we're in a Mexican restaurant."

"So what do you think of Santa Cruz so far?" said Thea.

"It seems . . . well," Libby paused. "I don't know. In my mind I thought it would be more like Los Angeles but with redwoods."

Vanessa eyed her niece who, against the backdrop of this casual scene, looked overdressed in her lacy leggings, black ankle boots, and belted sweater coat. "I like it here," she said. "Everyone is young and going to school and outdoorsy."

"For sure," Libby said, watching two salty-haired guys shoot tequila at the bar.

"And it's super laid-back," said Thea. "Not like the city."

Libby furrowed her brows. "But I sort of like the city. I mean, L.A. is really exciting."

The trio was silent for a moment. Then Thea shrugged. "Yeah, it's too quiet here. That's why I left."

"Thea!" Vanessa jerked her head in Libby's direction. "You're supposed to be telling her all the good things."

"Well, quiet's a good thing. When you're studying and . . . I don't know, hiking, hanging out. But after college I had to come back to L.A. I could never have done my work up here. I mean, Santa Cruz is beautiful and I'm glad I lived here, but I had to get back to civilization."

Libby giggled and Vanessa reached out and patted her niece's hand. "Don't listen to Thea. She likes shady characters and urban blight."

"Sleaze can be inspiring," Thea said and shrugged.

"And let's not prejudge anything," Vanessa was starting to sound shrill.

"I'm just being honest," said Thea. "Anyway, she needs to see the campus. I mean, she'd be living up there, not down here on the boardwalk."

Their drinks arrived and Libby's cell phone buzzed. Glancing at the caller ID, she shot up from the table. "I'll be right back," she said, scampering outside to shiver alone on a windy stretch of sand.

"Could you just not say anything?" Vanessa stared at Thea with exasperation. "I don't think we should influence her decision."

"Get real. Teenagers don't pay any attention to adults."

Vanessa licked the salt on the rim of her glass. "Oh, God. I'm acting like her mother in the absence of her real mother."

Thea swallowed, enjoying the bite of lime on her tongue. "It's weird being here. It seems more upscale now than when I was a student."

Vanessa was perusing the menu. "I think we should stick with the grilled entrees. Maybe the mahi mahi tacos?"

"Yeah, definitely not the fettuccine. What's that old saying? 'The closer you get to the water, the worse the food'?"

"What about that great Italian place near your house?"

"Yeah, well, Venice is its own special brand of beach town."

Vanessa set down her menu and reached for the chip basket. "Any resolutions for the New Year?"

"Get back to work," said her sister, loading up her tortilla triangle with green salsa. "December kind of derailed me. I'm out of my routine."

"Hmm," said Vanessa, licking her oily fingers. "So, are you going to give Cal a call?"

"That's your fantasy."

"He is just up the coast."

"Have you talked to Neil?" Thea fired back.

Vanessa tensed, then raked her hair. "He called this morning. But I told him . . . to just forget about what happened."

"And what did he say?"

"He said . . ." Vanessa tried to remain composed but then giggled. "He wanted me to come to his place and talk about it!"

Thea banged her glass on the table. "Talk about it? You mean fuck first, talk later. Did you go?"

"No, silly. I drove to Santa Cruz! *With my sister and my niece.*"

Pressing her nose against the window, Thea watched the winking lights of two boats out on the water. Then she spotted Libby, nestled in the sand, her head cocked over the cell phone.

"I guess," she said quietly. "I guess our time for trysts and heartbreak and unhappiness has passed."

"Well, it's not like we missed anything," said Vanessa.

"We didn't miss anything," said Thea.

"It's sort of fun acting like girls again."

"I was tormented as a girl." Thea glanced away from the window.

Oh, please, you were not, Vanessa was about to snort. But there was something in Thea's face, something haunted, that made Vanessa pull back. "We need to eat," she said quickly, searching the room for their waitress. "I think we've got low blood sugar. Will you go get Libby? I'm going to flag down Tattoo Surf Angel and order dinner."

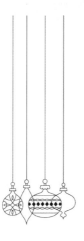

14

This is the darkest goddamned forest I've ever seen in my life, Thea worried as the beams from her headlights darted wildly through stands of towering redwoods.

At just past midnight, the road through Samuel Taylor Park was virtually deserted. Thea glanced fearfully at the fuel gauge: a quarter of a tank. Why hadn't she filled up in San Francisco? There was no way a gas station would be open out here.

Earlier that evening, she had left Vanessa sleeping soundly in their hotel room and crept down to the lobby to use the guest computer. Somehow her fingers had Googled Cal

Hawkins and then, somehow, she wasn't quite sure, MapQuest had showed her the way.

To Point Reyes.

She hated that she had succumbed to the worst possible urges: neediness, heedlessness, craziness.

But she couldn't stop herself.

Why didn't she just call him and catch up? Because she was afraid to talk to him. She wanted to see him first and look at his house. Get a visual.

She wanted to know if he was happy. *Happy without her.*

I haven't loved anyone, *that way*, since him. It was his art. I always wanted to dive into his pool of creativity and never come out.

Stop being so melodramatic, she scolded herself. You've loved other men. Running down possible candidates she nominated Adrian, a commercial director, who worshipped suede coats, all things Japanese, and cocaine. Too bad he gave up drugs and converted to Scientology, she thought ruefully.

And then there was Sergio, who never missed an art opening. She'd admired his leonine profile and his wicked sense of humor. Sergio gave me the best head of my life, she moaned appreciatively, as the tingling memory of his virtuosity darted from her pelvis up her spine. And I would've loved him longer, except that his interest in art didn't extend much past arty girls.

Yes, Adrian and Sergio were both amazing men, Thea asserted. They were smart and sexy and wild and . . .

Not Cal Hawkins.

Oh, just shoot me now, she thought morosely. I've become

a cliché in a magazine article. "Women Who Stalk Ex-Boyfriends but Pretend They Don't."

Oh, well, she didn't care.

Wasn't she entitled to act crazy every fifteen years?

Fuck, she panicked, I should come up with a good reason I'm here. Let's see . . . I'll tell him that I'm driving through on my way to . . . She searched frantically through the California road map in her head. Unfortunately, Point Reyes wasn't on the way to anywhere. In fact, it was out of the way of everywhere.

Okay, I've got it, she decided. I'll say I'm driving up to Napa but I wanted to take a day trip to see the ocean. And someone told me you were living up here, so I thought as long as I was in town, I'd see if you were in the phone book . . . and since it's the holidays you might be home . . .

Was it too much explanation?

She was only about ten miles away now, if you could believe Internet cartographers.

So what was the plan?

Ring his doorbell? And then hide?

Wait till he ambled outside to howl at the moon, smoke a cig, identify the constellations?

She refused to stop and think rationally. She was compelled to do this. Besides, she couldn't stay in that claustrophobic hotel room listening to the *tick, tick, tick* of the clock radio and the steady breathing of her sister.

Even if all I do is stare at his house and drive back, Thea thought, I will know something I didn't know before.

She clutched the wheel and longed for a cigarette. Fiddling with the radio dial, she found a quirky show from Canada and listened intently to their farm report.

At the crest of the hill, she gasped at the yellow half-moon hanging over the peninsula. With a fresh burst of energy, she traversed the backside of the mountain down into Point Reyes Station. Grabbing at the directions again, she took a right and then a left onto Bay Road.

There were no lampposts in this neighborhood and the street was dark. The car bumped noisily over the gravel and potholes, so she slowed down and switched on the high beams. She passed five or six houses separated by pastures and euca-lyptus trees. She strained to read the numbers on the mail-boxes. *I need one of those tiny flashlights on my key chain,* she thought suddenly. *Why the fuck do I sneer at people who have things like that?*

At the bend in the road was a wooden gate and her beams swept the address: 33.

His house.

Cutting the motor, she coasted past his property, rolling to a stop a way down. She didn't want to park directly in front.

He might see her.

For a minute or two, she remained still and wondered if she was going to faint, her heart was working so hard.

Thea, she coaxed, *you've come all this way. Get out of the car.*

Closing the door softly, she tiptoed along the muddy shoulder till she could see his house.

It was set back about a hundred yards. In the dim light she could make out a tin roof and casement windows. There was some kind of a barn off to the right—maybe his studio?

She smelled salt in the air and the funk of marshland. It

was damp and cold and ghostly quiet. No traffic, no neighbors.

There were no lights on in the house and it was too late to knock on the door and wake him up. It was then that an overwhelming fatigue batted her down. The adrenaline rush of the ride and the quest dissipated down the rabbit hole. She was a weary romantic, far from home, in a strange place with no one to welcome her.

Doubling back to the car she felt ashamed and ridiculous. Safe in the driver's seat, she noticed that the needle in the gas gauge had slipped into the red zone.

Even if she wasn't exhausted, she'd never make it back to the freeway on this tank. She'd have to wait till morning when, hopefully, a station in town would be open. Her watch said one A.M. Dawn was only a few hours away.

Zipping up her quilted black jacket, she pulled the hood over her ears and jammed her hands into the sleek pockets. She was so sleepy. If she just dozed for a little while, she'd have the strength to figure this out. She heard the distant hoot of an owl and closed her eyes.

"ARE YOU ALL RIGHT?"

Thea was awakened by a tapping noise. Sitting up, she realized it was morning and she was absolutely freezing.

A man was standing outside the driver's door.

Tall and rangy, he was wearing a black knit cap and some kind of high-performance rain jacket in sapphire blue.

He was Cal Hawkins.

Their eyes met and she saw a flash in his gray irises.

"Are you all right?" he repeated.

No, she thought, swiping at the drool at the corner of her mouth, I am not all right, I am pathetic. My God, what do I look like? One of those runaway women on Lifetime television?

Ducking her head, she prayed he wouldn't recognize her. "I'm fine," she mumbled.

But he stood there, staring.

A bundle of brown-and-white fur jumped at his side and she heard a bark.

His dog. He was out with his dog.

Say something, she thought. You've come all this way.

See it through.

Mustering up as much grace and confidence as she could fake, she climbed out of the car.

The dog, a panting, circling spaniel, clawed at her black wool leggings.

Cal dropped his jaw. "Thea?"

She nodded and bit her lip. "I guess you . . . didn't expect to find me here . . ."

But he swept her into a hug. An enormous, safe man of a hug. And then he was cupping his warm hands over her cold fists.

"What are you doing here?"

But she couldn't remember her story. What was it again? Passing through . . . a phone book, a side trip. Casting about, she noted the mist hovering over his field and the streaks of pink light in the sky above him. "I wanted to . . . see Point Reyes at dawn?"

He laughed easily. He was bigger, lighter, older than the last time she'd seen him.

"I can't believe it. How did you—"

The dog's barking echoed through the quiet lane.

"Buttercup!" Cal snapped his fingers sternly. "Sit!"

"Buttercup?"

"I know," he said sheepishly. "My daughter named her."

His daughter. Oh, my God, he has a daughter.

"Look, if we don't walk she'll wake the whole neighborhood. Come on." His eyes were shining.

Thea glanced down at her suede clogs sinking slightly in the soggy earth. Perfect, she thought. What's a quest without a muddy path?

They fell into step, cutting through a wet field and working their way up a gentle slope.

"When was the last time we . . . I saw you?" Cal's stride was strong. Purposeful.

"Maybe fifteen years ago? The bar at Musso's?"

"Oh, yeah." He shook his head. "My second home."

"I don't drink anymore." She shrugged.

"Really? I probably shouldn't. Look, this is just so . . . strange. Tell me everything. Why you're in Point Reyes. Where you live now. What you're doing."

They had reached the top and below them was a dramatic view of Tomales Bay and Inverness Park on the other side. Traversing the spine of the ridge, they headed north, passing a few horses and cows out for their first taste of dewy grass.

As they hiked, Thea ran though the highlights of the past few years, all the while wishing it was Cal who was doing the talking.

Stopping abruptly, she grabbed his forearms and faced him. "Okay, look, the truth is I came here to see you. I haven't come across any of your work lately and I just wanted to know what you were doing."

He gazed up ahead at Buttercup. Thea noticed faint lines in his forehead and tiny flecks of gray in the stubble on his chin.

"I live here with my wife and my daughter, Pearl," he said. "Karina works in the city and I do . . . a variety of things. Help at the co-op, take care of Pearl . . ."

Thea was stunned. "But you're still painting?"

"I'm taking a sabbatical," he said a little too grandly. "I'll get back in the studio, but right now there're other things going on. You could say my life is my art . . ." His voice wavered and Thea sensed a danger there. Don't press it, she warned herself. Just don't press it.

A few yards ahead, there was a wooden bench overlooking the bay. "You want to sit down?" he said. "It's a pretty great view."

He whistled for the dog and she returned to his side. For a few minutes they all watched the morning fog drift above the water. Cal pointed out the oystermen down on a dock below. Thea searched frantically inside her for some kind of reaction. Was she happy to see him? Thrilled?

Did she still love him? She worried that things were happening too fast.

"I've seen your work in *Art News*," he confessed softly. "And one of your pieces was up here at MoMA in that show . . ."

"'Reflections'?" she said.

"Yeah. The collage with the illuminated text. I thought it was really good." He paused and she could see he was choosing his words. His mouth was more tender now, less set than it used to be.

"You're always reinventing yourself as an artist." He shook his head. "How do you do it?"

"Let's see. I obsess, I make myself miserable, I make everyone else miserable . . . then whatever's left I spin into art," she said ruefully. "Don't you remember?"

"Yeah, well, looking back, I think being with you scared the shit out of me. Living with those . . . expectations. I wasn't that focused, you know?"

She didn't know. Didn't know what the hell he was talking about.

"I couldn't take all that craziness. L.A. New York. The competition, the criticism. The whole art scene. Nah," he reached down to stroke Buttercup. "I like living here, next to the bay, with horses and cows, a small town."

Thea suddenly recalled the cowboy bar in Valencia. The place he'd taken her that Halloween night. How she had thought it so retro, so artfully unhip and square.

Maybe that was Cal.

Maybe he was unhip and square.

"Remember that night at the Golden Spur?" she said. "You told me you liked country music. I thought it was just backlash hip."

Cal laughed. "Yeah, well, I probably played it that way. Knowing me then. I was such an asshole. What did you see in me?"

Tears suddenly welled in her eyes. She hated them, tried

to compose herself. "God, Cal." Her voice quavered. But she didn't trust herself to go on.

"Well," he said sweetly, "you're the one I remember from that time. You're the one who got away."

"Got away?" A sharp pain bit her numbness. "You pushed me away."

"Come on, Thea, we both did some stupid things. Please don't hold that against me."

Cal folded his arms defensively and Thea took a deep breath.

"No," she said. "I don't."

He lowered his eyes. "Look, when you didn't come back to New York, I got pissed. I was young . . . we were both young, and I . . . well, it's different now."

He searched her face. "Why are you really here?"

A pair of geese sailed overhead and she pulled the collar of her coat around her neck.

"I wanted to see you."

"You could've called."

"You know I'm a visual person. I need to see the whole picture. I just . . . for some reason I was thinking about you, wondering what you were doing, what you looked like."

"But why now?"

"I don't know. Maybe it's the holidays. They make me feel melancholy and nostalgic. Do you remember the Christmas where you cooked dinner for everyone in that apartment with no furniture? We sat on the floor and ate off paper plates."

"That was a great place," he said. "Except for the parking. I think I got a hundred tickets living there."

"Street cleaning," they said in unison.

"Well," she sighed. "That was one of the best Christmases I ever had."

They watched a blue kayak skim across the water towards the Inverness shore.

"It's really beautiful here," she said.

"Yeah, I'm lucky. Look at this. You could travel the world and never find a place as amazing as Point Reyes. I love it. And we didn't want to raise Pearl in the city." He glanced back at her. "So, what about you? Are you married?"

"No. No husband, no kids."

"That's got to be tough."

Thea bristled. "Why do you say that?"

"Because life would be hard without family."

"Life can be hard with them too, you know." She grew defensive. This is freaking me out, she thought. He seems sort of . . . conventional. Did I ever know him?

He stood up.

There was nothing more to say, really. *About them.*

On the way back, they exchanged gossip about people they used to know and reminisced about things they once did. It felt shallow but somehow satisfying. This must be what it's like to go to your high school reunion, thought Thea, having never been to one.

Then they reached his house.

"Do you want to come in?" he asked awkwardly. "I'll make coffee. I'd love you to meet Karina and Pearl."

"Thanks, but I have to be at UC Santa Cruz by ten."

He raised his brow.

"My sister and her niece are there," she said simply. "But before I go, I have to find the nearest gas station."

* * *

THE DRIVE BACK THROUGH THE REDWOODS wasn't nearly so haunting. In the morning light, with the birdsong and the lacy ferns, the forest was inviting and peaceful.

Thea sipped a triple espresso Cal had bought for her at the Feedlot, the meet-and-greet place for everyone in town. Just down the block from the gas station, the cavernous red barn housed a yoga studio and an organic co-op along with the livestock supplies. She took another taste and licked her lips. It was an amazing cup of coffee . . . and all the more amazing for being steamed right next to bales of hay and sacks of grain.

Before she'd climbed back into Vanessa's car, Cal had leaned over and kissed her on the cheek.

"It was really good to see you."

"If you're ever in L.A. . . ."

"Nah, I never am."

They'd smiled and she'd pulled away.

That was it.

I never would have guessed, she thought, idling in backed-up traffic in San Anselmo, that he'd be so different.

Fifteen years ago, he'd been the center of the indie universe. He hung out with underground bands and conjured up sets for low-budget films. He knew everyone and went everywhere.

Then one day, he was bored with all of it. I can't stay here, he'd said, and then, after he decamped to New York, taunted her for not joining him in "the city of real fucking art."

But she had prospects here. A group show at LACES

downtown. Not much money, not prestigious. But it was enough to give her faith in herself and keep her going.

And she wasn't going to turn that down for a loft on Warren Street, in lower Manhattan, with three underemployed art majors.

No, he had changed but she hadn't. She was still the same driven, reaching girl she'd been fifteen years ago.

With considerable success.

She had never imagined that maybe it was she who was too much.

Not him.

She visualized his weathered house, the pasture, the cows grazing on the land above Tomales Bay.

She could never picture herself in such a place.

With a man like Cal.

Baking bread. Grooming a horse. Or whatever it was that he did all day.

Jeez, she shivered, heading south on the 101. That was a narrow escape!

He wasn't the one who got away.

He was the one she caught and released.

Coming up on the Golden Gate Bridge, she turned a critical eye. It was an amazing feat of engineering, soaring, improbable. Yet she had always hated the paint job—that dull rusty-red color and flat finish. What if it were wrapped in gold leaf? she pondered. That would be much more of a statement.

Stopping at the toll booth, she paid her fare, snatched her cell phone, and dialed Vanessa's number.

Voice mail picked up and she left a message.

There was no way she'd be back for that ten A.M. tour.

RAYMOND PATEL WAS DOUGHY, WITH MASHED-DOWN black hair and wire-rimmed glasses. In jeans, Velcro sandals, and the ubiquitous fleece vest, he faced Libby and Vanessa on a windy hillside at UC Santa Cruz.

"So I thought we'd conclude our tour with the dorms," he said in a mumbling monotone.

"Finally," mouthed Libby to Vanessa.

The two women had dutifully followed Raymond through the university's libraries and science centers, a bookstore and marine biology lab. The campus was empty and quiet this holiday week. A few dedicated bikers and joggers were out on the single-track paths, but mostly it felt deserted.

Raymond led them up a winding street through a grove of redwood trees. "All undergraduates reside in one of ten colleges," he panted. "Each is its own small community offering social and academic support systems."

"So what are you saying?" Libby asked pointedly. "That if you don't get into a good dorm, your social life sucks?"

"Not at all. The university has designed living arrangements with the students' needs in mind." Raymond seemed curiously unperturbed by this pretty teenage girl. "This is Crown." He pointed to a sleek white apartment building. "Where I live. Our focus is science and technology. What's your major?"

Libby hunched her shoulders. "Maybe environmental studies?"

"Do you mean Environment and Society or Environment with a Worldview?"

Vanessa smiled at Libby's bemused look. "Why don't we see both?"

"Perhaps I should clarify," Raymond said earnestly. "There's College Seven, which supports environmentalists working within the system. And then there's College Five, which are your basic ecoterrorists."

They approached a cheerful-looking terrace dotted with blue umbrellas and sturdy metal tables.

"Are you interested in a theme floor?" he said.

Vanessa and Libby exchanged puzzled looks.

"We have single gender, queer questioning, substance-free, or diversity awareness."

"Any just co-ed?" said Libby.

"Of course."

"College is so fascinating now," murmured Vanessa. She glanced at her watch and felt slightly annoyed. Thea had said she would try to meet them, but Vanessa had doubts. On one hand, she was happy her sister had looked up Cal Hawkins and of course she was dying to know if they'd slept together.

But on the other hand, Thea could never be counted on to show up for any event involving children. Any children. Not even an adult one.

"Aunt V?" Libby threw a beseeching glance her way. Apparently, Raymond had run out of useful information. The tour was over.

Returning to the front entrance, Libby shook their guide's hand. "Thank you for showing me around. It was very helpful."

"Sure," he nodded.

"And we appreciate your doing this during vacation," Vanessa added.

"Oh, no problem. I saw my aunt and uncle in San Jose for Christmas," Raymond said. "But I needed to get back in the lab and check on my rats."

"Eeew," Libby winced.

"You should know that we are fully accredited by AAL-LAC, which is internationally recognized as having the most stringent rules governing animal welfare, and we have even taken additional steps to ensure—"

"Yeah, bye, Raymond," Libby cut in.

"Well, I hope you will consider Santa Cruz in your future plans," he said formally. Then he turned and ambled back to his substance-free floor.

"Raymond was . . . very thorough." Vanessa folded up the campus map.

"Loser," Libby said, shading her eyes and glancing back towards the dorms.

"This place is amazing." Vanessa dug through her purse for her cell phone. "I mean, the classes, the forest, the view of the ocean. And it's so great that everyone bikes."

"Mmmm," said Libby.

Vanessa dialed her sister's number, only to reach voice mail. "Hi, Thee, we're done with the tour. Are you coming to get us? Call me." She scanned the street in both directions and sighed. "I was hoping she'd be here by now. Maybe we should just take the shuttle back to the hotel."

"Whatever you want," Libby said absently. She had dropped down on the dry, patchy grass and was scrolling through her messages.

Vanessa settled down beside her. "So, Lib, what do you think?"

"About what?"

"Uh, about the university?"

"Oh, it's nice."

"Nice?" Vanessa frowned. "We've come all this way. Can't you give me a little more than that?"

Libby jammed her phone in the pocket of her sunburst-orange hoodie. "Sorry. It is really beautiful and I love that there's an ocean."

"The dorms are unique." Vanessa poked Libby's shoulder.

"Yeah, that was sorta weird."

Vanessa squinted at her niece. "You don't seem excited."

Libby rolled her lips together. "Aunt V, if I tell you something will you promise not to tell my parents because they'll say it's *Brian* but I swear it's not."

"Okay. I pledge total secrecy."

"Now I want to go to school in Los Angeles. I think I really need a big city. I've lived my whole life in a small town and I just want to go somewhere different. And Boston is not that different, no matter what my mother says."

Vanessa remained quiet. This is the great thing about being an aunt, she realized. All I have to do is listen and love and I don't have to parent.

"I want to leave the East Coast. And it's not because I hate my parents or anything. It's just . . . I want to be on my own. My mother is the only person in the world who doesn't get that."

Vanessa's maternal instincts rose up in defense of Patience, but she decided to ignore them. Better to be the good listener.

"Aunt V, do you understand?"

"I understand," she reached out and stroked Libby's hair. "And you want to know my secret? I'm hoping that you'll come to California so I can get to know the grown-up you."

"Really?" Libby grinned.

"Really. After all, you're the only girl I've got."

THE THREE TRAVELERS WERE QUIET ON the ride home. Libby was asleep in the backseat, and Vanessa, needing some company, was listening to an old Alanis Morissette CD.

Thea was dozing. Every so often she would glance out the window at fields of artichokes and gas stations and freeway exit signs. Any satisfaction she had felt at tracking down Cal had vanished. She was annoyed at Vanessa—she hated Alanis Morissette—and was growing resentful at having to listen to what she considered bombastic keening for another three hundred miles.

Vanessa peeked over her shoulder at her niece. "Libby's asleep," she whispered to Thea. "So tell me what happened with Cal."

Why should I tell you anything? Thea thought petulantly.

Opening her mouth to say *it was good*, she abruptly exploded. "Nothing happened! He's fine, I'm fine! But if you hadn't kept bringing him up, I would never have gone there!"

"Well, I'm sorry. I just thought he was still stuck in your mind."

"Well, he wasn't."

"Well, I'm sorry."

For a few minutes they each resolved not to speak to each other, then somewhere around Cambria and the turnoff to Hearst Castle, Thea struck again.

"He's married and he has a kid. Are you satisfied?"

"Oh, is that why you're upset?" Vanessa looked at her sister with pity.

"I am not upset! I'm exhausted and I hate Alanis Morissette."

"How can you not like her?" Vanessa jammed her index finger on the CD Eject button. "Anyway, don't get mad at me. I was just trying to be supportive."

"Yeah, right."

"Look, you didn't have to go. I didn't make you."

"You wouldn't let up."

"You could have told me you weren't interested."

"I did!"

"Well, I didn't make you drive there."

"Yes, you did."

"No, I said you should *call* him."

Thea felt her pulse racing. The irony about that castle, she thought, was that Hearst spent a billion dollars on it and Marion Davies was still unhappy.

"Anyway," Vanessa lapsed into the tone of the all-knowing mother, "don't yell at me because things didn't work out."

"Of course they worked out. I have a happy life and so does he. Everything is fine."

"You're not happy." Vanessa instantly wished she hadn't said this.

"And you are?" Thea sharpened the knife. "You're thinking about fucking some tortured writer, that's how happy you are."

Vanessa glanced fearfully in the rearview mirror, praying Libby was still asleep. "I didn't do anything," she hissed. "And it's mean of you to bring that up now with you know . . ." she jerked her head towards the backseat.

Thea knew she was skating on cracking ice but she didn't care. "I'm perfectly happy with Marcus. Why can't you accept that?"

"I never said you weren't happy."

"You said he's too young for me."

"What I meant was that he isn't your equal."

"What the fuck does that mean?"

"Let's just forget the whole thing," Vanessa said tearfully. Speeding past the royal blue REST STOP $\frac{1}{4}$ MILE sign, she swerved into the exit lane.

"And PS . . . he's not tortured!"

Inside the Ladies' room, Vanessa peed into an institutional, stainless-steel toilet and then washed her hands at the institutional, stainless-steel sink. Why do public bathrooms have to be so horrible? she fumed. What does that say about us, as a society?

Returning to the park outside, she heard the chatter of blue jays in the stark liquidambar trees. Thea was stretching her calves on a circle of dying grass next to the row of parked cars.

Sidling up to her sister, Vanessa struck a diplomatic tone. "I don't want to argue. I want us to be happy."

Thea rolled her neck. "Then don't pick a fight."

"You started it." Vanessa longed to slap her sister's smug face.

"I came up here because you needed me. What are you bitching about?" Thea dropped her shoulders huffily.

"Oh, I should be grateful because you do this one little thing? I hardly ever ask you to do anything. And I practically have to beg you to see the boys."

"I told you I'm not good with kids."

"They're not *kids*—they're your *nephews*. And for your information, it's really wonderful being an aunt." Vanessa noticed Libby heading their way. "We can't talk about this now."

"Good," said Thea.

"I'm just going to go pee," Libby yawned.

"Sure," said Vanessa. "We'll wait."

As Libby scuffed to the restroom, the sisters pounded back to the car and writhed angrily in their seats.

"You know," said Vanessa, eyeing Thea hatefully, "I always show interest in your life, I'm always supportive of your work, I go to all your shows."

"Okay, then you win. You're a better person than me."

"No, it's just . . . Oh, I can't talk to you. I just . . . please just shut up for the rest of the drive," Vanessa said.

"No problem." Flinging open her door, Thea annexed the backseat.

I hate Vanessa, she thought. I hate how she always brings up men and kids. She tries to make it seem like that's much more important than a career. I hate that she wants me to act like her. This wanting, she thought, helplessly. This wanting me to be something else. It stands between us. It keeps us apart.

Feeling a hardness against her butt, Thea dug her fingers into the crack of the seat and unearthed an iPod. She scooped it up along with Libby's hoodie and dumped them into Vanessa's lap. "I think the *niece* should sit next to her *aunt* for the rest of the way."

Then, coiling into a fetal position against the backseat, Thea shut her eyes and retreated into her icy igloo.

LATER THAT NIGHT IN HER PARENTS' hotel room, Libby lounged in a padded armchair with her feet propped up on her father's side of the bed. Nestled side by side against the headboard, Patience applied hand cream while Richard flipped through the TV channels.

"Mom, I've decided that I really, really should apply to USC," Libby said, checking her phone for messages.

"Isn't it too late?" Her mother fluffed the pillow and, yawning, switched off her table lamp. "Weren't all the applications due before Christmas?"

"Some schools aren't due till mid-January," said Libby. "I'll go online right now and check out their website."

"Oh, Libby, stop! Would you just not fiddle with that phone for five minutes?" Patience heaved a martyred sigh. "Richard? Richard? Will you weigh in on this please?"

Reluctantly, Richard dropped the clicker on the bed and faced his womenfolk.

"Now she wants to apply to USC. I think it's a little late in the game. She's made her choices—good choices with a college counselor—and she should stick to them."

"Dad, don't you see? She's trying to control my life."

Patience smoothed her cuticles. "Well, you didn't want to come to Los Angeles till you met Brian."

"That is so not true!"

Richard shrugged. "If she wants to apply, apply. If she gets in, *then* you two can argue about it."

"We'll talk about it in the morning," said Patience. "Those twins wore me out. And you must be exhausted from the drive down."

Libby frowned. "Not really. I slept most of the way."

"Well, I'm turning in." Patience opened the drawer of her bedside table and removed a black satin sleep mask. Adjusting it over her eyes, she pulled up the blanket and rolled over on her right side. "Good night, I love you both."

Libby leaped from the chair. "Dad, can I sit next to you?"

"Sure, Pumpkin, snuggle in right here." Richard flipped back the covers and hoisted his left arm, drawing Libby in close beside him.

"What's on?" she said, staring blankly at the TV.

"Not much."

"Let's see if *Jaded* is on."

Richard groaned. "Do you still watch that?"

"It got better this season."

Pressing the remote, he clicked to the channel guide, and, for a few minutes, they watched the night's offerings scroll by.

Libby waited for the sound of her mother's steady breathing to be sure she was asleep. "Daddy," she whispered, "you want me to be happy, right?"

"I want all my girls to be happy," he whispered back.

"You know I don't want to come out here just because of Brian."

"I know."

"I like it here."

"I like it here too," he said. "You can play golf in January."

"So you understand why I've changed my mind."

"I understand," Richard said, hitting mute. "But I also expect my daughter to consider the bigger picture. Beyond the Brian."

Libby's nostrils flared. "It has nothing to do with that."

"Good," Richard nodded. "By September, you might not even be interested in him. Who knows? You might meet someone else."

Not possible, Libby thought.

"I may be just an old man"—her father kissed the top of her head—"but I know a little bit about love."

"You met Mom when you were young."

"That's true. But we didn't get married until a few years later. I went to medical school and she worked in Boston. So if it's right, if it's meant to be, it will happen."

Libby sniffled. Richard looked down at his sorrowful daughter. "Liberty, your mother and I want what's best for you, even if you don't believe that. We're not against Los Angeles, or Brian, or your happiness in general. We want to make sure that you choose a school that's right for you. Does that sound reasonable?"

Her eyes brimmed with tears. "I don't want to go back to Wenham. What if when I leave, Brian finds someone else?"

"Oh, honey," Richard gave her a reassuring squeeze. "How could he find anyone as wonderful as you?"

"You're saying that because you're my dad."

"And as your father, I'm in a position to know that it's true."

"So, can I apply to USC?"

"Let's just finish our vacation in peace." Richard hesitated. "Then, when we get back home, I'll speak to your mother."

"Thank you!" Libby kissed her father on the cheek. "You're the best dad ever."

"The best sucker ever," he sighed.

Patience began to snore.

"Oh, look!" Libby grabbed the clicker gleefully. "*Jaded* comes on at ten."

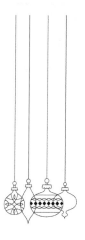

15

I can't believe it's December thirtieth." Patience gazed up at a towering saguaro cactus and a seamless blue sky. "Back home in Wenham it's snowing!"

Patience and Vanessa were visiting the Huntington Gardens, a mere forty freeway minutes from the Channing house. Having thoroughly consulted the visitors' guide, they had made their way over to the desert section, an arid landscape of rocks and cacti that looked like an old Western movie set.

"I thought you preferred snow at Christmas," Vanessa said teasingly.

"Did I say that?" Patience peered at a spiny, globular succulent. "I've never seen plants like this. They're eerie, don't you think?"

"Definitely," said Vanessa, who, despite initial misgivings about spending an afternoon with her sister-in-law, was beginning to enjoy herself. This was a good idea, she thought with relief. We're outside, enjoying nature, and we're not sitting around the house talking about dinner or—she racked her brain for other, mutual topics—the holidays.

"Okay, I'm bored with cactus. Let's go over to the conservatory." Vanessa pointed towards a glass building. "There should be greener things in there."

The moist air inside the hothouse seemed to oxygenate Patience's vocal cords. She oohed and ahhed over the array of exotic flowers and plants and fondled every leaf.

"I had so much fun yesterday with Alex and Ethan," she said, reaching out to touch a vanilla orchid. "I'm so jealous of your sister, living so close, getting to see them allthe time."

No need for jealousy there, Vanessa thought with a twinge. "Actually, Thea doesn't spend much time with them."

"Really? Well, she's an artist. And single. My sister, Hope, has girls, too, so I don't have much experience with boys. I was a little worried about what to do with them, but they're awfully self-sufficient. They wanted to go to the skatepark and when we got there, they just ran off with the other kids and had a grand time. I have never seen so much energy. Libby was never that active. And those ramps! They're terrifying. I just had to hold my breath."

"Welcome to my world," said Vanessa. "Anything that could send you to the emergency room must be fun."

"No, really, they're such good boys. And they're very polite! I can't remember the last time I cooked dinner for such an appreciative audience."

A small rain cloud passed over Vanessa's sunny day. "What did you make?"

"Nothing fancy. Just spaghetti with my homemade ragu sauce."

"Sounds delish." Vanessa tried to sound appreciative, but really! If Patience ordered pizza once in while, they'd probably be better friends.

Laying her hand on Vanessa's forearm, Patience hesitated. "Do you think maybe Ethan and Alex could come out and visit us this summer? I would love to take them to Crane Beach and of course they could ride horses at the stable."

Reflexively, Vanessa opened her mouth to decline but the expression on her sister-in-law's face gave her pause.

"I hate that we live so far away," Patience was saying. "I don't really know my nephews. And it all goes so fast. Who could believe Liberty will be off at college this fall? Anyway, do you think they'd like a week with their aunt and uncle?"

My God, Vanessa realized. For years I've been wanting Thea to spend time with the boys, and right here, under my nose, is the aunt I've been waiting for.

"Oh, do you think they're too young to travel?" Patience mistook Vanessa's silence for reluctance.

"No, no," Vanessa rushed in. "I was just . . . I think they'd love a vacation with you."

"You're welcome to come too, of course," said Patience. "But I thought if you needed a break or . . . I didn't want you to feel you always had to fly to Wenham. And I promise to take very good care of them both."

"I'd never worry if they're with you, Patience, you're a great mom. And it's really, really sweet of you to offer."

"You'd be doing me a favor." Patience gave a small half smile. "I mean, Libby's always off somewhere. She doesn't spend much time with her parents these days."

"Oh, I see," Vanessa said softly. "It must be hard, letting her go."

"It is. I don't know what I'll do without her."

A group of fawning orchid lovers crept up behind them and invaded their privacy.

"Let's head over to the Tea Room," said Vanessa, leading the way towards the exit.

"All right." Reaching into her pocket, Patience withdrew a tissue and dabbed her eyes.

They strolled companionably past velvet green lawns, Greek statues, and the Shakespeare Garden. Vanessa identified what few native plants she knew and Patience marveled at a stand of creaking bamboo.

The Tea Room, a white pavilion with columns and French windows, overlooked the rose garden. There was a queue outside the door, and the Channings took their turn to wait for a table.

"You know, initially I didn't want to come out here," said Patience, shading her eyes from the waning winter sun. "I guess it's no secret that I'm a homebody. And I was worried I'd miss all my Christmas traditions. And my Open House. And Beau. But now I'm glad I did something different."

"Well, unfortunately, I don't throw a party like you do,"

said Vanessa. "I'm just not great in the holiday department. I guess I'm more of an everyday person."

"What do you mean?"

"Oh, that I'm better at everyday life. Holidays just confuse me."

"I'm definitely a holiday person," Patience said merrily. "I like to look forward to things. Special days. It keeps me going."

"I have an idea," said Vanessa. "From now on, you should do the holidays and I'll stick to regular life."

"Oh, that's silly." Patience waved off the suggestion. But she looked pleased nonetheless.

"Two for tea?" said a lethargic hostess with pale lips and a clacking tongue stud. "I have a window next to the rose-bushes."

Vanessa and Patience limboed through jabbering relatives and frenzied toddlers, circled a buffet of sandwiches and pastries, and landed at a table with a view.

"Enjoy," clacked the hostess, handing them two menus.

"This is so elegant," said Patience, admiring a fireplace and a beveled mirror on the far wall. "It sort of reminds me of Europe."

A flabby granddad in too-short shorts bumped their table. "Well, maybe by way of Vegas," Vanessa said.

The busboy set down a basket of scones. Patience reached out and poked one. "Mmm, still warm!"

The ladies exchanged polite smiles and then turned to their menus. "It was awfully nice of your producer friend to invite Richard and me to his party," Patience said. "I mean, he doesn't know us at all."

"Oh, don't worry. Gary loves a big crowd—it makes him feel more important."

"And Liberty has promised to babysit the twins. It's the least she can do, after you drove her to Santa Cruz."

"Well, I won't say no to that. It's practically impossible to get a sitter on New Year's Eve." Vanessa set down her menu. "I think I'll order a pot of the Russian Caravan."

"That sounds good." Patience examined the gold-rimmed teacup on her right. "Will Neil be there?"

Neil? Vanessa tripped. She hadn't thought of Neil for, what? At least six hours. And wasn't it strange? Everything that happened at Christmas seemed like years ago.

"I don't know," Vanessa said airily. And what if he is there? I'll be with JT and Richard and Patience and a hundred of Gary's closest friends and if I see him I'll act charming but professional. She smiled dreamily, imagining her upcoming stellar performance.

Patience leaned forward. "You know, I think he has a little crush on you. There was something in the way he looked at you on Christmas."

"What? No," Vanessa sputtered. Her performance got a little less stellar. "We're just, er, colleagues."

"Well, he seems lonely to me. Does he have a girlfriend?"

"We hardly ever talk about personal things." Vanessa wriggled slightly, then pointed towards the crowd swarming the buffet. "Should we go over?"

"Neil is a man who needs someone to take care of him," Patience continued. "Like JT. JT would be lost without you."

"He would?" Vanessa suspended her preoccupation with

Neil in favor of her husband—apparently a man bereft without her.

"I can't believe how upset I was when he broke up with
Amanda. Well, she was all wrong for him. She turned out to
be a little bit of a snob."

"She did?" Vanessa cast a sudden, magnanimous warmth
towards her sister-in-law.

"Oh, yes. Amanda wanted a certain kind of New York life
with the right schools and the right friends. No, I realize now,
you and JT are perfect for each other."

"We are," Vanessa agreed heartily. *Of course, we are. Neil
was nothing more than a momentary flirtation, a whim, a
holiday.*

*And haven't we determined that I'm not really a holiday
person?*

Vanessa smiled serenely. She had a complete sense of clo-
sure about that whole silly episode. *Yes, for me, it's best to
stick to the everyday,* she conceded.

And leave the holidays to the professionals.

"Let's get our food," she said, leading Patience to the buffet. Wending past the drones circling the chocolate mousse
and raspberry tarts, she seized the serving tongs and offered up
a lovely chicken tarragon sandwich to her dear, dear sister-in-
law.

Even though she had announced her intention to get
back to work, declared herself ready to work.

Thea wasn't working.

She was reading and napping. She was wandering around her house. She was watching TV.

And she never watched TV.

This morning, she'd risen early to walk to the beach with Marcus. Six A.M. and six P.M. were the best hours for waves. And Surfline had predicted a northwest five- to six-foot swell in Venice.

As Marcus paddled out into the roiling Pacific Ocean, Thea burrowed into the sand, a fringed saffron-colored shawl wrapped tightly around her black turtleneck and leggings. Despite the sunshine predicted for later in the day, it was foggy and chilly this early in the morning.

Thea enjoyed watching Marcus and the rest of the we suit posse ride the ocean range. She admired their balance and graceful movements on their boards. They made surfing look easy, and she knew, firsthand, that it wasn't. Marcus had tried to teach her once, insisting that she had the perfect body for it: Her limbs were taut and muscular from years of walks on the beach and weight lifting at Gold's Gym. But Thea didn't care about waves; she lacked the drive to harness their power for the triumphant ride to shore. So she opted instead to be a spectator, even though Tina mocked her endlessly for being a *goddamned* surfer girl.

After about an hour of riding, Marcus was spent and they returned to her house for breakfast: toasted raisin bread with apricot jam and rich, frothy espresso.

They sat across from each other at the kitchen table. Marcus scanned Surfline and Yahoo! News on his laptop while Thea read the *Los Angeles Times* on hers. She started several feature stories but nothing seemed compelling. It was the end

of December drivel: best and worst of the year movies and restaurants and people, warnings about drinking and driving and
CHP checkpoints, retail sales figures, reheated articles filed
before Christmas so the reporters could ditch work and play
like the rest of the world. The news was uninspired and boring. Everything's boring the last week of the year, she decided.
Especially me.

"I feel so draggy," she said. "These last hours of December."

"Fuckin' A!" Marcus was grinning at the three-day surf
forecast. "I'm driving up to Ventura tomorrow."

"But it's New Year's Eve," said Thea. "I thought we were
making chili."

"Yeah, well, sorry, six- to seven-foot waves, baby."

"Hmmm," said Thea, thinking that there were indeed limits on how interesting surfer boys could be.

"Come with me." Marcus slurped his cup of java.

Thea considered his damp corkscrew curls and his tapping
fingers. She felt removed from him, his breath and his bones.
Somehow, seeing Cal again had thrown Marcus into . . . well,
while not an unflattering light, certainly a crystal-clear one.

There was no getting around his youth and youthful out-
look. Marcus didn't have the weight of an older man. The heft
of an older man. A man like, oh, say, Cal.

Why are you even comparing them? she admonished herself. Compare and despair. Nothing good ever comes of pitting
people against each other. Or against yourself.

But still, in the forty-eight hours since she'd returned from
Point Reyes—the forty-eight hours she'd realized that time
had passed and years whizzed by—something *had* changed.

Something in her and with her, and it had dragged Marcus down with it.

She glanced over at him. "Nah, I want to stay here and ring in the New Year with Mel and Tina and chili and the uncut version of *Children of Paradise*."

"Baby, are you sure?" he said consolingly, as if he couldn't imagine such a horrible fate for anyone.

What's the expiration date for *baby*? she mused. Is it similar to the one for *surfer girl*?

AFTER MARCUS LEFT FOR WORK, THEA dawdled on her bed upstairs and thumbed through some old sketchbooks. Flipping through her drawings of locals, tourists, and canal life, she listened to a jazz anthology program on the radio. She watched seagulls and a few egrets troll for sustenance in the water down below.

I need a project, she thought despairingly. I need my art to consume me.

At lunchtime, she rummaged through her refrigerator and, hopelessly discouraged, ventured out for a decent meal. She headed over to Abbot Kinney Boulevard and one of those tasty sandwiches at the new, overpriced deli.

It was a mile walk and there was a larger than usual crowd out on the street. She imagined that most of these people had the week off. And they were spending it browsing in the boutiques and dining in the restaurants with their relatives from Chicago and New York—happy to escape the cold climes.

She bought a tomato and mozzarella panino and then sat, cross-legged, on a bench outside the store, enjoying the sun on her face and the sweet bite of basil on her tongue.

There was a whole crop of younger, slightly cleaner-looking locals in Venice these days. As she ate, she watched them struggle past with their babies and strollers and coffee and bags. With their dogs. With a red wagon. With their beach cruiser bikes.

What's wrong with me? Thea puzzled. That I don't want what everyone else seems to want. A child, a stroller. I don't even own a rescue dog.

Was Cal right? Was life hard without family?

She wasn't sure if she loved her life right then, and wondered if anyone felt much of anything on the 364th day of the year.

But Cal had triggered something in her.

Perhaps it was love.

Did she want love?

More than just sex-love with beautiful men?

She licked the creamy pesto mayo dressing from her fingers, crumpled up her paper bag, and tossed it into a nearby trash can. Crossing the street, she cut through the alley and over to the bike path to walk the long way home.

I'm bored with Marcus, she admitted, passing the busker who played the recorder and the woman who roller-skated in a thong and a Lakers cap. Maybe there's something else, something *older* in the year to come.

ON NEW YEAR'S EVE, LIBBY ARRIVED at her aunt and uncle's with a downturned mouth and pink, swollen eyelids.

"Sweetie, what's wrong?" Leading her niece into the living room, Vanessa tossed aside the Xbox controllers, two baseball mitts, and a broken candy cane and sat her down on the couch.

Libby hid her face in Vanessa's sheer black, ruffled blouse. "They're so mean!"

"'They'?"

"She means us," said Patience sharply. Following them into the room she dropped stiffly into JT's armchair. "Liberty, stop making a scene."

"Brian has to work tonight," was Libby's muffled reply. "But Aunt V, he said I could hang out with him at the hotel. And it's New Year's Eve!"

"Oh, I see." Vanessa looked at Patience. "It is an important night. Why don't I stay home with the twins?"

Libby lifted her head hopefully.

"Nonsense," Richard boomed. He was planted firmly in the archway, unwilling to entangle himself in the living room drama. "We are not changing our plans now. Liberty can spend an evening with her cousins. There'll be plenty of time tomorrow to bid adieu to Romeo. They'll have to part eventually."

Vanessa grimaced. She hated the idea of being the cause of so much angst and misery on a night already primed for that sort of thing.

Libby broke out in a fresh set of tears. My parents are the most horrible fuckheads in the world! she wailed silently. Making me babysit on New Year's Eve. I will never, ever forgive them!

A sudden rush of cool wind interrupted her inner tirade,

and then a tornado of blue flannel with muddy feet was circling the coffee table.

"Libby," Alex cried, "come see the fort we built in the backyard."

Peeking out from the safety of Vanessa's torso, Libby came nose to nose with her impish cousin.

"Libby, Libby, you have to see. We made it for you."

Somehow, the sight of this adoring fan softened her. She felt the flame of guilt—how could she be mean, be so selfish, and cry in front of him. "I would love to see the fort," she croaked bravely.

His arm shot out and, grabbing her wrist, he dragged her outside to a byzantine nest of blankets, patio furniture, and cardboard boxes.

Vanessa turned to Patience and Richard and groaned. "I feel terrible."

"Don't," Patience said tersely. "She should spend a few hours with Alex and Ethan. After today, she'll be gone—off to college, off to her life, off to—"

"Oh, for God's sake, P," said Richard, "let's not take this into the future. Where's JT?"

"He's right here." JT appeared in jeans, a beige fisherman's sweater, and a gray wool cap. He smelled faintly of lime shaving cream.

Vanessa rose, smoothed her blouse, and fluffed up her hair.

Patience followed Vanessa's slim skirt and kitten heels as she crossed the floor. I feel so dowdy, she thought, staring down at her blue gabardine trousers and argyle cardigan.

"You are so gorgeous," said JT, giving his wife a squeeze.

"I guess we're the fuddy-duddy relatives," pouted Patience. She glanced at Richard's stodgy blue blazer and Top-Siders—perfect for a night at home with scotch and Scrabble, but not right, she felt, for a party with theater people in Los Feliz, wherever that was.

"I haven't been out on New Year's Eve in years," she said dolefully. "I'm always tired after the Open House and Christmas dinner. Plus there's nowhere to go in Wenham."

"Well," said Vanessa, "do you want to borrow something?"

Patience looked up at her sister-in-law. Something in Vanessa's gesture, the playfulness, ignited a girlish yearning. "Do you think I'd fit into anything of yours?"

"Let's see."

Tapping briskly to the bedroom, Vanessa threw open her closet door. "You always look classic," she said, noting Patience's neat hair and prim attire. "Do you want to try something completely different?"

"Not completely." Patience hesitated. Peering into Vanessa's wardrobe, a narrow tunnel hopelessly mired in separates and accessories, Patience felt like she had stumbled into a fifty-percent-off sale. The only thing missing was harsh fluorescent lighting.

The shelves were jammed with sweaters and plastic storage containers. Here and there a sleeve or a belt cascaded down like jungle vines. The wooden pole sagged from the weight of coats, pants, skirts, and dresses of every length. The floor was littered with mismatched shoes and dirty laundry.

Patience zeroed in on the Talbots box peeking out from under a pile of JT's wrinkled shirts. Don't jump to conclusions, she cautioned herself, you don't know that Vanessa didn't like your present.

"Didn't you like my present?" she heard herself saying.

"I love your sweater," Vanessa said quickly. "But I haven't had time to put anything away. Look"—she pointed towards a duffel bag next to her bed—"I haven't even unpacked from my one night in Santa Cruz. Now, let's concentrate on you."

Vanessa plucked a sleeveless sheath in a bright geometric print and held it under Patience's chin. "What do you think?"

"Oh, no," Patience flinched. Maybe dress-up wasn't a good idea.

"Yeah, you're right. I'm sick of this look now that all the teenagers are wearing it."

Rummaging past a cache of black, Vanessa seized a taffeta skirt with gold embroidery and a vermilion silk dress with a mandarin collar and frog fastenings.

Patience fingered the skirt. "Oooh, this is pretty."

Vanessa nodded. "That would look stunning with a wide belt and a short cardigan. Very fifties, very elegant . . . Hey, I know!"

Opening up the Talbots box, Vanessa held the persimmon sweater next to the skirt. "Your classic style—but updated and dressier."

Patience grew excited. The sweater and skirt did look great together. "But I can't wear your present."

"Why not?" Vanessa separated footwear on the closet floor. "What size shoe are you?"

"Six and a half," said Patience.

"Okay, these will be a little big, but we'll stuff the toes."

Vanessa pushed simple gold pumps into Patience's arms. "You have such a tiny waist. I have just the belt for it."

Patience sat down on the bed and bounced giddily a few times. She remembered one particular snow day when she and her sister, Hope, had sneaked into their mother's closet and tried on her clothes. When Mrs. Polk returned from the market and discovered Patience in her fanciest black cocktail dress and heels, she'd given her daughters a stern lecture about permission and privacy and banished them to their rooms.

"Did you play dress-up when you were little?" asked Patience.

"All the time. With Thea. My mom had a ton of clothes and we were always going through her stuff. How did you know?" Vanessa laughed.

"I guess all girls want to do that. Liberty loved a particular robe that I wore—blue velvet with lace cuffs. And she'd put on high heels and ropes of pearls and a sun hat."

"I'll bet she looked adorable."

Patience had a vivid memory of Liberty at three or four, wrapped in that robe and climbing into bed with them for "cozy" time.

Her stomach fluttered and she forced herself back into the present. "I think I'll change in the bathroom."

Vanessa glanced at her sister-in-law sitting modestly on the bed. "Stay here, I'll go out. Let me know if anything doesn't fit."

Waiting in the hallway, Vanessa recalled how she and Thea loved playing with Barbie and that dressing her doll was the best part. Once Barbie met Ken at the imaginary beach or dance, the sisters would end the date and whisk her back to the dream house to style her again.

Thinking about Thea made her feel guilty. They hadn't spoken since the ride back from Santa Cruz. She hadn't even called to wish her sister a Happy New Year.

Well, she could have called me, Vanessa thought defiantly.

Patience opened the door. "What do you think?"

In the fitted cardigan and full skirt, and her short legs elongated in three-inch heels, Patience was gorgeous.

"It's perfect!" said Vanessa.

"You don't think I look too, too . . ."

"Too glamorous?"

Patience beamed before the mirror.

"It makes you look younger," said Vanessa. "This style is good on you."

"I like it."

"I love it," said Vanessa. "But we should get a move on. We're going over the hill, and traffic through Hollywood can be a nightmare."

"WHERE ARE WE AGAIN?" ASKED PATIENCE. She was peering out the rear passenger window at a winding street with beautiful, eclectic houses and dramatic landscaping.

"Los Feliz," said Vanessa, riding up front with JT. "It's kind of an old L.A. neighborhood. There're still a few houses around that were built by the silent-movie stars in the twenties."

Old, thought Patience, thinking about the Whipple House, back in Ipswich, which must be going on four hundred years.

JT pulled up to a valet stand in front of an exquisitely tarted Spanish gem.

"Jeez, our car's so dirty," moaned Vanessa.

A blond goddess in running shoes, a gold lamé baseball cap, and tight sequined vest opened their doors. "Happy New Year!" she said.

"A girl valet?" Patience whispered to her husband.

"Happy New Year indeed," said Richard, admiring Valet Girl's two best assets.

They headed up the front walk, past olive trees laced with twinkle lights and Moroccan lanterns. The baroque front door was open and music and laughter drifted from the rooms beyond.

"Vanessa! JT! Happy New Year!" Conner Kaplan, Gary's partner, kissed them on both cheeks. "And this must be The Family."

Vanessa introduced her in-laws, and Conner bestowed more continental kisses on a shocked Patience and Richard.

"Vanessa said you're from Massachusetts. I love love love New England," Conner said as they sailed through a tiled foyer with an undulating wrought-iron staircase. "So completely untouched by tacky tacky hands!"

Patience thought she had never seen such white teeth on a man. And was he wearing Lancôme bronzer?

The house was the most beautiful place Patience could imagine. Beckoning velvet couches in topaz and ruby. Gleaming coffee tables with satin runners. Flickering candles and bowls of candy-red apples. A barrel ceiling with lacquered beams and, high above their heads, a cascading crystal chandelier. Patience longed to linger, but their host was speeding into a courtyard with a fire pit, its rising flames creating a sense of urgency and passion. Along the perimeter, guests were lounging on chaises and daybeds under awnings of nutmeg-colored canvas.

"Here," Conner said, patting a king-sized mattress covered in paisley silk. "I want you to have the best seat in the house."

"Conner, this is amazing," said Vanessa.

"Imagine!" Patience gasped. "Sitting in a cabana outside in December."

"It's why we live here," Conner said airily. "Slumber parties all year-round."

JT and Vanessa kicked off their shoes and crawled onto the bed. Richard reluctantly removed his loafers and sat stiffly against the wrought-iron footboard with Patience.

A bulked-up young waiter in tight tight black arrived with a tray of champagne flutes.

"Thank you, Tristan," said Conner, reaching for a glass. "Everyone, before you take your drink, you must tell me one wish for the New Year."

"Stay healthy," joked JT.

Conner looked him up and down. "You look pretty healthy to me."

"Spend more time with my shoes off," said Richard. He was wiggling his toes and suddenly enjoying the breeziness of it all.

"What about you?" Vanessa said to her host.

"I pray my listing on Glendower *finally* sells so I can get some sleep at night." Conner tipped his glass at Patience. "Tag, you're it."

"I hope to spend more time with Liberty, my daughter, before she leaves for college," she murmured.

"Aww," was the collective sigh.

Conner turned to Vanessa. "Okay, last one."

"I should probably clean my closet." Vanessa glanced guiltily at Patience.

Conner rolled his eyes. "Well, let's not set the bar too high."

Patience giggled like a schoolgirl. "This is fun!"

"More than fun," said Conner, and with a jeté towards another sparkling arrival, he disappeared.

The waiter passed out their drinks.

"Happy New Year!" They all clinked and took a sip of their champagne.

"Do you know all these people?" Patience said.

"Well, some of them are from the play and . . . oh, there's Gary," said Vanessa, noticing the producer making his way through a sea of guests. As usual, he looked tense and anxious.

"Dear Vanessa." He leaned into their cabana and kissed her cheek. "Thanks to you, the show will go on."

"Oh, please," she said, coloring slightly. She made another round of introductions and then squeezed Gary's hand. "What's wrong? You look worried."

"Of course it's Conner. He always says he'll take care of everything, and then at the last minute he hires the most incompetent, most expensive caterer." He glanced at his watch. "I don't know how we're going to get this dinner out."

"We could help you," said Patience.

Vanessa shrank back, hoping the *we* meant *she*.

"Oh, no," said Gary.

He means, *oh, yes*, thought Vanessa. And I just got here!

"It'll be easy," Patience was saying. "I mean, you probably just need some extra hands for getting things to the table, right?"

"She's a saint," he murmured, laying a hand on Vanessa's forearm.

"Besides"—Patience was already sliding off the bed—"I'd love to see your kitchen!"

"I'm not really that good at cooking," said Vanessa.

"But this poor man," said Patience.

Vanessa reluctantly handed her glass to JT. "How come guys never volunteer for kitchen duty?"

LIBBY WAS IMPRISONED IN HER COUSINS' fort. Holding a flashlight, she was sitting on the cold grass reading one of the Lemony Snicket books with both boys cuddled up against her.

An hour before, she'd felt depleted from hating her parents. But somehow the cousin love zinging her way had lifted her spirits. They really were so sweet.

"Lib, can I get you a bowl of ice cream?" Alex tugged her left arm.

"Or microwave popcorn?" Ethan tugged the right.

"Are you guys bored with reading?" She laughed.

"Is it time for the ball to fall?" Alex said. "Maybe we should check the TV."

Reaching out, she knighted each boy in queenly fashion. "Sir Alex, you check the TV. Sir Ethan, you make the popcorn."

The boys crawled out of the tent and Libby stretched her legs. Her neck was cramped from hunching over. The ceiling of her makeshift castle was only about two feet high.

"Libby, Libby!" Alex threw open the blanket flap. "Someone's at the door!"

"We're not allowed to open it!" cried his brother.

Libby frowned. Who would come over on New Year's Eve?

She followed them across the damp lawn and into the kitchen.

"It's an ax murderer!" Ethan grabbed her hand as they crept towards the front entry.

"Hello? Libby?" came a familiar voice.

"It's Brian!" Libby rushed to unlock the door.

What was he doing here? Sweeping her into a hug.

The twins were crestfallen. A handsome suitor had stolen their fair maiden out from under them.

"Brian, these are my cousins, Alex and Ethan."

"Hey, guys, high five." Brian held out his palm for a slap. The boys remained stationed at their big cousin's sides.

Libby looked down at them with compassion. "We were just about to have popcorn in Fort Channing," she said to Brian. "It's amazing. The boys built it. Want to see?"

"If it's okay with the guards."

"We're knights," said Alex.

Brian stroked his chin thoughtfully. "I see. So there's probably a secret knock that only knights use to get in?"

Alex's eyes grew large. "A secret knock a secret knock a . . . yeah. Eth"—he grabbed his brother's arm—"we'll go in first and then you come"—he pointed at Brian—"and give the *secret knock*."

"Whew," Libby sighed, watching them tear through the dining room. "You almost didn't make the cut."

Brian leaned down and kissed her. Again and again.

She pushed him away. "Stop it! I'm supposed to be babysitting."

"Mmm, the babysitter. That's so hot."

Libby giggled. "I thought you had to work."

"I got off early," he said, circling her back with his right arm. "The perks of nepotism. Plus, there was nothing much going on."

How could she resist him? His skin was so silky and he was making her feel spongy and moist. Like a luscious layer cake, with butter cream frosting inside.

"Libby!" A plaintive cry reached them from the kingdom beyond.

For the next hour, Brian and Libby conjured every game they could think of to tire out the twins.

There was hide-and-seek, driveway skateboarding, and broomstick jousting.

Just when the boys' eyes were rolling back into their sockets, Libby announced bedtime and they staggered, like zombies, to their room. There wasn't even an argument about brushing their teeth.

Engaging automatic pilot, she read them one last chapter about orphans and a wicked uncle, while silently obsessing about her virginity. She had always wanted to lose it in a *special* way. With someone *incredible*. Wouldn't it be *amazing* to lose it on New Year's Eve? Why should I wait? she thought urgently. Who would be better than Brian?

Closing the book, she kissed her cousins, snapped off the light, and raced to the living room, diving in next to her boyfriend on the couch.

Picking up the remote, Brian clicked off the TV. "When are your parents coming back?"

"Not till after midnight."

The kissing began.

During the oxygen break, Libby checked the time on her phone. "Eleven o'clock! We don't want to miss New Year's."

Brian reached around her back, slipped his hand under her T-shirt and unhooked her bra. "I don't care about that."

She pulled off his shirt.

He unbuttoned her jeans.

She unzipped his cords.

The clothes were off.

The couch was warm and cushy. The room was aglow from the sparkle of the Christmas tree lights.

Brian touched her, again and again. She was so aroused that when he waved the square foil package in front of her she didn't hesitate.

"Yes."

"Are you sure?"

She opened her thighs and shifted around him. "I want you."

Slowly, gently, he entered her, just a little. She held her breath. There wasn't any pain, it was kind of strange, but she liked it.

He was inside her, but touching her too. In all the right places. "Brian," she gasped. How does he know? How does he know me like that? And then, before she could mark, for all time, the exact moment of Losing Her Virginity . . .

She was coming.

She was coming.

She was coming.

Happy New Year.

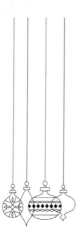

16

Tina looked tough and fearless in a lacy purple slip and motorcycle boots, but she cradled a plastic tumbler of wine like it was a sippy cup. Beside her, on a white folding chair, was Thea, her colored braids unleashed for the evening and an arc of silvery glitter fanned across her eyelids.

They hovered at the edge of a portable dance floor at the Venice Art Guild. It was hot and airless in what was really the basement room of a crooked Victorian manor. It had been converted to a community center in the '70s, and as a venue for poetry readings and local art, the guild was always on the brink of demise.

So every New Year's Eve, for a retro fifteen-dollar cover charge, the Venetians quaffed watery wine and felt virtuous about saving a historic site that they seldom patronized.

Having been ditched by their respective lovers—Marcus chose Ventura over Venice, Mel chose Samantha over Tina— the friends had decided that a night alone in Thea's loft making chili was too gloomy and domestic. So they'd walked down Venice Boulevard, past the homeless encampment under the sycamores, and the merrymakers on the streets of Abbot Kinney, to a destination they hoped would be lively and anonymous.

"Mel is a heartless bitch," Tina was shouting over the harsh braying of a recently reunited L.A. punk band. "She says she can't be with someone who's not out. She doesn't understand my family. Do you think she's right?"

"I'm here to support you," Thea shouted back. "And I can't take sides. You guys could get back together again in an hour."

"But tell me the truth," Tina begged, snapping the adjustable strap on her lavender bra.

"There is no truth." Thea patted Tina's arm and scanned the crowd, mostly skinny, sweaty young men and women in thrift clothes and body art. Here and there she recognized an old neighborhood stalwart: the Rasta guy who sold incense on the boardwalk and the seventy-something potter with the gray chignon who taught ceramics at UCLA.

"If you love someone, you're patient and . . . you understand that sometimes she needs time to work things out." Tina's bright red lipstick was bleeding around the edges.

"Remember the time I did the performance piece as Boudica here?" Thea groaned. "I think there were five people in the audience."

"I don't believe it." Tina caught sight of Mel entering the room on the arm of a tall woman in cowboy boots, a buzz haircut, and three nose rings. "She came with Samantha! Well, I'm not going to hide from them—I'm going over."

Thea glanced at Mel, who looked awfully cute in a slouchy beret and fuchsia cat glasses. "Maybe you should talk to her tomorrow . . ." she said, knowing full well that Tina would ignore her advice, ". . . when you're both sober."

But Tina was already pushing past the twenty pogo-ing dancers and provoking a scene.

Thea escaped to the makeshift bar—two banquet tables littered with wine bottles, soft drink cans, and tubs of melting ice. A clean-cut sort of guy in his early forties stood opposite her, pouring himself some chardonnay.

"Can I refill your glass?" he shouted.

"It's club soda," she shouted back.

Searching through the assortment, he plucked the Canada Dry and topped off her drink.

"I'm Jason," he continued. "I just moved to this side of town."

Oh, no, Thea thought, midlife crisis. "I can tell," she said, pointing at his crisp white shirt, tie, and jeans.

"Yeah, I guess I'll have to get native pretty soon," he smiled, showing off perfectly straight teeth. "How long have you lived here?"

"Around fifteen years." Jesus, she thought, how did this Boy Scout wander off the path?

"I was living in the Valley."

Did I ask you for your life story? "And let me guess," she said dryly. "You're divorced, and you always wanted to move to the beach."

"Okay, so it might be a little cliché. But I'll bet you could boil yourself down to one too."

Thea paused. Jason didn't seem the least bit offended by her—how intriguing. She decided to play along.

"I'll take that challenge. I'm a liberal, feminist artist who dates . . ." She was on the verge of saying *younger men,* but then, realizing Jason was around her age, censored herself. ". . . men," she finished.

"Men?" he said. "So I guess you're not a cliché, then. I had you pegged for a liberal, feminist artist who dates Labradors."

Angling around the table, he closed in on her. What's he doing? she thought. He's so . . . hopelessly square. But he smelled so good, so clean, and his skin was glowing, healthy. Like a Renoir, she decided.

"What's your name?" said Jason.

Thea opened her mouth just as a compact body heaved itself against her backside.

"Thea," whispered Tina, "I have to talk to you."

"Uh, excuse me," Thea said to Jason.

"But you were telling me your . . ."

Tina dragged her friend back to their former seats, which were now occupied by a pit bull in a party hat and his owner, a Hispanic man in clogs, sunglasses, and braided soul patch.

"Those skanks deserve each other." Tina lunged at Thea, clutching at her shoulders and staring hungrily at her best friend's mouth. "They can rot in hell," she blubbered. "Why aren't you my lover?"

"Okay, no more wine." Thea confiscated Tina's glass and, with a beseeching nod at Soul Patch, handed him the drink. "You've wandered into drunken logic land."

"But you said you slept with a woman."

"That was in art school," Thea said. "Everyone's bisexual in art school."

"Why didn't I go to *your* school?" Tina was crying big crocodile tears now.

"Come on, Betty, let's give the ladies some privacy," said Soul Patch, moving away with his dog.

Tina gazed longingly at her friend. "I've always loved you. I want to be with you! We'd be perfect together. Why won't you fuck me?"

Thea contemplated Tina's swollen mouth and seductive cleavage. Although she wasn't attracted to women and wasn't taking Tina's overtures seriously, Thea wasn't immune to the temptation of New Year's Eve and the desperate need to hook up, forget, damage, and destroy.

It would be nice. Having someone new desire me, thrill me. To be adored and ravaged. She took a moment to scan the room, seeking any other possible partners for the night. She noticed that Jason was now chatting with Soul Patch and patting the pit bull. He glanced over at her and she quickly looked away, embarrassed at being caught. God, if that's the only available guy in the place . . .

"Okay, time to leave," Thea grabbed Tina's limp arm. "Can you walk?" It must have turned midnight, for as they stumbled down Pacific Avenue, cars began to honk and slurring voices high up in the apartment buildings chanted, "Happy New Year!"

"Happy fucking New Year," Tina whimpered, and, grasping at Thea, began to moan. "I feel sick."

Goddamn it, we should have stayed in, Thea groaned, enfolding her right arm around Tina's waist and steering them down the block. Nothing good really happens when you go out on this night.

They reached Thea's studio and managed to scale the outside stairs before Tina threw up on the front door.

"I'm sorry!" she wailed. "Please, please don't hate me."

Pushing Tina into the guest bathroom on the right, Thea flipped up the toilet lid just as another torrent of bile spewed into the bowl.

Tina sobbed and clung to the seat. Thea gently twisted back her friend's hair: thick, wavy black tresses, soft and dense, like molten chocolate cake.

"I love Mel so much." Tina was heaving and choking through her tears. "How could she be with someone else?"

"Oh, sweetheart." Thea gazed at her image in the mirror over the sink. With her tumbling, unbraided plaits, she resembled an unkempt warrior princess. Her forehead was high and strong; her eyes were clear and wise. I am Boudica, she thought. Ready to fight my way through another year on the urban battlefield.

Having purged thoroughly, Tina was now muttering about her breath and mouthwash and a facecloth.

"There's some Listerene in my upstairs bathroom," Thea said.

Tina curled up on the cracked cement floor. "I'll wait right here."

*   *   *

THEA MADE UP THE LIVING ROOM couch and Tina, now cleansed and scented, stretched out on a gray-and-white pin-stripe sheet.

"You're so beautiful Thea," she said. "I love your hair . . ."

Thea leaned down and kissed her forehead. "Yeah, time for sleep."

"I feel so bad about everything."

Thea tucked a beige cotton blanket up around her friend. "Don't worry—you'll feel even worse in the morning."

"Did I say anything embarrassing?"

"Well, the next time I need an orgasm, I'll call you up."

"Okay," said Tina. She closed her eyes and Thea tiptoed from the room.

In her bedroom, Thea sat at the window and peered down at the canal. The fog was creeping in and there were no stars visible in the sky. She heard the faint murmur of traffic and party music—some rap, some salsa—and watched the reflection of house lights shimmer in the water below.

Well, Thea thought wryly, it's New Year's Eve. I went to a loud, ugly party where I didn't meet anybody, someone's barfed, and now I'm alone. All is as it should be. It'll probably be a good year. She flashed briefly on Jason but dismissed him vigorously. Please, she sighed. A divorced guy like that? *But he was sort of sexy*, a feathery voice cooed inside. *In a completely icky totally straight way.*

She hugged her knees and thought about the sex of New Years past. Last time, she and Marcus had gone to Joshua Tree, but she couldn't visualize their doing it. Oh, no, wait. They'd gotten up early to hike in the park and had some pretty wet hands-over-clothes rubbing behind a craggy rock formation. And they'd stayed in that funky stucco motel that smelled of cigarettes and carpet cleaner.

She couldn't recall ever meeting someone on New Year's Eve. There had been parties to get through, a few times she'd gone away.

Her last New Year's Eve with Cal had been in New York. She had come to stay with him in his loft, a drafty, unfinished building with a maze of corridors that made her feel skittish, like a rat.

Cal shared the space with three other guys—each man commanding one corner of the floor—and there was little privacy behind the plywood walls, Japanese screens, and flimsy curtains.

So the two lovers had retreated to Times Square to be alone among the thousands, just strolling and holding hands. Hanging close together against a storefront, they kissed and waited for the ball to fall.

"Let's get married," Cal whispered, his breath tickling her neck. "I love you. I'll never love anyone but you."

"Yes," she said. "Yes!" For it was romantic, she did love him, and she was swept up in the moment.

Then she'd flown back to L.A., where she immersed herself in work for her upcoming show and landed a review in the Friday Arts section. Somehow the city had wooed her, lassoed her, and corralled her in Venice Beach.

Where she was now tied to herself.

She hadn't moved to New York as she'd promised.

And when Cal had flown back to find her, she was already

sleeping with that film editor—what was his name? She shuddered, remembering they'd done a lot of drinking and they were terrible in bed.

Why did I do that to Cal? she thought remorsefully. Because I was young and callow?

And . . . she bit her lip. I didn't really want to get married. Ever. I liked the idea of it, the panorama of it, but I didn't want to lose myself that way.

I guess I'm just a selfish bitch, she thought. Less sentimental than your average girl.

Not willing. Not willing to be his wife.

Pressing her cheek against the window, she felt ashamed of the way she acted and the pain she caused. Noticing a few final revelers stagger down the street, she thought, Oh come on, Thea. If you had to do it over, you'd still get on that plane.

She flashed on the woman with the gray chignon, the potter she'd seen around Venice for years, who was often with a different man. Gray Chignon certainly gives the impression that she's enjoying herself. And maybe I'm like her, one of those women who'll never marry.

Was that so terrible? A life to be pitied?

There are worse things in life than a string of lovers. Art and success and a view of a Venice canal.

Art and success.

Thea stripped off her clothes and lay naked in bed.

She felt alive and warm against the sheets.

She was going to greet the New Year in her bare skin.

*   *   *

GARY'S KITCHEN REMINDED PATIENCE OF SOMETHING you'd see on a television cooking show.

It was professional yet homey, sleek yet comfy. The silvery stainless cookware dangled, like twinkling ornaments, over the center island. There was two of everything: refrigerators, sinks, ovens, dishwashers, coffeemakers. She was sensing a Mediterranean theme, from the majolica serving dishes and the royal blue hardware on the cabinets. There were alcoves and nooks for breakfasting and computing and floral arranging and personal training. The kitchen was so all-encompassing that one could live a rich and full life within its boundaries. It extended outward, like the suburbs, into an entire second living room with couches that could seat twelve, a flat-screen television, and a flickering fire inside a glass fireplace. Patience swooned, imagining herself sautéing onions with a studio audience cheering her on. She'd be wearing signature jewelry and a colorful shirt—like all TV personalities—and sipping wine and joking with her amiable cohost.

Right next to Patience, Vanessa was gulping her champagne and scanning the room for an out: Voilà! There he was! A roly-poly chef in jeans, T-shirt, and white apron, a red bandanna bound around his graying temples.

She sidled over. "It looks like you've got everything handled," she said to him. "So I think I'm going to . . ."

"This is a nightmare," said Steve, the caterer. He grabbed her free hand and held on tightly. "My two best guys, Manuel and K.K., are both down with the flu—or drunk, who knows?—and I couldn't find anyone else at this hour. I mean, New Year's Eve, Hello, the town is booked."

"Well, don't you worry," Patience smiled eagerly. "We're here to help."

"Give me something easy," Vanessa said flatly.

"Come." Steve led her into one of the alcoves, a curtained, beribboned hideaway, where she came face-to-face with Neil and Ashley, the stunning actress who played the sister in the show. Ashley's blond hair was loose, and her small, triangular breasts jiggled merrily inside the bodice of a jade-green ballerina frock.

"Well, hi, you two." Vanessa blushed to her hairline. She cast a furtive look at Neil, so handsome in a black-and-white pinstripe shirt and dark jeans, his intense gaze fixed on chopping tomatoes.

"Vanessa," he said. Their eyes locked and loaded.

"Oh, hi!" Ashley giggled. She was tearing up romaine lettuce leaves in portions fit for a pachyderm.

"That Gary! He has us working for him, even now," Vanessa forged on. She felt awkward, like the ex-girlfriend at the ex-boyfriend's engagement party. She glanced at the food on the table. "What do you want me to do?"

"Maybe the Parmesan?" Teetering on silver lamé ankle straps, Ashley pushed a hunk of cheese, a box grater, and a platter across the table.

"How're your boys?" Neil turned towards Ashley. "Vanessa had me over for Christmas Eve with her family."

"Oh, how sweet. You have kids?" Ashley tossed the enormous leaves into a mustard-colored bowl.

The way she said "kids" made Vanessa feel like a grandmother. "Yeah, twins. So what have you guys been doing over the holidays?"

"Well, we just drove back from Big Sur," Ashley rubbed herself against Neil. "It was awesome! We hiked and had massages and stayed right on the cliffs over the ocean."

He took her away, Vanessa thought jealously. For sex and . . . more sex. She was about to chime in, *I went up north too, to Santa Cruz*, when she realized, What am I going to say about that? That I toured the college with my niece and sister? With that guide Raymond, majoring in dorkiness? How unromantic, how boring and stupid . . .

"I'd never seen that part of California," Neil was adding. "It's incredible. The coastline is spectacular."

"We have to go back there," Ashley purred at Neil. "Maybe when the play's over?"

Vanessa flashed a too-big smile and lobbed the Parmesan back into Ashley's court. "I think you have things under control here. I'm going to ask Steve what else needs to be done."

PATIENCE WAS DEFTLY ARRANGING A PLATTER of chicken tandoori and scented rice when Gary fluttered over. "That looks stunning," he said approvingly.

"Do you have a matching bowl for the yogurt and the chutney?" asked Patience. "We could nestle them side by side."

"I don't know where anything is," Gary said, flapping open the cabinet doors. "We never stay in any kitchen long enough to arrange things permanently."

"What do you mean?" Patience was now crisscrossing the chicken legs into something akin to the Eiffel Tower.

"We move every two or three years."

"Why?" Patience ceased the construction on her chicken coop.

"Conner flips houses."

"He what?"

"He buys a fixer-upper. Then we move in, we redo it, and we put it back on the market and sell it—hopefully at a profit. Although these days, I'd better learn to love my kitchen."

Patience looked aghast. "I would hate to move every two years. I've been in my house for twenty and I feel like I'm just getting to know it."

"What a lovely sentiment," said Gary, not meaning a word of it. "But Conner is more of an artist, really, he has to be creating. So our life is best when Conner is busy restoring and designing. And luckily, he has exquisite taste. People fall in love with his houses."

"I know." Patience breathed. "This is the most beautiful house I've ever seen! It makes me feel like I'm on a movie set."

"Well, it's for sale, we're always for sale," said Gary. "And heaven knows I'm not complaining. These houses support my life in the theater. I could never afford to do plays like Neil's without Conner and West Coast Contractors."

VANESSA SLIPPED UNOBTRUSIVELY THROUGH THE CROWD in the kitchen. She wanted to put as much distance as possible between herself and Neil and his Cute Thing.

Entering the foyer, she climbed the staircase to the second floor on the pretense of finding a bathroom.

She circled the master bedroom—more outsized furniture in shades of chocolate, more flat-screen TV—and stepped out on a balcony that overlooked the courtyard. Leaning on the wooden railing, she spied JT and Richard down below—it was funny how they looked more alike as they aged—and then watched as they ceased conversation, midsentence, to oogle Ashley, who slithered past with a martini.

I wonder what happened to the salad making, she thought peevishly.

"Vanessa."

She felt a thrill, aware of him behind her.

"I just saw Ashley down there," she said, not turning around. "I had no idea you two were a couple."

Neil came up beside her. "Vanessa, I'm really sorry about what happened," he said, leaning back against the railing. "I feel like I created a mess. Like I opened Pandora's box. Please forgive me?"

Of course I forgive you, she thought. It's me I can't forgive. For fantasizing, for . . . prolonging the agony. If I were the least bit grown-up, respectable, loving even, I would have never kissed you back.

"You're mad at me." He brushed against her shoulder and she sucked in her breath. Slowly she turned to face him.

His mouth was so gentle, his eyes too. "I'm not mad," she said. "I guess . . . it's just a hopeless situation."

"Look, I promise I won't bother you again." His face was gray. His shoulders slumped, but he moved in closer.

Vanessa stood still. She was remembering an article she'd read at the dentist's office. A profile of some anthropologist who was studying a lost tribe on a remote island that could only be reached by boat at a certain time of year—something about ocean currents or tides or the moon. What was it called? Tangoray? Kambali? Lost Horizons?

And on this island, on one day every year, everyone was free to sleep with whomever they wanted. With no repercussions. No guilt. No scarlet letter.

Why can't we do that here? she wished fervently. On New Year's Eve! Oh, that would be the day, the perfect day, for a tryst! It might give some *real* meaning to this holiday, she thought sensibly, and make it worth living through.

But she wasn't a member of a dwindling tribe. She didn't live on an island accessible only by boat. She didn't even know any anthropologists to corroborate this story.

And, more than anything, she loved her husband.

She pulled back. "Look, you can call me . . . if you get stuck with the play," she said, in what she hoped was a professional tone of voice.

Then, realizing the danger in that invitation, she glanced away to avoid his eyes.

For a moment, they said nothing. But there was a lingering energy between them. If I reach out and touch him, Vanessa thought, it could start all over again.

But she remained in place. And the moment passed.

Neil cleared his throat and moved tentatively towards the door, resting his hand on the wrought-iron handle. "I want you to read the Sunday *New York Times*," he said.

She cocked her head. "What?" She could hardly hear him over the wail of her inner grief.

"The 'Love Life' column. I wrote it."

"Oh," she said, confused. "If you want."

Then he was gone.

She felt curiously relieved and grateful to him for not pressing her. Not pursuing this.

For in another minute . . . she would have let him.

She searched for her husband down below and saw him chatting with Conner. In the New Year, she vowed, I'm going to love JT even more. I'm going to find a way to make us a little more special.

Neil had made her feel special again. Girlish.

She sensed someone come up behind her again. Anxiously, she spun around.

It was Gary, wagging a finger at her. "I thought I saw you up here."

"I was just . . . coveting everything you own," she said, spreading out her arms to encompass the house and garden.

"Well, keep that coveting to material things," he said cryptically. "I would hate to see your darling family compromised in any way."

Vanessa averted her eyes with embarrassment. Of course it was obvious! Obvious to Gary that there was something between her and Neil. She was a fool to think she could keep this sort of crush a secret.

"Gary, really, it's not what you think—"

"*I* think he's quite something," Gary interrupted. "I mean, look at me, I'm bankrolling his downer of a play. But best at arm's length, don't you agree?"

Vanessa hung her head like a guilty five-year-old.

"Sweetheart," he said, "don't you think I know how hard it is to be faithful? I'm a gay man . . . and that's not the half of it."

"I can't have this conversation with you," Vanessa glanced desperately towards the door.

"Why? Do you think it'll affect our working relationship? Please, half of the company has wet their panties over Neil."

Half the company! So she was just . . . one of the fan club. Just another silly schoolgirl throwing herself at the popular boy. Her shame suddenly doubled.

"Come on, let's go downstairs," said Gary, wrapping his arm around her. "It's too sad and mournful up here. It's New Year's Eve . . . let's drink and be sad and mournful with others."

"Okay," she murmured, allowing him to escort her down the stairs, find her another drink, and introduce her to his college roommate.

Then just before midnight, Gary and Conner assembled all their guests in the courtyard and passed out party poppers and horns.

". . . three, two, one," they counted. "Happy New Year!" The sky was suddenly ablaze with streams of confetti.

"Happy New Year!" Vanessa cried and kissed her husband, then Patience, then Richard. Looking across a sea of people, she caught sight of Neil and Ashley, in a tight embrace, on the other side of the fire pit.

Yes, if it were up to me, on New Year's Eve I'd be allowed to sleep with the popular boy, she thought wistfully. And then in the morning, I'd go back to my steady boy, and my predictable life, no questions asked.

*   *   *

An hour later, when the four tired Channings were driving over the hill, Vanessa suddenly remembered the rest of that story about the tribe and the anthropologist. He had slept with a native woman on that Sultry Adultery night, then sailed back to Rome. Two years later, he learned that she had borne his son, who was now growing up on the island, without a father.

I hope she got him for child support, Vanessa thought indignantly.

She glanced over at JT, who was watching the road and bobbing his head in time with the jazz on the stereo.

"I want you," she whispered.

"I'm available," he whispered back. "For you."

Later, when they were finally alone in their bedroom, JT carefully unbuttoned her wrinkled ruffled blouse.

"The big downside to New Year's Eve," he said, "is you have to live through a long tiring night before you go home and get the sex. Maybe from now on we'll skip the night and go straight to sex."

"Okay," she said, tugging at his jeans.

"Promise," he said, unzipping her skirt.

Afterward, lying on her side, with JT's strong arm curled around her middle, she gently closed the door on the Old Year. Sticking with your everyday love, especially when it's no longer mysterious and exciting, was sometimes hard, Vanessa conceded. But infinitely better than what could be unleashed from Pandora's box. Just having the fantasy is as far as any of us should go, she determined, as she drifted off to sleep.

On any day of the year.

*   *   *

New Year's Day was overcast and sort of blah, like a fuzzy hangover.

Thea was craving something hot and sweet. She ground a handful of fragrant coffee beans and then foraged in the recesses of her stark Swedish cabinets for that pancake mix she liked. And wasn't there a tin of real maple syrup from some forgotten gift basket? Continuing the search she struck gold. Honey buckwheat flapjacks. This would kick-start her year.

The front of the box featured a stack of steaming hotcakes and a quaint New England cabin. Why are pancakes always set in Vermont? Thea wondered. I've eaten thousands of them in California. Dumping the mix into a yellow bowl, she added an egg and water and stirred. Then she lifted a cast-iron skillet from the lower cabinet, set it on the burner, and turned up the heat.

Tina stumbled into the kitchen, wan and squeezed dry. "God, what did I drink last night?"

"Everything," said Thea. "Pancakes?"

Tina shuddered. "I'm not hungry."

While Thea minded her pan, Tina helped herself to coffee from the French press.

"There's half-and-half in the fridge." Thea flicked some water into the skillet and watched the drops dance across the hot surface. She added butter, swirled it, and then ladled in the batter.

"I can't remember the last time I barfed so much," said Tina, giving her coffee a liberal dose of cream. "And cried so much. What else happened?"

"Revenge, recrimination, regret."

"Did I say anything inappropriate to you like—"

"Forgotten," Thea interrupted. "What's a drunken proposition between friends?"

"But I do love you." Tina looked down. "I'm so desperate about Mel, I think I mixed up all my feelings."

"I was flattered," Thea winked. "I want everyone to want me."

Tina smiled with relief. "Did I heave on anything expensive? I hate New Year's Eve."

"Why didn't you tell me that before we went out?"

"I don't want another relationship." Tina rummaged through the drawers for a spoon. "I'm thirty-five but my love life is stuck at sixteen."

"Sounds like a pop ballad," said Thea.

"If Mel really loved me, she'd accept my situation." Tina slumped down at the table and hugged her coffee. "Not everyone's family is understanding. Her parents are shrinks, so she has no idea what the real world is like."

Thea carried the maple syrup, forks, and napkins over to the table. "What did she say?"

"That I'm too needy. But she's too distant and I perceive that as cold and uncaring. She's kinda like you—sort of self-contained and unavailable."

"Unavailable?" Thea resumed her place at the stove. "I don't think I'm unavailable. I've had lots of relationships."

"Besides that one painter, you don't get in deep. You just play with those boys."

"Boys are fun to play with." Thea scooped up a golden hotcake, flipped it onto a plate, and smeared some butter over the top.

"Is that for me?" Tina eyed it wantonly.

"I thought you weren't hungry." Thea poured more batter into the pan.

"Okay. I've decided my New Year's resolution is to focus on my work and not on my love life."

"Just turn your pain into arresting images. Worked for Van Gogh. And Kahlo."

"That smells amazing." Tina tipped some maple syrup onto her finger and licked it. "Isn't the New Year a time of fresh starts and new beginnings?"

"And a time for every purpose under heaven," Thea bussed the plate of hotcakes to the table. "You want breakfast with that syrup?"

She cooked up her own batch and then joined Tina, who, despite her hangover, was wolfing down her meal.

"I did a needy love thing," said Thea, pouring rings of golden syrup over her flapjacks.

Tina's eyes widened. "What?"

"I went up to see Cal Hawkins."

"Why didn't you tell me? Did you have sex?"

"No, he's married now. But it was weird. Not like I imagined."

"Oh." Tina laid a sympathetic hand over Thea's forearm. "Did you think you made a horrible mistake not marrying him?"

Thea snorted. "No."

"Because . . . now he's fat and bald?"

"No, he's still pretty handsome, but in an outdoorsy sort of Patagonia way."

Tina frowned. "Doesn't sound like your type."

"No, I guess not."

"Well, Marcus is sweet." Tina's voice trailed off. She reached over and cut a forkful of Thea's pancake for herself.

"Why does everyone say 'he's so sweet,'" Thea mimicked, "when they talk about Marcus?"

"Maybe they think he's a lightweight." It was hard to hear Tina through her mouthful of food.

"Just because he surfs?"

"And he's not really your equal."

"Why does everyone say that too?"

"Who's 'everyone'?"

Thea banged her fork on the plate. "You . . . and Vanessa. We had a big fight coming back from Santa Cruz."

"About Marcus?"

"That and . . . I don't know what it was about. She's pissed that I don't babysit her kids basically."

"She's right, you're a horrible aunt."

"Why do you say that?"

"You never do anything with them. I see my nieces and nephews all the time. They're adorable. And totally fun."

Thea jumped up and poured herself more coffee. "I can't believe you're giving me shit about that."

"Family's important. Plus, you're missing out on one of life's great pleasures—playing with kids and then giving them back when you're done."

"Look, I'm not a kid person and I'm just . . . tired of her mentioning Cal and marriage. It's . . . pedestrian."

"She can't help it. Straight people want everyone to live that straight married life."

"I know! Which is so hypocritical since half of them get divorced."

"Yeah, but why do you care? Why does this bug you?"

"Where are you getting this therapy talk?"

"Probably from Mel; she talks like her parents. But Vanessa is right, Marcus is a lightweight," Tina said in a singsong manner. "Definitely not deep, soulful material."

Thea planted her fork as a barricade against Tina's stealthy moves on her pancake. "Why don't you use all your new-found pop psychology on your art and not me," she said. "Let's see, you're heartbroken, your heart is broken, love has died . . ."

"Oooh, I like the 'love has died' thing." Tina's eyes grew wide. "What about bead to death?"

"Yeah, death has a lot of possibilities."

"I could bead a coffin! And get into the whole idea of endings, and finality, and darkness."

"Yeah, I love dark."

"And maybe do some Day of the Dead stuff—there must be a cultural grant for that."

"It's great, Tina. This is a really cool idea."

"I hate grant proposals," Tina groaned. "Will you help me write one?"

"Sure." Thea chewed her meal with relish. "We could go online now, see what's up for the New Year."

Tina pushed back from the table. "Uhhh, I can't believe how much I ate. I say we should go for a walk along the beach and maybe see a movie and then think about grant writing tomorrow."

*   *   *

LIBBY SPENT HER LAST DAY IN California with Brian, touring his world: his dorm, his favorite coffee house, the film school, the UCLA Student Union. It had been exciting and fun, but underneath she'd felt a queasy dread.

Anticipating the moment they would say good-bye.

Now it was almost eleven—Patience had insisted, in no uncertain terms, that Libby return to her room by eleven—and the lovers were entwined on "their" chaise by the pool. The very spot they'd first met. It was time for Libby to go upstairs, but they held together, like palms in prayer, consumed by plans.

"Couldn't you fly out at spring break," Brian said, "and visit your aunt and uncle?"

Libby nodded. "And maybe I could get a job and come for the whole summer. I could stay with them and babysit the twins."

"Or I could visit Presidents weekend." He kissed her again.

And again.

"You're not sorry . . . that we did it?" Brian whispered.

"No! I'm glad. It was . . . it was . . ." She stretched for words. Even though they'd declared their love, consummated their love, she still felt shy. Not quite ready to speak freely. "It was amazing."

Brian consulted his phone. "It's eleven," he sighed. "I don't want you to get into trouble."

"I'll call you tomorrow when I get back home."

They kissed. One last time.

Then she pulled away.

Upstairs, she could barely swipe her key card through the scanner, her heart was breaking so.

The adjacent door opened and Patience peered out into the hallway.

"Liberty, Sweetie, are you okay?"

"I'm fine," Libby said coldly.

"Do you want to talk? Let me come over and we'll talk," her mother said earnestly.

Liberty stared at the frown line between her mother's eyebrows. That worry mark could suck her in, and she'd be lost forever. "Just leave me alone!" she said, forcing her door open.

Patience reached out a little farther into the hallway, keeping her right foot wedged in the doorjamb. "But, Liberty, I love you, I want to help."

"Help me by leaving me alone!"

Safe inside her room, Liberty stumbled across the floor and cried freely. She unzipped her brown corduroy miniskirt and kicked it into her open suitcase.

Brian was the most amazing boy in the world. How could she live without him?

While removing her sweater and bra and panties, she pored over every moment of their day, and then, reaching further back into last night, every second of losing her virginity. So much had happened in twenty-four hours. They were so close—she felt like she'd known Brian forever.

And now that she wasn't a virgin, could people tell? Would they look at her and know? She seemed the same but she had this enormous secret inside.

After they'd done it and Brian had left, she had texted Sarah because her BFF should be the first to know. But then she'd thought of her mother and felt awful.

Shouldn't she have told her mother?

Changing into a camisole and peppermint-pink pajama bottoms, guilt washed over her in waves. She had wanted to confide, had wanted to sit on the bed and let her mother hug her.

But she couldn't.

What if her mother freaked out and told her dad? Libby didn't want him to know.

And if she confessed, Patience might forbid her to see Brian again! Or, worse, what if her mother called him up and said something horrible?

Dragging herself to the bathroom, she washed her sticky face with Tea Tree Foaming Gel, then crawled into bed.

Her life had changed, totally, and she was all alone with it.

Mashing her face in the pillow, she sobbed helplesslessly while fantasizing about *Romeo and Juliet* and how after *they* do it, they basically never see each other again and then they die.

At least after we did it we got to see each other again, she thought pitifully. Still, suicide by poison and dagger are really nothing compared to months of exile in Wenham, Massachusetts . . .

Without Brian.

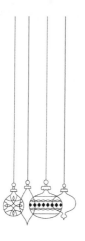

17

Early on the morning of January 2, before the commuters began their climb up and over the Muholland Ridge, Vanessa was ripping the ornaments off the Christmas tree while her family slept peacefully in their beds.

Clad in a clingy zebra-print nightgown and JT's fisherman's sweater, she was piling the red and silver balls, the handmade keepsakes, and the harp-strumming angels on the couch.

She wasn't the least bit concerned about breakage. Somehow, in the weeks between Thanksgiving and New Year, the

Christmas ornaments had lost all their sentimental value and had morphed into junk.

She was in a peculiar sort of frenzy. She felt directed by an unknown force to expel the tree and the discarded giftwrap and the tinsel from her house immediately. She was bearing down the way she had in childbirth. *Get this fucking stuff out of here!*

As she filled the cardboard boxes, one by one, her compulsion mounted. Sweat broke out under her armpits; her mouth grew dry.

"Honey?" A groggy JT, clad in his new flannel PJs, stood perplexed in the archway. "Is everything okay?"

"Don't just stand there staring at me," said Vanessa. "Either go back to bed or come help."

"V, we have the whole day to do this."

"No, I have to do it *now*," she said, tugging hard at a toy soldier that was holding fast to the brown, brittle tree branch. "I have to get this room back. My life back."

The string on the soldier broke and Vanessa stumbled back, smacking her knee into the coffee table. JT flinched from the snap and crackle of bouncing ornaments. "Okay, it's your insanity," he said, disappearing into the kitchen.

Working at the top of her game, it took only thirty-five minutes for Vanessa to jam every single bauble back into its foam packing, cardboard slot, or cellophane box.

But the tree. She would need help with the tree.

She had a fantasy of skillfully wielding a chain saw and hacking up her Douglas fir into neat piles of wood for the winter. But the intoxicating scent of freshly brewed coffee lured her to the kitchen, where she joined JT for breakfast at the island counter.

Her husband glanced up from the paper. "Okay, I get it. You're over the holidays."

Vanessa poured herself a bowl of stale wheat flakes and added milk.

"I'm not the only one."

"But you're certainly the earliest." He took a hit of java. "Look, we've got all day, all week to put stuff away. I'm not working, you're not working. The kids don't go back to school until Monday."

"Stop right there," Vanessa said between mouthfuls of dusty fiber. "I have to make room for something else in my life besides *all that*. Why do you think we're not working? Because we're doing *all that*. Well, it's time for *all that* to be over."

JT grinned. "You're *all that*." And, leaning over, he kissed the tip of her nose. "I guess I just missed most of the holidays between work and the deadly virus. But now that I'm awake and I'm caffeined up, I'll carry those boxes down to the basement."

"Really?" His willingness to help her was intoxicating. "Would you take down the tree?"

"Nothing would please me more," he said, inching his stool closer to hers. "You're so hot when you're whirling about the living room, cleaning."

"Oh, stop it," she giggled. "I am not."

"In fact," he said, reaching his left hand up underneath her bulky sweater and scaling her back, "why isn't there more housecleaning porn?"

"Maybe there is," she said, gently brushing her bruised knee against his thigh. "Maybe there's a whole genre we've missed."

"Maybe we should make some." He led her back to their bedroom and locked the door. "Okay, take off your clothes and dust."

"But the boys will interrupt us."

"Not a chance," he said, lifting up her zebra stripes, "with that new blood-splattering game in the Xbox."

"I thought it was rated E for everyone."

"I thought it was E for Exceptionally Violent."

She straddled him on the bed. "You know what I love about you? You're so good-natured."

"Great, you make me sound like a granola bar."

"I like granola bars," she pulled off his pajama top. "And you humor me . . . humor me in my madness."

They kissed, warm and sweet. Familiar. This is the man I love, she thought. In the bed I love. In the life I love. Thank God it's back.

A jolt of panic shot through her as she suddenly realized what she would have lost if she'd slept with Neil.

"Oh, honey," she clung to JT, tears welling in her eyes. "I love you so much. You know I could never live without you!" She gave a little sob and collapsed on his hairy chest.

"Vanessa?" He groaned. "Are you crying? No, no, no crying! Crying is bad for sex."

"But I want you to know how much you mean to me," she sniffled, nuzzling his left ear.

"I already know." JT rolled out from underneath and flipped her on her back. "And I love you too. But let's focus on the sex. You're the hot housewife, and I'm the granola bar."

"Okay," she smiled. "Dust me."

Closing her eyes, she felt his warm body envelop her. I've

got a 320-day reprieve from the holiday season, she calculated, snuggling up against him. I'd better make the most of it.

"COME WITH ME," MARCUS WAS SAYING to Thea. "It'll be awesome."

Resuming their everyday life with breakfast at the Dudley Street Diner, they had ordered the huevos rancheros and put the holidays behind them.

Marcus squirted hot sauce over his fried eggs. "Kingston knows this guy in Maui who wants to come to L.A., so they're trading places for three months. You should see his crib—it's fucking sick." Scrolling through the photos on his phone, he clicked on an image and held it up for Thea's approval.

"Wow," said Thea, squinting at a postage-stamp-sized picture of what looked like a garage door and a hibiscus bush. *What the fuck would I do all day in Hawaii with Marcus and his brother?*

Marcus catapulted a forkful of salsa and beans into his mouth. "Winter's the best time to go there. No tourists, big waves. You said you're blocked. So come to nirvana, Thea. Get hyped."

"I don't know." Thea was less than enthusiastic. She almost shuddered. "I'm not really a beach person."

"What?" He choked, practically spewing his food over the table. "You live in Venice."

She flipped back her braids, annoyed. "I guess I meant I'm not an *island* person."

Marcus sighed. "Thea, come on."

With keen precision, she bisected her egg-topped tortilla. "But you should go, really, you shouldn't miss this opportunity."

Marcus swallowed hard. "Dude, I do not get you."

Thea laid her knife and fork down on the plate. She glanced about the restaurant—it was quiet on the second day of the year. People were still hiding out, waiting to resume their normal routines.

"I thought you'd be stoked," Marcus was saying, "that I found us a place in paradise."

"I know, I'm sorry. But, well, it's just not what I want to do right now." *Or ever*, she added silently.

Marcus reached across the table and put a rough, calloused hand over hers. "Look, I can show you the island. All these places no one knows, just the locals. It'll be good for your work. And I know how crazy ass it's been for you. You're all about the art."

Thea raised an eyebrow.

Marcus grinned. "You think I don't know you, but I do. And it's cool. I love my fine art girl."

Jeez, Thea thought. Even Marcus, who can barely see past the waves, knows how much I need my work. "Fine art girl," she said. "Maybe that should be my website."

He pulled back from her and picked up his coffee. "Just chill on it. I'm gonna think positive. That you'll change your mind."

Oh, Marcus, Thea thought guiltily. It's not Hawaii.

It's you.

*   *   *

AFTER BREAKFAST, THEA DUTIFULLY accompanied Marcus over to the surf shop. As they passed the local library and the yoga studio, Thea drummed up some breakup courage.

Tell him now, she said to herself. Tell him it's over. Cut him loose, let him hook up with someone in Hawaii. *But he's on his way to work*, another, weaker voice whispered, *you should wait till he gets home.* Okay, she decided, I'll tell him tonight.

Marcus balanced the cruiser against a metal parking meter and faced her. "Look, Thea, three months is a long time. So while I'm gone, it's okay if you see other people."

Fuck, Thea thought, *he's* ditching *me!* "Three months is not that long," she found herself saying rather petulantly.

He leaned over the bike and kissed her. "Then catch a flight over."

Thea suddenly felt withered and ancient. Felt like fucking hard young bodies had actually hastened the aging process instead of keeping her young.

"Can we talk about this later?" Marcus glanced at his waterproof watch. "I've gotta go."

"Sure. I'll be home tonight." Thea turned away, heading back down Main Street towards home.

But with every block she put between herself and Marcus, her head grew clearer and her limbs grew stronger. She had loved Marcus . . . well, maybe not *loved*, but certainly *appreciated*. But what was she doing with him? She wasn't honoring him . . . or herself.

She quickened her pace, eager to get back to her studio, back to her canvas. With Marcus out of the picture, she could concentrate on her work.

God, she missed her work.

That was her real husband. Her real marriage.

I'm so predictable, she thought. There's always that pain, that angst, that unhappiness before any creative breakthrough. But I can never see it when I'm in it. I always mistake it for something else. Like Cal or emptiness or love. But it isn't any of those things. It's just the wandering and being with the not-knowing.

Arriving home, she began to outline a large canvas. For the first time in months, she had a very clear vision of what she wanted.

Then she had an image of Vanessa.

Fuck, what a buzz kill.

She tried to store Vanessa into some mental desktop file, but that didn't work.

Dropping her pencil, she seized her phone and scrolled down to her sister's number. Hovering over the Send button, she remembered how Tina had said she was the worst aunt ever. Continuing through her address book, she highlighted Tina's number instead.

She listened to the voice mail and pushed #1 to leave a message. "Hey, girl, it's Thea. I need to talk to you about Vanessa. And what do you do with kids anyway?"

ON SUNDAY MORNING, THE JT CHANNINGS decided to walk down to Ventura Boulevard for coffee and pastries.

Vanessa loved her neighborhood on weekends because traffic was light and it seemed more peaceful, more homey. The boys raced ahead, leaping up to smack the lowest branches of a sycamore. She waved at her neighbor Ron, who was up on his roof taking down a plastic Santa and his reindeer. The sight of his dry, discarded Christmas tree lying in the gutter made her smile.

Inside Coffee Cakes, the family placed their order and then moved to the pickup counter to wait for their drinks.

"Indigo!" the twins screamed, rushing up to their classmate, who was wearing a braided gold headband and dirty pajama bottoms.

Vanessa turned around and came face-to-face with Karen Maguire-Weinstock, looking unusually haggard with two-inch dark roots and no makeup.

"Oh, hi, Vanessa," Karen sighed. "Aren't you glad the holidays are over?"

"Yes?" said Vanessa, wondering if this were a trick question.

"I had *my* relatives and *Scott's* relatives and a new baby," Karen was confessing. "I don't know what made me think I could do both Hanukkah *and* Christmas, but it almost killed me. Really, it was insane. I can hardly wait for school to start tomorrow so I can get *her*"—she bobbed her head towards her daughter—"out of my hair."

"Triple nonfat latte and an orange juice!" The barista placed a coffee container and a plastic drink on the counter.

Karen grabbed her order. "Indigo, we've got to get to the drugstore." She smiled grimly at Vanessa. "Of course the baby was sick, too. Next year, I'm saying no to everything." With a tug on Indigo's sleeve, she swept out to the parking lot.

Through the window, Vanessa watched as Karen set her coffee on the roof of her car, and then jumped into the driver's seat. As she backed up, the cup toppled to the ground and exploded into a muddy, foamy five-dollar puddle.

Vanessa giggled guiltily. You'd better enjoy it now, she told herself. Because Karen will do Christmas just the same next year—and she'll probably go bigger.

VANESSA AND JT SAT ON THE leather couch in the living room section of the store. While they sipped their drinks and stared blankly into space, their boys conducted a heated burping contest in the club chairs facing them.

As they got up to leave, Vanessa noticed an erudite-looking couple in their sixties—both in glasses, khakis, and v-neck sweaters—nestled at a window table reading the *New York Times*.

The New York Times, Vanessa thought thickly. What was it about *The New York Times* I was supposed to remember?

Then it hit her. Neil. Something he wrote.

She checked the communal newspaper rack and rifled through a slew of free magazines with names like *On the Boulevard* and *Valley Style*. Who reads these? she wondered. Since they're always here on the shelf.

She was about to concede defeat when Erudite Husband walked over and deposited his *New York Times* into the wooden slots.

"Excuse me," said Vanessa. "Are you done with your paper?"

"Yes," he smiled. "Do you read the *New York Times*? The L.A. papers are just a waste of wood pulp, don't you think?"

"Uh, definitely," said Vanessa. "Do you know what section 'Love Life' is in?"

"Sunday styles," he said. Unfolding his paper he plucked it out for her. "And it was excellent today. A New York playwright, of course."

"Of course," she said, swiftly tucking the section under her arm.

As they trudged up the hill towards home, Vanessa fell behind, quickly scanning the pages for Neil's byline.

"What are you reading?" said JT.

"Neil said they were doing a piece about the play," she mumbled.

At the corner, the boys jumped off the curb into the street.

"Ethan! Alex! Stop!" JT yelled, dashing up the block. "Honey, I'll meet you back at the house."

Vanessa's gaze landed on "Over the Holidays," by Neil Cohen.

"*A few years ago, I fell in love over the holidays. It was a fairy tale, and like all fairy tales it ended with a kiss between the star-crossed lovers. She was married . . .*"

Vanessa was livid. That asshole! So he'd had an affair before. With another married woman!

"*I fell in love with her despite the fact that she questioned my work and she seemed uninterested in me—not the sort of spark that has ever led me into romance. Our affair was textbook: furtive glances, longing, an impossible situation. And, of course, it was the holidays, a time ripe with heightened expectations and attendant regret . . .*"

She crumpled up the newspaper and then it hit her: What

if Neil had veiled the story in the past to protect *her*? To protect their kiss.

Oh, she melted, tenderly smoothing out the page. *Oh* . . .

Back in his memoir, Neil imagined her naked body and the way they'd linger together the morning after sex. He imagined the cities they would visit: Paris, for love; New York, for culture; Orcas Island, for whales. *(Whales! How utterly fanciful!)*

"*I'll never know how perfect we'd be, how painful our fights, how deep our relationship would take us. What our children would look like. That will remain a fantasy, like a perfect holiday, an image that warms me in the winter and amuses me on a summer day. But what I do know, the part of the story that's real, is that I adored her and loved her once upon a time.*"

When Vanessa finished, she clasped the paper to her heart. Neil had sent her a gift that she'd cherish forever . . . he had given her a secret admirer.

HOURS LATER, WHEN SHE AND JT were back at the kitchen counter—he paying bills, she writing thank-you notes—he stretched his arms over his head and then ambled over to the fridge.

"Hey, I read that piece by your playwright," he said, extracting a hunk of Vermont cheddar. "He's a good writer but, come on, why didn't he just sleep with that chick? He sounds gay."

"Gay?" said Vanessa sharply. Nervously, she cleared her throat with a little shrug. "I didn't get that."

"Yeah, well, Gary's producing his play." JT snagged a box of Wheat Thins on the counter. He rummaged deep to the bottom and came up with a fistful of broken pieces. "She sounded hot, come on! If he wasn't such a pussy, he'd have nailed her."

"JT, you're such a pig!" She was on the verge of defending Neil, trumpeting his chivalry, his sensitivity, and his goddamned moral high ground when she realized how foolish that would be.

"You're probably right," she conceded. "Maybe he is gay."

"No maybe about it." JT hacked at the cheese with a butter knife and then balanced the crumbly pieces on the cracker bits. "Are you going to work with him this week?"

"No," she said. "We're done. I don't think there's anything more for us to do together."

"What did you say his play's about again?"

"Brothers, a father's death, and a family secret."

JT whistled. "Throw in some incest and you've got a Pulitzer."

Later that afternoon, Vanessa stole away to her cluttered desk in the corner of the bedroom. She pulled out the lower left drawer, which was packed with hanging file folders. Running her fingers across the blue plastic tabs, she landed on V.C.C. LETTERS.

Unlike the rest of the files, this one was old and frayed, its once ruby-red color faded to a dullish pink. But the sight of it thrilled her and she laid it gently on the desk.

Inside were love letters she'd saved from every boyfriend since junior high. And tucked in with them was a plastic bag filled with withered petals from long-ago bouquets. Yellow

roses and tiger lilies proclaiming love and desire and atone-
ment. The decaying flowers took her back, instantly, to forgotten lovers and sweet kisses and sweeter forgiveness.

Last, in the very back of the folder, were photos she didn't
want to share with the family albums. The one of her at
twenty-one, in jeans and a cloche, on her first trip to Paris;
at twenty-five, lying topless on the beach at Lamu; at twenty-
seven, in a navy peacoat, somewhere (Union Street?) in San
Francisco; at seventeen, in her black strapless prom dress at the
Universal Sheraton Crystal Ballroom.

Into this sentimental soup, she dropped Neil's article.
When I'm really old and really wrinkled, she thought warmly,
I can go through my file and remember my secret admirer.
And all my past boyfriends. And know that I've been loved.

This treasure trove made her feel giddy and peaceful at the
same time. Then, securing it away for that future pick-me-up,
she slammed the drawer shut.

THEA DABBED SUNSCREEN ON HER FACE and hands and then
slipped into gray yoga pants and a zippered sweater. She
wrapped an Indian-print scarf around her neck, laced up her
sports shoes, and headed downstairs to her studio.

Because she liked to think about her work during her
morning walks, she took a peek at her canvas before heading
outside.

She had painted a winter scene—a traditional house with
a wreath and a sleigh. Through the picture window was an

ordinary family assembled around the tree, each isolated in a golden halo—daughter, mother, and father. They seemed distant, unconnected, bereft. It was Currier and Ives through the fright lens of Hieronymus Bosch.

Satisfied with her progress, she closed the front door and turned west towards the ocean, passing a hodgepodge of shingled cottages hemmed in by überarchitecture. As she crossed the alley, a blue hybrid whizzed by and then slammed on its brakes. Jeez, he almost clipped me, she thought.

Suddenly, the driver was jumping out of the car and rushing towards her. Was this some kind of nut job? Her spine tensed. But this nut job was wearing a suit, a very nice cut, sort of grayish, and he was waving at her.

"Hey! Hi!"

Shoving her hand in her pocket, she gripped her cell phone in case she'd need 911.

"New Year's Eve," he was saying. "The Art Guild. We shared some cheap wine in a basement. Actually, you had club soda."

Oh, that guy, Thea remembered. She uncoiled her fingers.

"You're an artist, right?"

"Did I tell you that?"

"Artist, feminist, doesn't date Labradors."

Thea rolled her eyes. "Oh, yeah. You're a divorced guy who moved to the beach."

"There's more than one of us?" he joked.

Thea thought he looked oddly out of place in his jacket and tie in this grungy alley that smelled of sea salt and urine and featured an amateurish mural of Bob Marley surfing a cannabis leaf.

"So, you live near here?" she said.

"About two blocks down," he pointed.

He was just standing there, staring at her. She had an instinct to flee, but something kept her nailed to the spot. "So," she hesitated. "That was a dismal night."

"You left too soon," he grinned. "The band got into a gnarly fistfight."

Gnarly? Thea warmed slightly. What was it about this guy that was so weirdly . . . weird?

"I'm Jason Mills." He waited for her reply, then gave her the prompt. "And you are . . . ?"

"Oh, uh, Thea Clayton."

They stared uncomfortably at each other, then Jason's cell phone rang.

"Uh, I gotta go," she mumbled.

"Wait," he said, switching off the ring.

"What do you do again?" Thea couldn't believe how stupid she sounded.

"I'm a lawyer," Jason said.

"Oh, right." She looked underwhelmed.

"But the good kind. I do a lot of pro bono work. In the arts. I have a thing for art."

And a thing for artists? Thea suddenly hoped.

He pulled his wallet from his pants' pocket and extracted his business card. She noticed that his movements were very fluid, like an athlete's.

"Have dinner with me?" he asked. "I'll take you to a club where the band plays together . . . or not, if you prefer jazz."

Thea considered Jason's hazel eyes. He was certainly a real

grown-up, but thankfully there *was* something boyish about him.

Old habits are hard to break, she thought wryly.

She took his card and lowered her chin flirtatiously. "I'm free Friday night."

"It's a date," he said, walking backward to his car. "Promise you'll call."

"I promise," said Thea.

"If you don't," he continued, swinging open the driver's door, "I'll have to camp out in this alley till I catch you again." He pointed at the mural. "Right next to that really bad Bob Marley."

He gave her a wave and then drove off.

Thea fingered her braids and then resumed her trek to the water's edge. The beach was fairly deserted this time of year. A few surfers were bobbing out on the water, waiting patiently for a killer set of waves. There were seagulls circling overhead, scanning for discarded fast food, and two tourists in bright new active wear were racewalking along the wet sand.

It's a new year and I've met a new guy and I have new work, Thea reflected. I feel like I've just had one big psychic colonic. I'm free of Cal and Marcus.

Except there's Vanessa, snapped a tiny voice. You can't get totally clean till you deal with her.

Passing the lifeguard station, she pulled out her cell phone and dialed her sister's number.

"Thea?" Vanessa's voice rang out into her ear.

"Yeah, hi," she said, plopping herself down on the ridge above the shore. "I'm calling to apologize."

"Oh, I'm sorry too," said Vanessa. "I can't believe we

screamed at each other. I've felt horrible the last week. And listen, you were right. I wanted you to be something you're not. But I'm going to accept the fact that you're not into kids and move on to someone else."

"What?" Thea's heart sank at the thought of being replaced at something she didn't want to do.

"Well, it turns out that Patience wants to spend more time with the boys. She offered to take them this summer and I think they'll have a good time. So just be yourself and don't worry about the other thing."

Thea frowned, watching the unfurling of the waves. I can't believe she's ditching me for that in-law, she thought angrily.

"Thea? Can you hear me?"

"But that's not what I want!" Thea pouted. "I called because, well, I hope that this year, things will be different."

"Okay," came the hesitant reply. "Like how?"

"For fuck's sake, Vanessa, I can be an *aunt*. The boys can spend the night with me too, you know. And Tina reminded me there's a surf camp here in Venice, and I was thinking maybe they'd like to come here and learn to ride. I mean, it's right down the street. And the kids in that group seemed around the same age. Around . . ." Thea racked her brain to remember the twins' age.

"Around nine?" Vanessa finished.

"Yeah, sorry." Thea dug a foot into the sand, feeling the cold earth slide down into her shoe. "Okay, nine. So, do you think they might like that?"

"I think they'd love it," Vanessa said. The smile on her face beamed through the wireless connection.

"And Vanessa," Thea pressed on, eager to finish up this

apology, "I didn't mean the stuff about you and Neil. You can fuck whomever you want. Have an affair. Who am I to judge?"

"I didn't sleep with him," Vanessa said. "But it's okay, I'm better off not entering the world of adultery."

"So you didn't get Neil and I didn't get Cal. Our holidays came to nothing."

"Yeah, but I decided I love JT."

"Yeah, and I decided I don't love Marcus."

"What?"

"Yeah," Thea said, momentarily distracted by a handsome young man in a wet suit shaking water from his glistening dark hair. "Uh, I met someone else."

"Who?"

"His name's Jason. He's a lawyer. Who knows if it'll work out. But he's kind of funny. And he's old."

"How old?"

"My age. It's good. I have a lot to look forward to."

"I love January." Vanessa sounded dreamy. "So blissfully free of holidays. And you know, I'm sort of grateful to Neil because it made me realize how much I love JT."

"Yeah, JT's a great guy." Thea glanced at her watch. Fuck, she thought. Now this is going to be a long, boring conversation about love and relationships and I have to get back to work. Jumping up, she listened to Vanessa blab on about life and the preciousness of it all as she scrambled across the sand. As she passed the parking lot, she noticed the guy with the wet hair lashing his surfboard to his roof rack. She took a detour and headed in his direction.

"Thea? You're not saying anything. I can tell you want off the phone."

"No, it's just . . ."

"I know you, it's so obvious. I'm hanging up now. If you want, you can come over for dinner on Sunday night and hang out. We can play games, like what are the twins' middle names and when are their birthdays?"

"Shut up."

"You shut up."

"They have the *same* birthday."

"In . . .?"

"March?"

"You're pathetic. I'll tell you on Sunday."

I have a lot to look forward to, Thea repeated to herself, once she and Vanessa had promised eternal sisterly love and finished the call. I'm not afraid of dating older men and I'm cool with the past and I'm working on stuff I like and it's a new year.

And maybe I'll even learn to like kids, she thought, resisting the urge to flirt with that dark Adonis who was now unzipping his wet suit and exposing broad shoulders and an unusually beautiful clavicle.

I mean kids who are related.

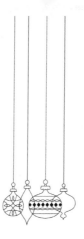

18

"Come on Beau," Patience clucked her tongue, coaxing her horse up the gentle hillside. "There's my good boy." She patted his gleaming coat and admired his firm gait. "Your leg is all better now, isn't it?"

They trotted back to the stable, wending through a stand of maples dotted with crimson and rust-colored leaves. When they reached the orchard, Patience smelled the sweet, winy tang of forgotten autumn fruit rotting under the naked trees.

She was eager to finish her morning ride and scoot back to her desk—there was so much to do. She and Richard had finally decided on a theme for this year's Open House—Christmas in

California. Tonight they would decorate the tree with miniature palm trees and fun movie tchotchkes she'd found at the gift
shop at LAX last January: I Love Lucy, Batman, E.T. She was
going to cover the front walk with green Astroturf and decorate
the *Bûche de Noël* with a miniature HOLLYWOOD sign. They
had floated the idea of just serving Margaritas, but Richard felt
the guests would miss her eggnog. So it was decided they'd do
both. Plus a really fine single-malt scotch.

At the Wenham Thrift Shop, she'd found a surfboard,
which she trimmed with twinkle lights. I'll plant it on the
lawn or hang it from my elm tree, she thought. That'll get everyone in a festive mood before they enter the house.

The guest rooms needed cleaning before the relatives arrived. And she had to finish the scarf she was knitting for
Vanessa—a beautiful moss-green wool just perfect for her
sister-in-law's coloring. But most important, she was picking
up Liberty this afternoon.

Yes, this Christmas would be the best ever.

PROMISING BEAU A LONG, LUXURIOUS GROOMING tomorrow,
she gave him a quick rubdown before dashing to the car and
speeding home. Circling around Wenham Lake she noticed it
had started to freeze over. Maybe we'll have a white Christmas,
she thought happily. They said there's a thirty percent chance
of snow later today.

In the kitchen, she curled up at her desk and checked
Libby's flight status: ON TIME.

Libby. Her beautiful daughter would be home for dinner.

This was the longest they'd ever been apart in over eighteen years. When Libby left for college last August, they'd planned on her returning for Thanksgiving break. But by the end of September, Libby had accepted an invitation to stay at her new friend Taylor's house in Manhattan Beach.

"It's only two blocks to the water!" Libby had said.

"But we haven't seen you since summer," Patience said woefully.

"Mom, it's only another three weeks and then I'll be home for Christmas. Please, please, I really want to go!"

"But you can't have Thanksgiving without your family." Patience had been incredulous at the thought of a holiday with strangers. "What about your aunt and uncle? I'm sure they want to see you."

So it was decided that Libby would drive to Aunt V and Uncle JT's for Thanksgiving Day and then go on to Taylor's. Patience and Richard were left to fend for themselves at her sister Hope's house.

But no matter how much Patience adored her two nieces, and how lovingly she'd tended to her cranberry caramel tart and pumpkin pies, she'd been utterly miserable without her daughter. Why she'd even sipped two full glasses of chardonnay just to get through the afternoon.

Tears filled her eyes. Never again, Patience vowed. I don't care how grown-up Libby wants to be. I'm never spending Thanksgiving again without her.

The day flew by and now, suddenly, here she was, at Logan Airport, thirty minutes late. It had started to snow and there'd been an accident on Route 128, so she'd been forced to take side streets. But it doesn't matter now, she thought, dashing into short-term parking and braving the steady beat of snow-flakes. Liberty's here and she'll be here for four weeks.

Baggage claim was a hive of holiday buzzing. Overcoats, steam heat, bags, parcels, crowds of relatives.

"Mom! Mom!"

Who was this young woman in jeans and flip flops—flip flops! It was nineteen degrees in Boston!—rushing at her? In a skimpy velveteen jacket and tissue T?

Hurriedly, Patience peeled off her light blue wool coat and threw it over her daughter's shoulders. "Liberty, put this on! You'll catch your death of cold!"

Patience hugged her and then stared down with horror at her daughter's bare toes and chipped black nail polish. "Aren't your feet freezing?"

Gathering up the two rolling duffels, they braved the whipping wind, loaded the car, and sped north towards home. As Patience maneuvered the maze out of Boston, Libby chatted about the seventy-degree weather she'd left behind, the English teacher she despised, her clean-freak roommate, Hannah, and her determination to switch dorms next year.

"How's Brian?" said Patience lightly.

"Oh, he's fine."

"I was sorry he didn't come with you."

"He had to go to his family's," Libby said. "But we haven't been seeing each other so much lately."

"Really?" Patience downshifted to nonchalance.

"He's always talking about film," said Libby with the distinct air of the uninterested. "And his friends are all film freaks too."

"Hmm," said her mother.

"I mean, there's more to life than just . . . retrospectives of Japanese directors. Anyway, I met someone else."

"You did?"

"In freshman English. We all call it English dumb-oh-one since it's totally stupid. But, whatever."

"And this boy . . . uh, person."

Libby smiled. "His name is Jean-François, but we call him J Frank. Poli sci. He's a Green Party activist." Her eyes gleamed. "Did you know that America consumes most of the world's resources? He says our country is totally corrupt."

Thank goodness that corruption doesn't include a University of Southern California education, thought Patience wryly.

"He's invited me home for spring break."

"Home to . . . ?"

"Paris."

"Paris!"

"Isn't that cool?"

"Uh," said Patience, nipping the urge to protest another holiday sans daughter. "Yes, very cool."

"So, Mom, could you please, please, please pay for my ticket?"

"What about the money from your summer job?"

Liberty squared her shoulders for the debate. "But Mom, going to France is not a vacation. It's seeing another culture and understanding the world. Don't you want me to have this experience?"

"I do," said Patience. "And I think that would be an excellent use of your money. It's exactly how I'd want you to spend your savings. On something educational. Like Paris."

"Oh, Mom!"

"How's Brian going to feel about this?" Patience stared ahead through the swipe of the windshield wipers.

"Brian doesn't rule my life. I mean, I love him, he'll always be special, but . . ." Liberty paused.

"He's special because he was your first?" Patience said quietly.

Liberty pulled her mother's coat collar up around her ears and scrunched down in her seat. "I wanted to tell you but . . . I don't know. I just . . . it was too weird."

Patience's chest felt tight. She suspected, she'd guessed, but she'd been too shy, too afraid, to say anything last year.

"It's kinda sad," said Libby wistfully, "that I don't feel that way about him anymore."

Patience nodded. "It's okay. He'll always have that place in your heart. He'll always be your first."

"Yeah," said Libby. "I'm glad it was him."

Patience concentrated on the road. Her palms were sweaty. Her girl was more than a college girl.

And now a French boy. Patience shook her head. Where did Libby come from? She's certainly not a homebody like me. She is my bold adventurer.

"Maybe your father and I could meet you in Paris?" she said hopefully.

"Uh . . . I'll be fine by myself."

"Of course you'll be fine," Patience said. "It's just that . . . well, I haven't been to France since my high school trip to Europe. I would love to go back. And I'd love to see it with you. We certainly wouldn't have to do everything together. We'd see a few things and then you'd go off with Jean-François."

"Hmm . . ." Libby hesitated. "If you came, would you take me shopping?"

"Shopping? Well, do you think that's a good idea? I wouldn't want Jean-François to think we're corrupt."

"Oh, Mom!" They both laughed.

Whoa there, girl, Patience chided herself. Pull back on those reins! Libby might be done with this boy by Presidents Day.

"It's so beautiful here." Liberty stared hungrily at the white flurries. "Snow is awesome. And I'm glad you're doing Christmas. I mean, no offense to Aunt V, but I think you do it better."

"I do?" Patience was flattered.

"Yeah, their stuffing was super dry at Thanksgiving. And she *bought* her pies at the store."

"Well, your aunt isn't that interested in cooking."

"That's why I'm glad I'm here. Are you making your cranberry tart?"

"If you want."

"And pancakes. I really, really, really miss your pancakes." Libby reached into her pants' pocket for her phone. A moment later her thumbs began to text.

Patience smiled happily at the steady, falling snow. A white Christmas, she thought gratefully. Cranberry caramel tart and homemade eggnog.

My daughter. My husband. My family.

We're going to have a wonderful time.

Over the holidays.

READERS GROUP GUIDE
OVER THE HOLIDAYS
SANDRA HARPER

This year, Vanessa Channing is NOT flying across the country to New England to spend Christmas with her in-laws. Determined to have a simple, meaningful holiday at home, she suggests to her husband they just stay in Los Angeles with the twins. But simple becomes complicated with the arrival of the Massachusetts relatives and, as plans go awry, Vanessa, her family, and friends search for the joy and goodwill of the season.

Discussion Questions

1. As sisters, Vanessa and Thea couldn't be more different. Vanessa lives in the suburbs of Los Angeles with her husband and twin boys, while Thea lives in vibrant, gritty Venice Beach with her art. How are these two sisters different in their approaches to life? Do they share any similarities?

2. Vanessa wakes up early one morning to find her husband JT making a spontaneous batch of cinnamon rolls (p. 22). What is the reason for JT's sudden need to bake so early in the morning, and how does Vanessa deal with her husband's stress?

3. There's a lot of fantasy and romantic images at the holiday season. How does that contribute to a woman's sense of herself and her well-being?

4. Vanessa comments that Patience's voice makes her "feel like she was standing in line at the soup kitchen" (p. 44). Why? How does Patience make her feel inferior? Do you think it's intentional, or is Vanessa being overly sensitive?

6. Thea is 40—twelve years older than her boyfriend, Marcus. Is there still a double standard about older women dating younger men?

7. Vanessa is called in by her friend Gary to help fix the play he's producing. But the playwright, Neil, is not happy with the decision.

How does Vanessa break down Neil's initial resistance to having her help him with his play? What assumptions does each person make about the other?

8. Patience takes her daughter Libby on a trip to historic Concord, Massachusetts, hoping to enjoy the holiday decorations and bond with her daughter. Unfortunately, things don't go as planned, and Patience breaks down and cries. Why is it so hard for Libby and Patience to communicate with each other?

9. Vanessa and Thea have a tumultuous relationship. Vanessa declares that Thea is "the worst aunt ever." (p. 108). Can the tension between married with children and happily single be bridged?

10. When Libby arrives in LA, she immediately falls for a local boy, Brian. How is her emotional roller-coaster over Brian indicative of her age and her feelings about her family?

11. Even though Vanessa and JT are happy, what is it about married life that causes Vanessa (or any woman!) to want to stray?

12. Thea finally works up the courage to visit Cal Hawkins in Northern California, but her trip doesn't go as planned. Is it a good idea to look up old boyfriends?

13. Vanessa and Patience finally find common ground getting ready for New Year's Eve. What are their new understandings about each other? How are they more alike than they realized?

14. What is it about the holidays that makes us believe our families will behave better and circumstances will be different from the rest of the year?

15. Patience clings to holiday traditions and Vanessa feels unsure of her beliefs. How important is it to stick to tradition? Is there room for change or improvement?

An Interview with Sandra Harper

What was your inspiration for writing this novel? Do you have special memories of Christmas? Growing up, was the holiday as chaotic for you as it was for some of the characters in this novel?
I like to write comedy and the holiday season is delicious material

for that! There's so much pressure and everyone goes a little crazy. My parents were divorced so when I was a girl we had to celebrate twice: once with Dad and once with Mom. That could be pretty chaotic.

Vanessa and Thea have a tumultuous relationship. How did your own relationship with your sisters influence your portrayal of Vanessa and Thea?

No one can love and fight like sisters! It's just the nature of the relationship. I was the oldest so I was the terrible bossy one.

Like some of your characters, you also live in Los Angeles. Do you prefer spending Christmas in sunny L.A. or have you ever tried spending the holiday in the snowy setting of New England? Where is your favorite spot to spend Christmas?

There's no question that New England is absolutely beautiful at Christmastime. But my holiday fantasy is to book a lovely little hotel in Paris, have café au lait and that wonderful french bread for breakfast, and then stroll along the Seine to Notre Dame. Please inform my husband.

The characters in your novel all struggle with the expectations of the holiday season. Do you see yourself more as Vanessa, frazzled and stressed out, or as Patience, focused and intent on having the best Christmas ever?

I sympathize with both characters. I myself have given up on the holidays but I understand the need and the desire that women have to create something meaningful. With any luck, no one will ask me to do them again.

Thea has an interesting and very personal relationship to her art. Do you feel the same way she does about being "married" to your art? Are you "married" to your writing?

Thea is my hero!!! I wish I was as focused as she is—I'd be so much more successful!! I love that she's bold and unafraid to give herself over to her art. Plus the idea of living alone and not having to compromise is so seductive, isn't it?

Is there any character you feel particularly close to in the novel, and if so, why?

I love all my characters for different reasons. When I begin a story, I sit down at the computer and wait for the characters to show up. I really enjoy getting to know them.

How do you see Vanessa's character evolving through the story? Do you relate to her on any level?

Vanessa struggles with the stuff of ordinary life: marriage, motherhood, and work. And because regular life can be tedious, it's a miracle that all of us aren't running away every day of the year.

A major theme of this novel is the importance of family and the need to communicate with one another. Do you think relatives come with certain requirements and expectations?

I'd probably need a Ph.D. to answer this. I can assure you that I'm highly unqualified.

Enhancing Your Book Club

1. Everyone in the book experiences a complicated mixture of feelings about Christmas and the holiday gift-giving season. Discuss your own thoughts and memories of Christmas with the group. Share any family traditions you have, or any that you wish you could get rid of. If the mood is right, have a craft day and make Christmas decorations. You can find ideas for crafts at www.marthastewart.com/christmas.

2. Vanessa and Patience have different ideas about the ideal Christmas dinner. Vanessa insists on a turkey, while Patience wants roast beef. Schedule a potluck meeting and have everyone bring in their favorite Christmas recipes. You can find ideas for good dishes at: epicurious.com/recipesmenus/holidays/christmas/recipes and allrecipes.com/Recipes/Holidays-and-Events/Christmas/Main.aspx.

3. Vanessa tries to educate Alex and Ethan with ideas about the ancient celebration of the Winter Solstice. Are there any alternative ideas for the holiday season that you and your family have experimented with? Have any been a successful cure for "Holiday Stress Syndrome," as Thea calls it?

Printed in the United States
By Bookmasters